THE BEAUTY IN DECEPTION

FELICIA STARR

The Beauty in Deception
Copyright © 2015 by Felicia Starr

Editing by
Catherine Stovall
Double V Editing and Proofreading
Cover Design by Bookfabulous Designs
Cover Model: Salvatore Fama Jr.
Cover Photography by Timothy Lucas

All rights reserved. Without limiting the rights under copyright reserved above, no part of this publication may be reproduced, stored in or introduced into a retrieval system, or transmitted, in any form, or by any means (electronic, mechanical, photocopying, recording, or otherwise) without the prior written permission of the author of this book. This is a work of fiction. Names, characters, places, brands, media, and incidents are either the product of the author's imagination or are used fictitiously. The author acknowledges the trademarked status and trademark owners of various products referenced in this work of fiction, which have been used without permission. The publication/use of these trademarks is not authorized, associated with, or sponsored by the trademark owners.

Published by Rockti Publishing
FELICIASTARR.COM

ISBN-13: 978-1512040661
ISBN-10: 1512040665

Other Books by Felicia Starr

Breaking the Darkness Series
(New Adult Paranormal Romantic Suspense)
Taken
Marked 1.5
Betrayed

Sacred Hearts Coven
(Steamy Contemporary Romance with a touch of magic.)
Dark and Stormy
Light and Sweet
Jack and Ginger

Hawk Creek Novel
(Psychological Thriller/Romantic Suspense)
The Beauty in Deception

Acknowledgments

First and foremost, I have to say thank you to my husband, mother, and my boys for all of their continued support. I also want to thank the people who have helped make this project possible. Thank you to my amazing editor, Catherine Stovall. Laura Hidalgo from Bookfabulous Designs, as always, blew me away with her creativity and perfectionism by creating a perfect cover. Thank you to my amazing beta team for helping me bring it all together. Thank you to my cover model Salvatore Fama Jr. and photographer Timothy Lucas. I must also honor and give many thanks to my Guruji, Rev. Jaganath Carrera, for keeping me spiritually grounded and helping me think about what is beyond me.

DEDICATION

This book is dedicated to Jean Bonanno.

PROLOGUE

One and a half years earlier.

EACH CORD OF TRINA'S ABDOMINAL muscles flexed with excruciating pain as she struggled to raise herself to a sitting position. Her screams were so loud they numbed her ears. In fact, she wasn't sure if the sounds that escaped her were real or in her mind. It didn't matter because the guttural shrieks continued to echo off the dark brick walls surrounding her. The darkness made it impossible to make out any details, and her eyes struggled to focus as she tried to look down at her body

It wasn't raining, but her clothes were soaked through and clinging to her skin with her every movement. Her hands trembled as she attempted to place them down on the hard pavement beneath her, and Trina rolled over onto all fours in an effort to find enough stability to get to her feet. Fatigued, her legs wobbled with the failed attempt at standing.

She wasn't sure if she was crying, yet she felt hot, wet beads slithering down her cheeks as she tried crawling down the deserted alley toward the lights of the random passing cars.

One hand in front of the other. Keep moving. Don't stop!

She forced her nearly broken body to push through the pain to get to the light. Small bits of gravel dug into her hands and knees, causing her to flinch so hard that her knees buckled underneath her. Her shoulder crashed agonizingly down onto the ground.

"Ahh!" The bellow came from a place deep within her gut. "Help me!"

Her cries went unanswered. Curling up in the fetal position, she rocked herself back and forth. The pain, confusion, and uncertainty of what had happened to her haunted every corner of her mind.

Trina never left the house without her purse or her phone. The realization that they might be somewhere within reach gave her an inkling of hope—unless she'd been mugged. Without any recollection of the preceding events, she couldn't know if they were close by.

Trying to push up again, enough to search the ground around her, she dragged her body, scraping the last layer of flesh from her forearms.

The sheath of salty liquid that filled her eyes impaired her sight even more, and while her vision was finally starting to adjust to the darkness, she still couldn't make out where she was. Sliding her palms out in front of her and to the sides, she searched for something, praying that she would either find her phone, or someone would hear her cries for help.

Her hand made contact with something soft, and thinking she had found her purse, a sigh of relief washed over her. However, when she attempted to pull it closer, it barely budged. Trina yanked again, but instead of it sliding in her direction, the weight of what she held onto pulled her forward.

Her hands still shook as she apprehensively stretched her arms out, feeling and searching to identify what she was touching. The object was rounded, like a log, but with a softness that started to concern her.

Her chest tightened, and she felt her brow cinch. She pulled herself up to a sitting position and wiped the tears from her face with the back of her hand before proceeding.

She held her breath, not wanting her hands to confirm her fear of what it was.

She couldn't really see, so she slammed her eyes shut and pulled her lips between her teeth, biting down on them as she searched the darkness in front of her. The cylindrical object was attached to something larger, and she felt the wet fabric that coated another body.

Frantically, she felt for the chest. The soft mounds of flesh that her hands skimmed over indicated that it was a female.

"Hello!" She shook the body. "Are you okay? Hello?"

No response.

"You have to wake up!" She continued to shake the body as she screamed out, "Oh God!"

She felt the body again. Slowing her pace, Trina released her hold on the limp arm. Her hands shook so hard that she felt the vibration coursing through them.

She didn't want to know, yet she had to be sure. Her hand slowly approached the female's body, stopping on her chest. There was no upward movement, and she forced her hand to the face to feel for a breath, but there was nothing.

"Oh. Fuck. Oh God! No!" She couldn't, but she had to continue. She took the arm into her lap and felt for a pulse, but again, there was nothing. Trina pushed the arm off her and scooted back. "Help!" her throat scratched out. "Please! Help!"

The dark alley brightened ever so slightly, and she looked up and saw lights flicker on in more than one window. She yelled again, hoping that they heard her.

"Help me! Call the police!" Her screams continued, over and over again, until her throat wouldn't allow it anymore.

⛤

It felt like an eternity that she sat there, crying out for help. Her body quivered from shock, fear, and the chill of the night on her wet clothing. Trina was alone, next to the body of a faceless woman who was not lucky enough to still have her life.

The sirens in the distance grew louder as they approached, and Trina tucked her head into her knees and held on for dear life. Sobbing, she rocked herself back and forth.

The vehicles she'd heard screeched to a sudden stop, at what was most likely, the end of the alley. She didn't want to lift her head to look. It hurt too much. At last, she could see the flashing blue and red lights illuminating the backs of her eyelids.

Several sets of footsteps pounded the pavement in her direction, and she listened to the familiar sounds of clinking and heavy leather belts rubbing against the legs of the approaching officers. It was a sound she wasn't sure she welcomed. She discerned the unsnapping of the gun holsters, counting at least three. There may have been more disguised by the sound of slides racking and the rounds being chambered in their standard issue Glock 45s.

The static sound of a radio switched on and off. "We have some kind of two-forty. Possible one-eighty-seven."

Ckkshsh... "Ten-four. Are you in need of an eleven-forty?"

"Yes, eleven-forty-one. You might want to send

over two buses. ASAP!" *Ckshhhh*.

The static cut in and out as the man's voice grew louder. Trina knew he was confirming that they needed an ambulance.

"Police! Hands up!"

Trina could sense that the officers were slowly getting closer to her, but their voices sounded as if they were miles away. Their words were muffled by the sounds of her whimpering.

"We are approaching you with our guns drawn. Please show us your hands!" The voice was loud and demanding. "We are here to help you, but we need you to show us your hands."

"Sir?" a woman's voice trailed behind him.

"I see it, Clark. Fall back and get some blankets and a first aid kit. I already called in a bus."

The man's voice was almost on top of her. Trina heard what he said, but she was about as frozen as a person who couldn't stop shaking could be.

"Ma'am, I am approaching you. Please, if you can hear me, please show me your hands. Are you injured?"

In Trina's mind, she could see herself releasing her legs and showing him her hands, but she couldn't connect the command to the action.

A second set of footsteps and the clambering of a gun belt rattled around behind her, and a sudden shot of pain on her shoulder jolted Trina into motion. She was too disoriented to realize someone had put their hand on her shoulder.

"Take it easy."

The man was no longer raising his voice, and she could feel him beside her.

"Here you go, sir," the female officer's voice sounded.

"I am going to put this blanket around you. My name is Officer O'Neil."

He draped the blanket over her shoulders, and the pressure from the shroud felt like pins and needles on her flesh. She wasn't sure if it was from an injury, or if her skin was so cold that it had become numb.

"Can you tell us your name?" he asked.

She slowly lifted her head. The intensity of the flashlights assaulted her eyes, causing her to blink repeatedly. Trying to focus was a struggle.

"Trina, Trina Hayes," her voice was just a whisper.

"Trina, can you tell me what happened here?" O'Neil questioned.

"Sir, we have a DOA here. The bus should be here any minute."

"DOA?" Trina's voice cracked.

With trepidation, her head turned to the officer who had said it. She looked at his face and couldn't help but think of how young he appeared. He must have been in his early twenties, but he looked like an oversized teenager.

How she wished she had kept her eyes on him instead of investigating her surroundings.

Her eyes fell down hard on a blood soaked body, only inches from where she sat. She scanned the woman's figure quickly, looking for injuries, and most importantly, her identity. Was it someone she knew?

Trina's hand escaped the shroud of fabric that was draped over her shoulders to cover her mouth as she gasped for air. She tried to back away, but she collided with Officer O'Neil.

"Do you know her?" he asked.

Trina turned into him and shook her head. He put his arm around her but did not squeeze her into an embrace. There was nothing personal about it, just a reassurance that she was in safe arms.

"The first bus is here, sir." Clark called over to O'Neil.

"Okay, let's get the squad over here and see if we can move Miss Hayes. Smith, you call in for the medical examiner to get down here." He commanded the two other officers that were standing beside the body, "Do a sweep of the area and tape off the scene."

"Miss Hayes, this is Officer Clark, I am going to have her ask you a few questions while the rescue squad checks you for injuries. I will be right here if you have any questions."

"No," she pulled on his arm as she looked up at

him for the first time, "stay. You can ask me the questions."

The pupils of his eyes were so big they looked black. His head was clean-shaven, and he wore a thick mustache over his top lip. She almost laughed to herself. He looked like a cop, one with the shoulders of a linebacker.

"If you insist." He rearranged his feet, so he could balance in a squatting position off to her side, leaving enough room for the medic to get in and do a quick assessment of her before they took her to the hospital. "Can you tell me what happened here tonight?"

"No. What time is it?"

"It is currently three am. What are you doing out at this hour?"

"I'm not sure. The last thing I recall is laying on the couch to catch up on my DVR list. I don't even remember leaving the house."

"So… are you telling me that you were taken from your home?" O'Neil asked.

"I don't think that is what I am telling you. I am

telling you that I don't remember anything after that. I would assume that I must have dozed off."

The medic flashed a light in front of her eyes, asking her to follow the beam, and grasped her wrist to check her heart rate.

"Excuse me, officer. Ma'am, I need you to remove the blanket, so I can see your arms and legs. Can you tell me where the pain is coming from?"

"Everywhere." Trina tossed back the blanket and looked down at her clothes. The last she recalled, she'd had on matching thermals with tiny flowers on them. She now wore jeans and what had once been a white sweater. It was torn through on the sleeves and covered in dirt and blood—a lot of blood.

"Whose...?" Her hand shook as she lifted it to touch her stomach. "Whose blood is this?"

CHAPTER ONE

"WHAT?" DEX GRUMBLED AT THE sound of his phone vibrating on the nightstand beside him.

Ignoring it, he tried to roll away from the mind-shattering noise and made contact with the warm body of the unsuspecting lady he must have picked up the night before. Sighing, he lifted his fingers to the bridge of his nose, squeezing in hopes that it would help alleviate the mounting pressure.

His cell phone was relentless, and he heard it beep twice, notifying him that he had a voicemail before the ringing started again.

"Alright, alright, I'm coming." He kicked his feet off the side of the bed and sat up, reluctantly opening his eyes. He looked down at the floral print carpeting and matching window dressings, realizing that he'd never actually made it home the night before.

Dex reached over to the nightstand, and instead of picking up his cell, he grabbed the pack of smokes and the Zippo that had once belonged to his grandfather. When he clicked open the small metal canister, he welcomed the smell of lighter fluid as he lit up a cigarette.

He sucked in a long stream of hot relief. There weren't a whole lot of things better than that first drag of a cigarette in the morning. He knew people thought that it was a death wish, but it made him feel alive. That, and attempting to keep the people of his little town safe, reminded him that he had something worth waking up for each morning.

He looked over his shoulder and enjoyed the view. He had no idea what her name was, or what her face looked like, but that was probably for the best. He wouldn't have a problem remembering her just as she was. Her soft creamy skin curved out and around the little bit of blanket left draped over a sliver of her body. He was tempted to run his hand over her ample, heart shaped ass, but he had a feeling he wasn't going to have time for that. His phone didn't blow up that often, and the few friends he had knew not to call him that early.

How early is it? He took in another long drag, swirling the smoke around his mouth before sucking it into his lungs. The phone sounded again, ringing for the third time, and he wondered how the chick didn't wake up from the ruckus.

Dex left the cigarette between his teeth and grabbed the phone. Leaning forward and resting his elbows on his knees, he swiped his fingers across the screen to wake it up. After he pulled another drag, he watched the embers shorten the paper casing before using his left hand to remove the cigarette from his lips as he blew the smoke out of his nose.

He debated on whether or not to listen to the voicemails. He knew the extension from the first call was from his partner's desk and the second and third had been from his cell.

"Shit." It had been a while since Johnny had called him that many times in a row. At that hour, and calling from both lines, it most likely meant that he was on his way to a crime scene.

Dex found his jeans on the floor beside the bed, but he was unable to remember if he had worn underwear the day before. Either way, his head hurt too badly to bend down and look for them. He stood up, pulled them on while being careful with the zipper, and put his phone and smokes in his back pockets. Searching for his keys, he found them on the table.

Luckily for him, he had not taken off his long-sleeve shirt the day before. He threw on his concert tee overtop the other shirt, and at least he didn't look as if he were wearing the same clothes. It was a fashion statement meant for a guy who wasn't on his way to work, but he was sure the alternative was not going to be an option.

He went into the bathroom and relieved himself of whatever whiskey remained in his system. Happy to find a complimentary tube of toothpaste on the counter, he put some on the tip of his finger and rubbed it along his teeth, doing the best he could with what he had.

Dex grabbed his keys and considered waking his entertainment from the previous night before leaving, but his phone rang again. He hit the green button to answer the call and closed the door behind him.

"Johnny, seriously, this better be good!" It was too early for pleasantries.

"I wouldn't exactly say it's good. Meet me at Moe's Diner. I am approaching the scene now." The call went dead.

Dex grabbed his quilted flannel, slid his smokes into his breast pocket, stepped out of his black F-150, and slammed the heavy door behind him. An array of emergency vehicles littered the parking lot, a sure indication that he was embarking on more than the usual breaking and entering call.

He shoved his hands into his pockets, to keep the chill

off the tips of his fingers. Dex followed the trail of officers, nodding at them as he walked past looking for his partner. Johnny was usually the lead detective in that part of the woods.

"Detective Preston." One of the uniformed men held out his hand for a shake. "The victim is at the rear of the diner. Detective Harrington is already back there. He said to keep an eye out for you. A few of the guys have money on whether or not you would beat the medical examiner here."

Dex closed his eyes before slowly nodding his chin in the direction of the uniform. "That's cute, you know, you're a real peach."

"Yup. As sweet as they come." His smirk was thick from the sarcasm. "The crime scene was intact upon my arrival. As far as we know, there has been no tampering with the body or any of the evidence." The uniformed officer led the way around the bright yellow police tape.

"Nice for you to grace us with your beauty this morning." Johnny never had a simple greeting.

Johnny Harrington was Dex Preston's partner, and had been since he'd made detective. He trusted him with his life, but there wasn't a day that went by that Johnny didn't bust his chops about something.

"Well, someone had to bring it. We can't all be brains, ya know." He snickered. "Shit, you know I only went to bed a few hours ago."

"Yeah and how much of that time was actually spent sleeping?"

"Johnny, it's like five-thirty in the morning. Maybe I'll let you know when I wake up." He stretched his long arms out behind him. "So what do we have here?"

"Stabbing. We have not identified the body yet. I have two officers combing the area, looking for a handbag or cell phone."

"Defensive wounds?" Dex asked as he squatted down in front of the covered body.

"Doesn't look like it. We are going to have to wait for the medical examiner's report. The victim is Caucasian female, mid to late twenties. They said the medical examiner should be here in a few minutes to take the body in. She is going to try to rush this through for us."

"Because she is so busy investigating other murders?" Dex interjected with a twist of the lips.

He lifted the white plastic tarp off the body. The victim had on a skirt that covered her knees and white stockings, splattered with crimson stains. The area was covered with so much blood that the metallic scent coated the back of Dex's throat, and he could almost taste it on his tongue.

"You said this was a stabbing, this woman has been butchered. You think they cut her throat before or after they attempted to gut her?" Dex dropped the cloth.

"I don't know, but for as much blood as there is on the body, there is not much around her. How long do you think she's been out here?"

"I don't know, but Mrs. Sinclair should be able to tell us. If she ever gets here."

"You know she hates it when you call her that."

"Well, that is how I know her, her doctorate, or whatever, hasn't changed that she is still Mrs. Sinclair to me."

"Lay off today. I don't want this thing carried out longer than need be. Be glad this shit doesn't normally happen around here. You and I, my friend, are going to have a shit ton of paperwork to do."

"I'm too hungry for this shit. Is this diner open, or did they shut the place down? We need to get some food before I pass out. You're buying, by the way."

"And why is that, Preston?"

"You woke my ass up way too early, that's why. I got lunch, don't get your panties in wad."

"Moe's is open. He is the one that called it in this morning, found the body when he opened the back door to take out some trash." Johnny ran his fingers over his short flattop of gray hair. Johnny was all cop.

"Hot breakfast sounds good, but we still need to chalk off the body and make sure all the photographs are properly taken and that there are enough. That shit pisses me off when I try to work a cold case and there are not enough pictures. At this point with technology, you don't have the cost of developing them, so just take the fucking pictures." Johnny pushed down at the edges of his mustache.

"You question him yet? Moe, that is." Dex pulled out his pack of smokes and realized he was down to the last cigarette in the small, red box.

"Nah. The first responder took a quick statement, and I quote, 'he didn't touch nothing.' Moe lost another waitress last week after she decided to move to the city. Another one that thought this town was too small for her. Figured, with him being short-handed, we could call him after breakfast, when things settle down."

"Any other witnesses or potential witnesses?" Dex flipped open his lighter and shut it a few times before he slid his cigarette box back in his pocket.

"Nope."

"Weapon retrieval?" Dex was getting annoyed with the one-word answers.

"Nope."

"Ok, so let me get this straight. We have no identity, no witnesses, no interviews, and no weapon."

Johnny nodded in agreement.

"So how could we possibly have paperwork to do? We have nothing. This shit is not going to fly with the captain." Dex had a sourness in his stomach that needed to be addressed. It could have been from the stress, or it could have been from the previous night's whiskey on an empty stomach.

"Well, we got an awful lot of uniforms here for nothing. What time is the M.E going to get here?"

"Any minute."

"She is late for everything. Guaranteed she has a fresh cup of coffee with her. Which, I need, by the way." Dex felt for his pack of smokes again but wasn't sure when he would make it to the store. No one else smoked, so he was going to have to wait for that too.

"Let's start getting some of these uniforms out of here. We don't need to draw this much attention. You know some of these people have nothing better to do than be nosey and gossip. These guys have more important things to do than racking up more overtime. That's our job." Johnny smirked.

Dex knew Johnny's weak attempt at humor was his way of coping. The case was going to take more than the nine-to-five they were accustomed to. He didn't miss being on the street in a uniform. He never much liked handing out tickets for things that he had always hated getting tickets for before he was a cop.

He knew that everything had its purpose, and whatnot, but there were some aspects of his job he wasn't big on.

Saving and helping people, those were the reasons he'd become a cop, not to worry about what kind of license plate cover someone has.

"Morning, boys." Dr. Shea Sinclair, the county medical examiner, sauntered up with her green and white to-go cup.

"Sinclair." Dex nodded to avoid having to give her a title.

Her long brown hair was pulled back in a ponytail beneath her blue cap, and her matching blue coat had her title emblazoned across the back. She dropped her small duffle bag next to the body.

"You're up early, Dex," she said as she squatted down to open the bag.

"Who says I'm not still up from last night?" He didn't appreciate her innuendo.

"That would explain the mature attire that you chose for today. Any idea how long the body has been here?"

"Not really. Moe said that she wasn't here last night. He said they closed up just after eleven pm," Harrington answered her, giving Dex a set of hard eyeballs. "He said he didn't recall seeing her in the diner for dinner either."

"Looks like I will have easy access to the liver, or at least what might be left of it," she commented as she lifted the white tarp. She slid a long thermometer into the woman's bloody abdomen. "I've never seen a body this bad around here."

"You're telling us. We got a real sicko on our hands here." Dex ran his fingers through his tousled brown hair.

"Looks like, based on the temp, I am going to estimate time of death between twelve, and four am. So this body is fairly fresh, especially with the cold fall temperatures out here. We can certainly assume that the knife wounds were the cause of death, but I will have to make a thorough examination before I can make that official." She slid the used thermometer into a sealed plastic bag before returning it to her small duffle bag.

"Are we good to move the body then?" Johnny asked.

"Yep. You can have her brought down to the morgue. I'll be by there after I get all my patients seen. Maybe six pm."

"You wear so many hats, Shea," Dex commented. It may have come out a bit more brash than he intended.

"Please, call me Dr. Sinclair when we are working. It isn't professional to call me by my first name." She tossed her bag over her shoulder.

"So I guess I shouldn't ask how little Abigail is or if you want to join us for breakfast... right?" Dex reached in his pocket and pulled out his last cigarette. He couldn't wait any longer. He tipped his head to the side as he flipped the brass cap of his lighter in front of his face but didn't lose eye contact with her for a second.

She just looked at him and rubbed her lips together.

In his peripheral, he saw Johnny turn away from the

scene. "Yup, that's what I thought. I guess we will see you later, Dr. Sinclair." Dex turned as he blew out a puff of smoke.

"Dex, wait..." her voice trailed off in the distance.

CHAPTER TWO

THERE WAS A CHILL IN the air that had come unseasonably early for that part of Oregon. Trina embraced the early onset of fall and cherished the colors of the ever-changing seasons. She had spent a few years living in Florida, but she'd missed having the opportunity to bundle up in big sweaters and fluffy scarves. The temperatures had not dropped quite that low yet, but she still needed a light jacket.

There were days that she missed the bustle of living in downtown Portland, but the memories, or rather the lack of memories had become too much of a constant burden. It had been about a year since she'd decided a more rural environment would be a safer place to live, both physically and emotionally. She'd moved into her grandfather's old farmhouse, which had been bequeathed to her when she'd turned twenty-five. She'd held onto it, not knowing for sure if it would be worth fixing up or not. The property values in the small town of Hawk Creek were nothing to get excited about, so selling it wasn't a big motivator.

It had been a tranquil retreat for her growing up, so it had seemed like the best option for her to move there. It wasn't much, but it was somewhere to go and explore until she decided where she belonged or found a better option.

She pulled her new economy car into the teacher's parking lot at the only elementary school in town. It was a short walk to the diner, and she enjoyed the early morning exercise. Trina flipped her collar on her coat, deciding to leave her bags in the car and grab them on her way back from a quick breakfast. She grabbed her purse and tossed her keys in the small bag.

Sometimes, she couldn't believe the extreme contrast between the fast-paced community she used to live in and the tiny town. The streets and businesses would have been filled to the brim by then in downtown Portland. In Hawk Creek, there were only a few folks just starting to drive to work, and it was too early for any of the shops that lined Main Street to be open.

She lowered her head as she walked down the street, looking through her handbag for her cherry-flavored lip balm. She'd accidentally purchased strawberry the other day at Simm's Pharmacy. Of course she found that one, but she had to have the cherry. Strange, because she could have sworn that she'd tossed the strawberry one in the trash the day before.

She didn't like to wear a lot of make up to work, and it never really made sense for her to wear lipstick to teach six and seven year olds. She suffered through the strawberry lip balm, it was either that, or she was going to start picking at her dry lips. A habit she wished she didn't have.

Breakfast was one of her favorite meals, but her least favorite to fix for herself. Moe's Diner had become an early morning staple for her. That morning, she hadn't been sure if she would have the fortitude to drag herself out of bed. She was surprised how early she'd managed to wake up after her night of drinking.

Trina had thought for sure she would awake to a hangover and exhaustion. It wasn't often that she got drunk, but she must have had too much because she didn't remember falling asleep. Either way, she was going to need a hot tea and a short stack of pancakes before work, to get her in the mood for a full day. The children in her class had an endless supply of energy.

Trina decided not to take the shortcut through the back alley and walked around the block. The twirling blue and red lights of two patrol cars immediately caught her attention. There were quite a number of emergency vehicles in front of Moe's Diner, more than she had ever seen in the short amount of time that she had lived in

Hawk Creek. She was concerned that something happened and the restaurant would be closed.

She approached the front steps of the restaurant and was relieved to see the orange open sign shining bright in the front window. The smell of fresh brewed coffee instantly made her feel more awake. She knew whatever was going on couldn't have been that big of a deal, if the eggs and toast were still on the griddle.

The bells jingled on the door as she entered the small eatery. Most of the tables were taken, which was okay for her. She didn't mind, in fact, she preferred to sit at the long breakfast bar that stretched the length of the small restaurant. It meant that she would always have a hot cup of coffee or enough hot water for her tea.

She took a seat at the edge of the bar closest to the kitchen. She was no fool, the waitress had to walk past her enough times that she wouldn't go ignored if she needed anything. There was a buzz in the building, but it was different from most days. The hum was more of a fuzz, since everyone was whispering back and forth.

"What can I get you, honey?" Becky was there every morning except Sunday because she wouldn't work on the Lord's day.

"Hot tea with lemon and honey, please. And I will have a short stack of pancakes. Is he making anything special today?"

"Not sure what you consider special. If you want your pancakes fancy, he's got blueberries or chocolate chips. Oh yeah, and we always got bananas." Becky snapped her gum as she scanned the rest of the room, taking inventory of the patrons' meals.

"I'll take blueberry, please," Trina said as she stood up to take off her coat. She left her purse on the counter and hung her coat by the front door.

Becky wrote out the ticket for the food and slid it across the food service window to Moe. He was approaching his early seventies, but that didn't stop him from coming in to run the business every day. She turned and served Trina a small metal pot with hot water and a mug with a tea bag set inside.

"So, what is all the commotion about out there?" Trina couldn't help but be a little nosy. "Did some vandals spray paint the back of the building again? I swear these teenagers need new hobbies."

"I wish," Becky spoke in a very low tone and hid her mouth behind her order pad. "I think Moe found a dead body back there this morning when he went to take out the trash."

Trina stopped stirring her tea and looked up. "There must be some kind of mistake. That kind of stuff doesn't happen here. That's why I moved here."

"I don't know, sweetie. I hope I'm wrong." She turned to

grab a pot of coffee from the burner behind her and made her way around the small diner to top off some empty coffee cups.

The spoon slipped and fell through Trina's sweaty fingers. She worked hard to surround herself with an environment that stimulated her mind with things that were not so dark. She had to come up with a scenario that made sense and would not cause her sense of security to unravel.

There were some fairly angry teens living in town that had a history of acting out. Everyone knew who they were, but Trina was sure that they were most likely the victims of their own bad circumstances. She tried not to judge people she didn't know, but she considered that maybe they were more disturbed than the rumors gave way to. Maybe the kids had killed a dog or something.

Animal cruelty wasn't something that she took lightly, but the alternative was not something she wanted to let her curiosity run away with.

The bells jingled on the door as it opened, letting in a short draft of cool air that tickled the hairs on the back of Trina's neck. She welcomed the distraction and turned to look back at the door.

In strode a man that looked as if he needed a cup of coffee and good night of sleep. Trina thought there was something familiar about him, but she didn't want to stare, so she turned back around to take a sip of her lukewarm tea.

She pulled up the sleeve of her gray sweater to check the time. It wasn't even six o'clock, and she didn't need to be at the school until seven thirty. She normally would have checked the time on her cell, but she knew from her search for the lip balm that she had left it in her car.

"You running late for something?"

She heard his question at the same time she felt him graze her arm as he sat beside her. She looked at him without a response, unsure he'd actually directed the question at her. His hair was messy, and he needed a shave, but his piercing blue eyes captivated her.

"So not only are you sitting in my seat, but you are rude enough not to answer my question," he huffed half-heartedly.

"Me?" she asked pointing to herself.

"Hey, Beck's, can I get two belly busters and two joes to go? I will take one for here too." He waved at the waitress as she walked by with an arm full of dishes.

"You got it, Dex."

"How am I sitting in your seat?" Trina asked the stranger sitting by her side.

"I usually sit there."

"That's funny. I have been here almost every morning for several months, and I have yet to ever see you. Either that, or you weren't memorable enough to notice." Trina snickered right to his face, her eyes ablaze with mischief. If he wanted to be snarky, she could return the favor.

"Dex, Dex Preston." He nodded his head and extended his arm in front of her.

"Nice to meet you, I think. My name is Trina. Just Trina." She didn't know him from Adam, and she sure wasn't about to hand out her last name to some creep at the diner.

Trina couldn't help but notice that he smelled of stale cigarettes and a faint stench of what was probably left over booze—and then it hit her.

"Did you have a good time at Kagley's last night?" she turned and asked him.

"Excuse me?" Dex fidgeted in his seat.

"When you walked in, I thought you looked a little bit familiar, but didn't think I knew you. Now I remember, though. I saw you at the bar last night. You were sitting by yourself." She knew that she might have had one too many drinks because there were a few parts of the night that she couldn't clearly remember.

"Oh yeah, I was there. I must not have seen you, or you weren't memorable enough to notice." He fidgeted with the saltshaker as they both waited for Becky to come back out of the kitchen.

"Touché. I don't usually sit at the bar. I usually just go there for take-out," Trina said, thinking that she maybe should not have mentioned anything about the night before.

The swinging door opened, and out came Becky with a full tray of breakfast orders. She stopped and dropped off a plate of pancakes. "I'll be back with your coffee in a sec, hun. Or you can grab it yourself. I know you're working. I don't want to keep you."

Trina squeezed the rest of the juice out of the lemon over her pancakes and watched the Dex guy get up and walk behind the stainless breakfast bar to fix himself a cup of coffee. His plaid shirt was just short enough to give her a good view of his round ass as he leaned forward to fetch a cup and saucer from the shelf below the coffee urn.

"You need more coffee, doll?"

"I am actually drinking tea, but it is cold. I can wait for Becky to come back." She used her knife and fork to slice away tiny bites of fluffy pancakes.

"I got this. I've been coming here since I was a kid."

He did seem to know where everything was. Within a few seconds, she had a fresh cup, tea bag, and a new pot of hot water.

"Thank you very much," she said as she dropped the tea bag into her new mug, "So you're working right now?"

"Indeed. Just grabbing breakfast for me and my partner before we head down to the station."

He apparently took his coffee black because she didn't

notice him put any cream or sugar in his mug. "You're a cop?" she asked wiping a drop of syrup from the corner of her mouth with her napkin.

"For the past fifteen years. How about you?" he asked.

"School teacher, first grade." She felt less concerned about telling him about herself, knowing he was a cop. "That is a crazy outfit you have on for work, what are you, undercover or something?"

"No." He chuckled. "Late night last night. I don't normally go in until the second shift. I am a detective, so I don't wear a uniform anyway. This coffee is strong today, you mind passing me one of those colored packet things?"

Trina reached over to the sugar caddy to hand him one of the blue sugar substitutes. She turned her body faster than she realized and the back of her hand caught the edge of her teacup, sending it flying in his direction. The cup missed him, but he wasn't lucky enough to avoid the hot, liquid content.

"Oh my God, I am so sorry. I am not usually this clumsy." Trina grabbed at the paper napkin dispenser and started to blot at his crotch until she realized what she was doing. "Oh, I... I'm sorry. I... here."

She handed him a stack of napkins as her cheeks flushed into a reddish hue. She could feel the burn at the tops of her cheeks. Dex looked over at her, and she held her breath waiting for his reaction.

His eyes squinted at the sunlight beaming from behind her, his lips curling up as he gave his head a short shake. "It's okay, really. It's not that bad." He laughed a little. "I needed to take a shower anyway. I always keep a change of fresh clothes in the ole locker."

"Really?" she asked, her voice barely audible.

"Really." He tossed the pile of damp napkins on the counter and looked around to grab the attention of the waitress. Lucky for them, Becky was walking out of the kitchen with a white paper bag.

"Uh, what happened here?" she asked as she placed the bag on the counter.

"No biggie. I spilled her tea on my lap. Can you grab her another when you get a chance, please?" Dex asked.

Trina looked over at him, and he shrugged his shoulders.

"Okie dokie," Becky turned and poured out hot coffee in a couple of to-go cups. "These are on Moe today. He said he will see you later."

"Thanks, Becks." He tossed a five on the counter for her. "Johnny and I'll be back at closing. If you're not working that late, it would be helpful if you could come back, so we can talk."

"Sure thing, Dex." She slid the five in her dirty, black apron and walked back into the kitchen with Trina's dirty plates.

"Nice to meet you, Trina. I don't usually do breakfast, but maybe I'll see you around town." He stacked the two coffee cups, carrying them in one hand while he put the white bag under his arm, so he could extend his hand again for another formal shake.

"Sure. Nice to meet you too, Detective." She smiled at him, wishing she had put on lipstick.

CHAPTER THREE

THE BELLS ON THE DOOR jingled behind Dex as he exited Moe's diner. He was tempted to look back over his shoulder to see if Trina was watching him leave. Too bad Johnny was parked in front, waving his hands and honking the horn.

"Take it easy," Dex said as he tapped on the hood of Johnny's police issue, black Impala. "I'm riding in with you." As he slid into the passenger side and sat the cardboard cups into the drink holder, he added, "I'll grab my truck when we come back to get Moe's and Becky's official statements."

"What the hell were you doing in there anyway?" Johnny looked over at Dex as he pulled away. "I really hope you didn't piss yourself."

"Very funny. Some chick spilled her tea on my lap. I was planning on hitting the gym and the showers when I got to the precinct anyway." Dex opened the paper bag and pulled out his sandwich. "You want yours?"

"Fuck it, might as well. You know there won't be any time for working out today, pretty boy, but I will cover for you while you shower and change. You look and smell like shit," Johnny said with his mouth half-full of the meat and egg sandwich.

"Why do they make the tops to these to-go cups so fucking hard to get and stay open?" Dex asked as he pulled the top off, tossed it in the bag, and sipped on the hot, black beverage. "So what did I miss?"

"Not much. The body has been taken down to the morgue, but we are going to have to wait for Dr. Sinclair to do a work up for us. I got one uniform stationed at the scene to keep an eye on it in case we have to go back and double check anything." He pushed a few buttons on the dash to get the heat going.

"Our team has been known to miss things before," his words were muffled into this cup as he took a sip. "We really need to identify this body. I can't believe her shit didn't turn up."

"I know. Maybe we will get lucky and someone will call in a missing persons report," Johnny responded handing him the empty ball of aluminum foil.

"That is not likely. Most people don't realize that their loved ones are missing until after at least a day or two have passed. They know something is off that first day, but talk themselves into a logical explanation about their whereabouts. Fucking sad shit, man. Not to mention the fact that if she has only been missing since last night, there won't be a MPR."

"Well we don't have much to go on or investigate. This has been the only death like this around here, but we can search some of the databases and see if we get anything that has the same M.O." Dex tuned the vents away from him. He wasn't a big fan of the cold, but he really couldn't stand hot air blowing on his face, be it from a vent or someone talking out their ass.

Johnny pulled around to the back of the police station. They didn't have designated parking or entrances at their small time operation, but their workout room and lockers were at the rear of the building.

"You should get a head start. I am going to make a call. I hope you are done by the time I come in." Johnny pulled out his cell and opened the tab on his coffee with no problem.

Dex twisted his lips to the side wondering why that never worked for him.

Dex showered and dressed in less than ten minutes. He actually had to wait for Johnny to come in before they went out onto the floor. He knew, the second they showed their faces, their captain would want answers.

They only had four detectives in town, Linder and Harts had their desks on the other side of the precinct. Captain Kard insisted that they had their own cases, and if she put the detectives all together, they would get distracted. Dex couldn't complain. He wasn't a fan of Linder. He wasn't a bad guy, at least not that he had witnessed firsthand. Something about him just rubbed Dex the wrong way, especially while hungover.

As soon as they sat down Johnny's phone buzzed.

"Detective Harrington," he answered the call as if he didn't know it was an in-house page. "Yeah, boss. We will be right in."

"She's ready for us," he said, looking at his watch. "It's only seven-thirty. She must have gotten called in on this too."

"Yeah, she's got someone in here that keeps her in the loop. Look how quickly she was on us. She has to know we have no paperwork done yet, right?"

"I don't know, man. Let's just get this over with, so we can get to work, we are going to need something to show her. And for heaven's sake, chew some gum. You still smell like cheap whiskey and cigarettes. You need to cut that shit out, by the way." Johnny slapped his hand on his desk as he tossed a pack of cinnamon gum to Dex.

"Mind your business. I don't tell you how to parent your kids, and I certainly don't need you treating me like one." He threw the gum back on Johnny's desk. "I hate cinnamon gum. Shit burns my tongue."

One thing was for sure, Dex liked that there was a long enough trip to the captain's office that she couldn't watch them from her desk. It was bad enough that his desk was butted face to face with Johnny's. He didn't much like being watched when he needed to complete a task.

Detective work involved a lot more paperwork than he'd ever imagined. He laughed at how romanticized television dramas were able to make his job look. Most of the calls that they went on were domestic disputes, theft, or drug related incidents, which often times involved the first two.

Captain Kard kept the water cooler and coffee pot just outside her office. It had floor to ceiling windows and doors, so she could see out over their small precinct. She didn't mind anyone drinking fluids. She actually encouraged it and made sure that they had a professional coffee brewing station and a machine that you could pop little pods into for quick cups of coffee.

Dex turned his nose up at the fancy coffee machine. Coffee was meant to be brewed so you could drink it black. It was supposed to wake you up, not take you for a gondola ride while vacationing in Venice. He would be grabbing a cup from the old fashioned drip machine on his way out of her office.

"Detectives, early morning today, huh?" All five feet of her stood up to greet them as they walked through the door. "You can close that behind you."

"Yes, ma'am." Dex said. He didn't like authority, but he respected it. He had to, it was his job, and he knew that he wanted the same thing.

"Please tell me that you have a lead or something to go on to help us identify this victim?" She walked out from behind her desk and leaned against it in a way that almost allowed her to sit on the edge.

"I wish I could say that we had something concrete, but that would be a lie. We need to wait to get back the results from the M.E. later tonight. The victim didn't have any identification on her. So—"

"So what? Get over and print the body. I am still trying to understand why that wasn't done at the scene. Run them through IAFIS and see if you get a hit." The captain crossed her arms and waited for a response.

"We were actually going to do that right after we checked for any matching missing persons reports." Johnny was quick to respond.

"Well, get it done before the word spreads that we can't do our job. I don't need the county sheriff sending in one of his special units to clean up our mess. This is our town, and we will get the recognition for closing this case and giving this woman's family peace of mind." She slapped her hands together. "So that wraps this up. Off you go."

Dex and Johnny turned to exit the office.

"Prints first, yeah?" She stood up straight and uncrossed her arms. She took the few strides to her closed office door and opened it for the two men, signaling them to exit.

"Yes, ma'am. Prints then missing persons," Johnny clarified and confirmed as they walked out.

⭒

"You know I was totally going to make myself a cup of coffee on the way out of her office," Dex said.

"Yeah? She would have had your ass on the chopping block. Today might be the one day you don't have time for coffee but need it the most."

Johnny was right. Dex was going strong, even with the lack of sleep, but he knew that the energy would start to fade if he didn't keep his caffeine intake on a steady influx. He really wasn't prepared for this kind of day. He'd known it could happen eventually, but he had hoped to coast through without facing that kind of brutality when he'd moved back to Hawk Creek.

"I miss the days when the morgue was located at the precinct," Dex cut the silence.

"I'm not sure that it ever was, and if it was, you probably

aren't old enough to remember that."

"Yeah, maybe I saw it on television and thought it happened. We are lucky we don't have to head out to the State Crime Lab for this." Johnny cracked his window. The air still had a chill to it, but the sun was shining through the windshield, cooking the stale air in the car.

"Maybe we should kick it over to Homicide and Violent Crimes Unit at the County Sheriff's Office. This might be out of our league. I don't want this girl's family to be left without answers to her whereabouts, or worse, without resolution as to who and why someone murdered her." Dex bit the skin around the edges of his thumbnail.

"We are capable, you are a good cop. You need to let things from the past go. We got this," Johnny said with conviction. "We won't stand for this crap in our town."

"Sure man. You're right." Dex moved on to his middle finger as he looked out the passenger window.

"Besides, Captain Kard would never stand for us letting this go. I don't have a lot longer until I hit my pension, I am not pissing her off now."

"I really need a pack of smokes. You think we could stop at the mini-mart? We can grab coffee too," Dex requested.

"Let's get the prints first, I don't really want to drink my coffee in the presence of dead bodies. We can stop after and grab lunch to take back to the station with us. Besides, we are already here," he said as he pulled into a designated parking spot for law officials.

The county morgue was located at the local hospital, with a separate room designated for bodies that needed to be autopsied or were left unidentified. The room was kept separate from normal hospital deaths and the locals that had died from natural causes.

They took the elevator down to the lowest level of the hospital. The morgue was located at the furthest point, past the radiology rooms, and even past the storage rooms. A receptionist worked the small desk just outside the elevator, helping to direct people to their destination. Dex was glad that he hadn't had to come to the morgue often enough for her face to be familiar.

"Good afternoon. How can I help you boys?" She was a tiny plump woman that looked as if she must have been close to eighty, and she moved almost as slow as she spoke.

Dex admired her tenacity to still get up every day and go to work. "Detectives Harrington and Preston." They both showed her their badges. "We are here to sign in to the morgue."

"Sure thing, honey." She reached into the drawer next to her and pulled out a binder. "Just log yourselves in here. Do you need me to call down a doctor or the medical examiner?"

"No, sugar. We have access keys." Dex winked at her as

he signed in. "Are you here every day?"

"I am here Monday through Thursday like clockwork." She smiled at him.

"Do you take your coffee as sweet as your smile?" Dex had a way with the ladies, and age was no deterrent to his charm.

Her pale wrinkled cheeks turned pink. "I do." She giggled a little, closing the binder." You boys need anything, you just let me know."

"Thank you, ma'am. You have a good afternoon now." Johnny was never without his schoolboy manners. "What is wrong with you?" he asked Dex, slapping him on the arm as they walked down the long hall.

"What do you mean? Next time we come here, we are bringing her coffee. What is the big deal?"

"You will flirt with anything that has a pair of tits."

Johnny might have been right, but Dex knew that he'd made her smile, and that was really what mattered.

"I don't flirt with anyone under the age of thirty, maybe a few twenty-something's slip through the cracks, but I am no pervert."

They slid their access cards through the small locking mechanism attached to the solid door that read, 'Morgue'.

"Man, I get the creeps every time we have to come here." Dex wasn't afraid to admit it.

"I would be more afraid if it didn't bother you. Death

isn't something we should have to get used to." Johnny opened the next set of doors that read, 'Law Officials Only'. "This won't take us long."

"You sure that Shea isn't going to get mad that we are tampering with the body? What if we corrupt any evidence that might be on the victim's fingertips?" Dex followed behind him.

"I think we are losing time searching for this killer by waiting for her to finish her day of work to come down here and start analyzing the body. I do what my boss tells me to do. The better question is, why didn't anyone do this at the scene?"

"Good question my friend, good question." Dex watched Johnny open the small kit he'd brought with him that had a small pad of ink and a finger print card.

"You can stare at me all you want, you are still helping me do this." He put the kit on the metal counter closest to the refrigerated body drawers. There were only three drawers in the room, so it wasn't hard to figure out which one she was in.

It made sense that the deceased would be in the middle drawer, since it was the only one that was easy to access. No need to bend or reach up to investigate the body. Johnny put on a pair of latex gloves and handed a second pair to Dex. He opened the door and pulled out the sliding metal slab. The victim was still in the black vinyl bag.

"You unzip it, and I will hold the ink pad and paper for you while you press her fingers for the prints," Dex offered, although he wasn't sure that was really the best deal.

The smell of death and decay assaulted his nose with such ferocity, that he was glad that he'd taken Johnny's advice about waiting for the coffee. Even though the odor of disinfectants was strong, it smelled like no one had ever cleaned the place.

"Yeah sure." He opened the bag. Normally, the feet would be at the end with toe tags to label the body with a name or Jane Doe. However, to Dex's surprise they were greeted by long blonde hair.

"What a shame. Her hair is still perfectly styled. It looks as if she was maybe out on a date or something. But what the hell would she have been doing behind Moe's at two or three in the morning. He closes up at ten, and even if he gets late stragglers, I don't think I have ever driven by there and seen the lights on at midnight. You?" Dex asked.

"Nah, but you know if I'm not working, the wife and I are in bed before ten." Johnny made sure the bag was open far enough down to access her hands. "Come over here and let's get this over with."

"Her body is still in rigor, I think that freaks me out the most." Johnny said lifting her arm slightly.

"Do you think we should take some quick pictures of her

clothing? Maybe we can look them up on Google, possibly something she was wearing came from a specialty shop or something?"

"I guess, maybe we should wait for the M.E. to show us what they bagged. I wouldn't know how to look that stuff up," Johnny said as he pressed her fingers onto the card.

"I have dated enough women to know about that kind of stuff."

"Is that what you call it? Dating?"

"I have dated women." Dex dropped the inkpad on the floor. He leaned forward to pick it up and hit his head on the bottom of the drawer. "Crap, for Heaven's sake. Can we get out of here please?"

CHAPTER FOUR

DEX WAS BUSY EMPTYING A packet of sweetener into the cup and gave it a quick swirl. He looked down at his hands, and although he had washed them and used hand sanitizer several times, he felt as if he could still see the stains of death.

"Dex," Johnny called out as he nearly came running over to him at the coffee station. "I got it. She was in the system. Tammy Larazzo, and I have an address. Can someone please explain to me why she wasn't printed at the scene?"

Dex shrugged, it sure wasn't his job. As far as he knew, all the necessary evidence was collected at the scene before the body had been moved. All he could really think about was getting a cup of coffee and some well needed rest. He was still struggling not to drag his ass, but the busier he stayed, the less likely he would start to crash.

"Looks like we got somewhere to be." He pounded the

hot coffee in one, long gulp and tossed the foam cup in the trash. "Does she live here in town?"

"She lives about two miles out from that Karaoke bar you like to go to. I got a cell number and a landline for her. We can call before we drive out there. See if she lives with anyone, or if she has someone looking for her." Johnny handed him a small slip of paper.

"That sounds like a better plan. We will need someone to come down and identify the body as well. Shit." Dex palmed his forehead before he pushed back his hair. He didn't want to deal with the emotional breakdown that would ensue when they came in.

His dark strands of hair kept falling into his eyes. He wished he had enough energy to be pissed that he'd forgotten to replenish his hair products in his gym bag. There hadn't been anyone else to borrow from in the locker room that morning when he showered.

"I got the number for her employer too, some insurance company in Portland. How about you call them, and see if you can set up an appointment for us to meet with her supervisor tomorrow. I will call her home and cell."

"That sounds like a plan. I'm going out for a smoke after this," Dex declared on the walk back to their corner of the station.

"You might as well hold off on that, we might be cruising out to her neighborhood. She wasn't wearing a wedding band, but she is young enough that she might have a roommate or a live-in boyfriend."

They both slid into their desks. Dex wasn't a fan of the way their desks were butted up against each other. He felt as if there was no escaping his partner. He would have preferred they had cubicles, but it wasn't a cubicle kind of job.

"You need this?" Dex asked Johnny, holding up the paper with the list of contact information.

"Nah, I made two copies." He waved his own slip in his hand as he started to dial.

Dex took in a deep breath, and the air created a rough sound as he exhaled through his nostrils and started to dial.

"Thank you for calling Jaguar Insurance. How can I direct your call?"

The high-pitched sound of the receptionist voice went straight to his temples. "Can I speak to someone in Human Resources please?"

"Of course, that would be Victoria Stein. Whom may I say is calling?"

He pictured her having very big blonde hair and bright pink lipstick. "Detective Preston, HCPD."

"Thank you, Detective. Can you please hold? I will transfer you now."

"Yes, I can hold." He wished that the line had been silent,

but instead, an automated message repeated several times about some of the things that their company offered new and long-standing customers. He pinched at the upper bridge of his nose where his eyes met.

"Victoria Stein, can I help you?" Her voice was deeper, more monotone, and a welcomed reprieve from the receptionist and the robot woman that had spoken to him while on hold.

"Yes. This is Detective Dex Preston from Hawk Creek Police Department. May I ask you if Tammy Larazzo is currently employed with you?"

"Detective Preston is it?"

"Yes, ma'am."

"Can I call you back at the precinct in a few minutes? I'm sorry, but I will need to verify whom I am speaking with before I can disclose any information pertaining to our staff."

"Sure. You can call me back at the precinct. I understand. I will talk to you in a few then." Dex hung up the phone and sat back in his chair. The wobbly old thing gave him a little bit of bounce back before he settled back.

"That was quick." Johnny held the receiver away from his face. "She work there?"

"The lady in HR is calling me back here. She wants to verify that I am with the police department before she gives out any information on whether or not anyone is employed with their company."

"Gotcha."

"How about you? Anything?"

"No answer on the cell. After this call, I am going to see if we can triangulate the GPS in her phone. I will talk to the guys in tech services."

The light on Dex's phone started to flash.

"Here we go." He pushed the red light and picked up the receiver. "Detective Preston."

"My apologies for having to call you back. I hope you can understand that it would be against company policy to disclose personal information about an employee without confirming your identity. I figured the easiest way would be to call you direct."

"Yes, that is fine, totally understandable. Thank you for calling me back."

"So you need to know if Tammy Larazzo works here?"

"That's correct, Tammy Larazzo."

"She has worked here for the past two and a half years. We have not had any issues with her. Is everything okay?"

"She is currently employed there. She hasn't shown up for work today, has she?" Dex asked.

"Hold on a second, I will check and see if she is logged in at her desk." She coughed a few times, but she didn't sound sick when she was talking. "She has not logged in, and her status is marked as a no show today."

"Does she make a habit of missing days?" Dex asked.

"Not that her file says. I can certainly check in with her manager if you want."

"No, I didn't think so. I am going to need to make an appointment to come down and speak to you and her direct supervisor tomorrow."

"Did she do something wrong?"

"I am not at liberty to say just yet." Dex took the lighter out of his pocket and leaned forward on his elbows as he repeatedly flipped the top open and shut.

"We can accommodate you any time tomorrow. Just let me know what works best for you."

"We can come in before your regular operating hours to be discrete about our presence. We don't want to alarm any of your employees or make them uncomfortable if it can be avoided."

"We start our day at nine, but most of the managers are here at eight. I can make sure that her manager and I are both here for you. How does eight thirty work for you?"

"Eight thirty. Yes, we can be there."

"It isn't too early, is it?"

"It's no problem. We work whenever we are needed. We will be there."

"I will have a conference room waiting for us when you get here."

He was really glad that she was so cooperative.

Sometimes, when they needed to interview people, it was like pulling teeth. "Thank you, we will see you then." Dex hung up the phone, shut the top of his lighter, and gave his partner a thumbs up, since Johnny was still on the phone. Dex was glad that he had made contact as well. That meant they were two steps closer to uncovering the truth about what happened to Tammy Larazzo.

The plastic wrapper that the small, red box was enclosed in smacked into the palm of Dex's hand as he packed a fresh box of cigarettes. It sounded like a hammer echoing off the empty walls of his mind. The slapping sounds did nothing to improve the throbbing at his temples that he had not been able to shake all day.

He knew, chances were that it was going to get worse before it got any better. He had at least one too many whiskeys the night before, and he was coasting along on maybe three hours of sleep. No bit of food or coffee was going to make him feel better. He needed a good night of sleep, but it had been years since he'd had one of those.

He pulled at the small red strip to open the plastic sheathing that kept the cancer sticks fresh. He loved smoking, but he had no patience for stale tobacco. He hated the way it sounded when he rolled a stale cigarette between his fingers. The thought of crinkling hard bits of tobacco made his skin crawl. He half-smiled to himself, knowing that he wouldn't have to add that to the list of shitty things he had to accept for the day.

He flipped the brass lighter open, lit his cigarette, and sucked in a long slow drag. He closed his eyes and listened to the crackling of the burning paper as he drew in the hot soothing relief. He blew the smoke out of his nostrils before he opened his eyes again.

"Thought I would find you out here." His partner wasn't a smoker, but he often took advantage of following Dex out for some fresh air.

Dex had just settled into his spot against the brick wall of the back of the precinct. His foot was bent up behind him, resting against the wall. He didn't bother moving when he heard Johnny. He intended to not only finish his smoke but to enjoy it too.

"Here I am. So...?"

"So, turns out that Tammy has a roommate. They had plans to meet for lunch today, and Tammy was a no-show. She said it isn't like her to not show up without calling or texting. She said she has been calling her cell all day, even tried her at work. She has been worried and waiting for her since noon," Johnny explained, re-tucking his shirt in and pulling his pants up over his slightly pudgy belly.

"Did you tell her yet?" Dex slipped his lighter in the front pocket of his jeans.

"No, I would prefer to tell her when she arrives in about twenty minutes." Johnny stood straight with his legs parted.

"That's probably for the best. You call about the cell yet?" Dex asked, dropping the butt on the ground and smashing it with the tip of his boot.

"I left Sam a voice mail, waiting for a callback. We have to go in and update the captain. She might want to sit in on the interview."

"I will make sure she is with us, could behoove us to have a female officer in there when we have her identify the body. Since we have the victim's identification confirmed with fingerprints, having the roommate identify Tammy by photograph should suffice. We can crop it, so she only has to see her face." He bent over, picked up the smashed butt, and tossed it in the trash as they walked back into the precinct.

"That's fine with me, as long as the captain is okay with it. Why don't you email me the photo from your mobile, and I will crop and print it off, so it is ready when she gets here."

"Alright, Harrington, I will forward it to you now." He pulled his phone out of his back pocket and loaded the image into an email as they walked. "I'm going to grab a coffee and try to maintain my chipper personality. I will bring the captain up to speed while you get that pic. I want to make sure we are ready when this roommate gets here."

They split off in different directions. Johnny went back to the corner that housed their desks, and Dex walked through the center of the precinct floor. There was not nearly as much of a buzz in the precinct as he would have expected, considering such a major crime had just taken place within their city limits.

Most of the uniformed cops were out on the street. There wasn't really a need for too many cops in the precinct. Two uniformed officers and a dispatcher always sat in the small office at the front of the police station to handle anyone that came in off the street.

"I hope you are working as hard on this case as you are at making yourself coffee, Preston." Captain Kard sat behind her desk with her arms folded neatly in front of her. Her face lacked an expressive indicator as to whether or not her comment held anything other than sarcasm.

Dex stirred his lukewarm coffee with the small wooden stick, contemplating an appropriate response. He was on edge and lacking the proper sleep and nutrition to maintain his cool vibe most people were used to seeing.

"Mind if I take a seat?" he asked, trying not to let himself be baited into a reaction.

The captain waved her hand out in front of him,

granting him permission.

He looked around the small room, although the captain didn't display many personal effects, she did make a small attempt to brighten the outdated space with a fresh vase of flowers. It was always there in the corner, on the rusty, dented, green filing cabinets that lined the wall behind her desk. He often wondered if she purchased them for herself, or if they were a gift from her husband. It wasn't something you asked a person, and it certainly wasn't something you brought up to shoot the shit about with the fellas.

"It's been a long day. I am under the ruse that the coffee is making it easier to get through." He took a sip. Man, it pissed him off when people didn't know how to make coffee. It was bad enough it wasn't hot, but the burnt bitterness caught him at the back corners of his mouth. He forced the sip down as if it was medicine.

Captain Kard didn't speak. She was never one for many words. He'd heard her say, on more than one occasion, 'You should make it count if you have something to say. Too many people just talk to hear themselves talk,' and she wasn't one of them.

"We have identified the vic. She is twenty-nine-year-old Tammy Larazzo. Detective Harrington has made contact with her roommate. She should be here sometime in the next twenty minutes. We are going to have her ID the body via photograph. We would like for you to sit in on the interview." Dex rubbed his free hand over his knee, drying the clamminess from the palm of his hand.

"What else do you have? Are we going to get a report from the medical examiner today?" She flipped open the top to her reusable water bottle and took a small sip.

"If we do, it will be late. I am thinking it will be sometime tomorrow. I plan on heading back to the morgue tonight if we don't get caught up with too many interviews."

She leaned forward, elbows on the desk. "I sincerely hope that you have more than one interview for this case."

He didn't like the tone of her voice. It was hardly above a whisper, but still harsh and demanding.

"We have an interview with her manager and the human resources director at her place of employment tomorrow at eight thirty in the morning. We also are planning to swing back over to Moe's around closing time. Hopefully, the roommate knows where Miss Larazzo was last night."

The captain nodded at him. Dex really wanted to toss the full cup of coffee in the trash because he couldn't bring himself to drink it. Perhaps he wasn't as desperate for the caffeine as he'd thought.

"So are you in?"

"I can be. Do we know anything about the roommate?" she asked, easing back, but not back far enough to look comfortable.

"Nope. Harrington is the one that spoke to her. I was on the phone with the HR lady. We are going to prep our interview now. I think having a female in the room with us should make her feel more at ease."

"I don't mind keeping a close eye on this case, but I shouldn't have to tell you that you should have a female officer with you anyway. I don't want it to get kicked to HVCU. We are going to close this case. We will get the credit. Do I make myself clear?"

"Yes, Captain, crystal clear."

CHAPTER FIVE

DEX WALKED OUT OF THE captain's office, his eyes narrowed at the beverage station as he chucked the stale coffee in the receptacle. He wanted to kick the thing really, but what would that prove? He felt the captain's eyes still on him, no chance he could stop to make himself a fresh cup.

He looked down at his watch in an attempt to deny the fact that he didn't have time to go anywhere and grab a cup. He had a few minutes at best to get with his partner to prep for their interview with Miss Larazzo's roommate.

His eyes followed his scuffed up boots as he walked back to his desk. He wasn't sure how Johnny had managed to score the case, but he really wished that it had gone to Linder and Harts. Dex preferred to deal with drug dealers and the idiots that were stupid enough to steal from others. Those were the kinds of cases that were black and white to him. If those perpetrators got rough, he didn't mind a tousle with them.

He thrived on knowing that he had the red-handed bastards in his grips. A foot chase and resisting arrest were just the things he needed to get his blood pumping and to make him feel something. However, those kinds of cases were still rare in their quaint little town.

Forcing thoughts of past crime scenes was something that Dex continued to cope with. The built up anger stored at his core was difficult to keep cool at times. He'd recently started sparring at a local gym in an attempt to have a place to drive those emotions. It felt good to thrust his fists against the bags and his opponents. He felt his fingernails imprinting on the palms of his hands, alerting him to the tension escalating inside of him.

"Preston, where you been? Our girl is in the lobby. They are about to buzz her in." Johnny didn't let him make it back to his desk. "I thought we should meet her at the door, Becker said she's a looker. Which doesn't surprise me, Tammy was quite attractive. They do tend to stick together, don't they?"

"I guess." Dex wasn't sure what Johnny was talking about. He'd never dated a girl who wasn't at least a nine, and in his experience, women all had a best friend that was more like a five. "I was in with the captain. She said she wants in on the interview." A breather was not something he was going to get. He pressed his eyelids together and then released them as he followed close behind his partner.

"I'm going to buzz the captain real quick and tell her that the roommate is here," Dex said grabbing the phone on the closest desk in his reach.

"Hurry up." Johnny straightened his shirt and pulled up his slacks while he waited for Dex.

"She said not to use the interrogation room, and she would meet us in the conference room. She wants this girl to feel at ease."

"Works for me." Johnny wanted to make captain at some point, so he never rocked the boat. He went by the book and her command without question.

Dex, on the other hand, cruised a thin line of expected behavior, and he didn't care.

The thick, steel, bulletproof doors that separated the station from the entryway buzzed and clicked as they opened.

Dex was so busy looking down at the nail marks on the palms of his hands that the first thing he noticed about the woman walking through the doors was her long legs. She wore a pair of black pants that looked as if they could have been painted on. The leopard print heels only elongated her legs, making him work at finding his way up her body to her face.

Her skin looked like fresh cream, and her cheeks looked

as if they were kissed by a cherry from the dropping temps outside. Her hair was as black as a midnight sky on a new moon, with bangs hanging straight across her brow line, nearly covering her chocolate brown eyes.

Dex couldn't help but think that her lips looked as if they were coated with blood, they were so red. The longest eyelashes he had ever seen on a woman enhanced her dark eyes, and he wondered if they were fake.

"Oh my God, Dex!" she said as her arms flew around him.

Johnny's eyes questioned her behavior. As Dex's face twisted off to the right and his shoulders lifted up in confusion.

"I didn't know you worked here or that you were a cop. You are a cop right?" she asked him as she took a step backward.

"I am, detective, actually." Dex searched her gorgeous face trying to put the pieces together. There was something slightly familiar, but he couldn't quite place it.

"I'm Detective Jonathan Harrington. How do you two know each other?" Johnny was a champ like that. He might have been married for what seemed like forever, but he still knew how to be the perfect wingman.

"Oh, well, we don't know each other that well. We actually just met last night." If her cheeks were pink before, her milky complexion was now flushed. She smiled coyly at Dex.

Shit, she must have been the woman he'd spent last night with. If he could have high-fived himself, he would have, because she was smoking hot. Except for the part that she was their first witness in his pending murder investigation.

Shit. The captain was going to be pissed.

"Can you tell me what's going on? Why did I have to come down here?" she asked.

"Of course, we are going to go into the conference room over here, so we can have a little bit of privacy," Johnny explained, guiding her to the room that was situated next to the captain's office.

The room was big enough that it held a medium sized conference table with ten chairs, and the back wall had a large dry erase board. The wall next to the door was lined with windows that looked out onto the station floor. The semi-private room was not completely ideal, but the only other option was the interrogation room. Windowless, small, and intentionally cold looking, it was meant to make the person on the other side of the small table feel uncomfortable and nervous.

Captain Kard was waiting for them when they entered.

"Bethany, this is Captain Kard. Captain this is Bethany Kingston. If at any time you think you would prefer to speak to her privately, just let us know," Johnny said with sympathetic eyes.

There was an unmarked manila folder on the table. Dex eyeballed it, wishing they didn't have to show her what was inside. He felt a twinge at the center of his chest knowing that she wasn't going to take it well. Who would?

"How do you do?" The captain held out her hand for a shake. "Please, take a seat."

Dex sat beside Bethany. He'd contemplated sitting across from her to avoid any awkwardness between them in front of his boss, but he hoped that his presence would give her an extra sense of safety. They needed her to have a clear head, so she could give them something to go on—like how her roommate had found herself lying dead behind the local diner.

"Can someone please tell me what's going on? Has something happened to Tammy?" She didn't take off her coat, and her arms clutched the handbag on the table in front of her.

Sitting across the table, Johnny pressed the record button on the small recording device that sat in the center of the table. "I want to let you know that I will be recording this conversation. It is to protect both of us and will be held onto for reference as needed. What you say can be used in the court of law, you are not in any trouble or being arrested, but you are welcome to have an attorney present with you if you so desire."

"Okay, that's fine, I'm fine. Well, I don't know if I'm fine, but I'm fine with the recording I mean," she said as she stared at the black electronic device on the table.

"Okay then, let's get started. Can you tell me where you were last night?" Detective Harrington didn't beat around the bush. He needed his facts, so that was what he asked for.

"Yeah, of course. I was with Dex last night. We were at the Karaoke place until it closed and then... well we were together the rest of the night," her voice trembled slightly.

Captain Kard's head turned so fast in Dex's direction that he was surprised that she didn't give herself whiplash. He'd expected that kind of reaction, so he was ready for her disapproving look.

"And what time were you with Miss Kingston until?" The captain's voice sliced through the air.

"I left Kagley's around six, and was at the Karaoke bar by seven, at the latest. We started talking very shortly after I arrived. I was with her until I got the call from Detective Harrington around five in the morning." Bits and pieces of the night were coming back to him. The more Bethany spoke, and the more he looked at her full red lips, the more he remembered.

"When was the last time you saw or spoke to your roommate?" Harrington asked as he recorded notes on a small pad.

"Gee, I don't know. Maybe dinnertime last night. I skipped dinner, but she fixed herself a small salad. She always does that before she goes out to eat. She says it helps her make smarter dinner choices. She is always watching her weight. I don't know why, she has a body to kill for." Her choice of words couldn't have been any worse.

"Is that so?" Captain Kard asked. "Do you think that someone would have had a reason to want to see her dead because of her body?"

"No! What? Why? I was just saying..." Bethany's eyes darted around the room between the three officers, clearly searching for an answer as to what had happened to her friend. She turned to Dex. "Has something happened to Tammy? I can't take it anymore, please just tell me."

"Detective Harrington is going to show you a picture of a woman. Do you think that you could take a look at it and tell us if you recognize her?" Dex sat in the chair next to her with his legs spread wide apart, so that his body faced hers.

Johnny pushed the file folder across the table to Dex, and he slid it in front of Bethany. He was tempted to grab the box of tissues that resided beside the black mesh cup filled with pens and markers, but he thought it best to wait. There was a chance that the dead woman, wasn't her roommate, or at least he pretended there was an inkling of hope for her.

"I am going to open the folder. Please take your time looking at it. We need you to be sure whether or not you know this person. Okay?" He put his hand over one of hers. "You ready?"

Bethany nodded her head once very slowly. Her brows cinched together as she braced herself. Dex wished he didn't have to open it, but he did. He kept his eyes on her instead of the contents of the file. Her face scrunched up as she gasped, and her hands instantly covered her mouth and nose as she shook her head.

Dex didn't want to rush her.

Face contorting behind her hands, and her head still shaking back and forth, her whispered denial was nearly inaudible, "No." She turned to Dex, her eyes pleading for him to tell her it wasn't true.

"Do you know who this person is?" he asked her.

"It looks like... Tammy. Please tell me it isn't her. She isn't—"

"Can you please tell me her full name?" Johnny interrupted her, so he could record her statement.

"Huh? Larazzo, Tammy Larazzo. Dex?" She turned back to him with a look of desperation.

He could see the tears starting to fill her eyes. "I'm sorry, Bethany. Her body was found this morning. We have identified her by her prints, but needed someone else to confirm that it is her. She was murdered."

"Oh my God. How? Why?" There was no stopping the tears pouring down her face like a summer storm. She wasn't even crying aloud.

The captain pushed over the box of tissues.

"That is what we are going to find out. Can you think of anyone that would want to hurt Tammy?" Jonny asked her.

"No, God no. She is the nicest person ever. She is…was so laid back. She wasn't the kind of person to cause friction, ever."

"You said she was going out to dinner last night, can you tell us with who?" Captain Kard asked.

"Yeah, this guy Sheldon. I am not sure what his last name is. This was only the third date they were going on. I haven't even met him yet." She took a few tissues and wiped her face.

"Do you think you could help us get his contact info?" Dex asked, his hand still on top of hers. "We haven't retrieved her cell phone yet. We can put in for her phone records, but it will take some time to cut through the tape."

"Sure, do you need her parents' phone number too? I can't bear the thought of having to tell them this news. I guess they are going to have to come and get her things from our apartment. I can't believe this is happening." Bethany leaned into Dex, her tears dampening the fabric covering his shoulder.

Dex put the palm of his left hand on her back in an attempt to console her. He looked over at his partner and his captain, who both stared at him. This was an all-new form of crashing and burning for him. He was used to things turning out like shit, but he was often the reason for it. It wasn't his fault that the woman's friend was murdered, but the helpless feeling building inside of him made him chafe.

He wondered if he had not sweet talked Bethany into a cheap motel room and been too drunk to remember most of his antics, would Tammy still be dead. Facts might be facts, but for some reason, he felt sick to his stomach knowing that he was connected to the witness.

Dex may have slept around, but it wasn't because he had a lack of respect for women. He looked at it as a mutual need being met without having to tie a string to it. Women had needs too, and he was happy to help them meet them. He was no good for anyone, so why would he put a woman through the pain and suffering of getting to know him.

He hadn't even remembered Bethany's name or face when he'd walked out of their motel room that morning. He'd never expected to see her again. He hadn't said goodbye to her, he hadn't left a note or a phone number. Now she was practically sitting in his lap, balling her eyes out.

What was he supposed to do or say to her? He couldn't very well start dating her now. Would she expect him to call and check in on her? Wasn't that a part of his job as a detective?

Dex reached over to the box of tissues and pulled out a small handful. He offered them to her, hoping that the distraction would help her to regain as much of her composure as possible. "Here, tissues."

"Bethany, we are also going to need to search through some of Tammy's things. Do you think we can set up a time with you for tomorrow?" Johnny asked.

Dex breathed a sigh of relief that he didn't have to be the one to ask her.

"Oh, really?" Bethany sniveled. "You can come any time. I think I will need to take a few days off from work. I am going to need to move, I can't stay there anymore. Not without her."

"Just take it one step at a time, Miss Kingston. We have a grief counselor that you can talk to, and I strongly recommend that you take advantage of the service. We can also have a uniformed officer see you home if you would like?"

Dex had never heard Captain Kard speak with such softness. Her words were the most tender he had ever heard. She rolled her eyes to meet his, and the ice-cold stare made him wonder if she knew what he was thinking.

"I think I'm okay. I can call you if I need anything. Right?" she asked, her face still in and out of the bunch of tissues.

Dex wasn't sure if she was speaking directly to him or to the group as a whole.

Johnny slid one of his cards across the table. "Here, take my card. If you dial my extension the voicemail gets directly sent to my cell."

"I can grab you one of mine too on the way out. I don't have any on me." Dex sat back and rubbed both of his palms over his knees.

"Do you need to know anything else? I really would like to go now, if it's okay." Bethany stood up, and her posture not quite as elegant as it had been when she'd walked in. Her body hunched forward slightly as she put her handbag over her shoulder and clutched it against her body with both hands as if it was a lifeline.

"If you need anything, or think of any information that you think might help us with this case, no matter how small, please feel free to reach out to me or either of my detectives." Captain Kard shook Bethany's hand before she excused herself from the conference room.

CHAPTER SIX

TRINA'S DAY WENT BY SO fast it was as if a storm wind had blown it away before she had a chance to catch a glimpse. It was a day of review, so she was on autopilot with the kids. They were able to work independently while she helped the few that needed a little extra help for their upcoming standardized testing.

It was a good thing that the day was a smooth one, because she could hardly get the cop she'd met at breakfast out of her head. She kept replaying the image in her mind of seeing him walk in through the diner door. She never would have taken him for a cop—maybe a contractor, carpenter, or even a steel worker.

Something about his gruff exterior had her intrigued. He was nice enough, but cocky in a standoffish kind of way. His hair had been messed up, but it had still looked good and had made his leftover summer tan look darker than it would have on someone else. Perhaps, it was that he had a more olive complexion than she did and that had stood out to her.

She laughed aloud a few times throughout the day, picturing herself spilling her tea in the poor guy's lap. *Who would attempt to dry off a perfect stranger's crotch?* She had, but it'd been more of a reflex to the situation than anything else.

She wondered if she would have allowed herself to do that had he not had those fuck-me-blue eyes. When he'd looked over at her, she'd felt a tingling sensation swirl around in her stomach that had branched off in quick waves down her arms and legs.

Some girls would have blushed and shied away from his overly charismatic personality. She wouldn't let herself be one of those people. She had come face to face with death and it had looked her dead in the eyes. Trina chose to grab life by the reins and live in the moment.

She still had not heard a word about what had happened at the diner. It had been quite a long time since she had seen that many emergency vehicles in the same place at once. It was surprising, because normally rumors spread through their little town like wildfire.

Part of her wanted to know what all the commotion was about, but even more, she wanted another glimpse at seeing the detective again. She wasn't sure if he would actually be in the station house, but she figured it was worth a shot to stop by. What cop didn't love a good cup of coffee and a doughnut?

The aroma of fresh, yeasty doughnuts and coffee filled her car. She stared at the two boxes of doughnuts she'd picked up from Mickey's, tempted to steal one, but who drops off a box of eleven doughnuts? She was starting to regret not getting her own to indulge in.

She pulled into a spot in the non-emergency parking lot. Trina thought it was strange and a little bit cute that the police station was not attached to the municipal building. Hawk Creek was a small town and the people didn't allow for too much to change. The brick and mortar police station was probably as dated inside as the outside looked. There was something to say about the historic feel of the building being entirely brick, unlike modern construction.

She lowered her visor and made sure that the little bit of mascara she'd put on had not smeared and coated her lips with a sheer gloss. She didn't want to look as if she'd gone out of her way to doll herself up just to drop off doughnuts, but she did want to make enough of an impression that she would entice the detective into wanting to bump into her again.

She rubbed her lips together and fluffed her long blonde hair. *Now, for the real challenge, carrying two boxes of doughnuts and two boxes of coffee into the police station unassisted.*

Trina walked around to the passenger side and grabbed a white shopping bag from behind the seat. She carefully slid the boxes of doughnuts in and managed to hold the bag in a way that the doughnuts didn't get all jumbled and smashed. She grabbed a cardboard coffee box with each hand and shut the door with her butt.

Trina looked up at the sign tacked over the entryway that read, 'Hawk Creek Police Department'. Even the wide steps were made out of brick. She really appreciated the little things about the small town that were a delightful contrast to the busy city she was accustomed to.

"You need a little help with that?"

Trina jumped a little and looked back over her shoulder.

"You are bringing those inside?" the uniformed officer asked as he took two steps at a time to catch up with her.

"Yes, thank you." She let him take the bag of doughnuts and handed him one of the boxes of coffee.

"So what's the special occasion?" he asked as he held the door open for her.

"Nothing special. I actually spilled tea on one of your detectives this morning, so I thought I could make it up to him by dropping this off for you guys." She thought it sounded silly once she heard her words aloud.

"Oh man, you gotta tell me who your victim was. We eat that kind of stuff up," he asked half-laughing.

"You mean you want me to tell you, so you can bust on him. I am not even sure what his name is," she lied. She had been repeating his name in her head all day long. "I'm not looking to stir up your testosterone games. You do want one of these fresh doughnuts, don't you? I think they are still warm, and the coffee is hot and fresh." She smiled at him, toying with his taste buds.

"Yes, ma'am. You drive a hard bargain. Are you sure you don't know who the cop was? I can see if he is here, so you can drop them off to him, instead of just dropping them," he offered as they stopped in the lobby.

"He was one of the cops at Moe's Diner this morning. If he isn't here, it's okay." She desperately wanted to catch another glimpse of the detective, but she would never let him know that, not yet anyway.

"Becker, are Harrington and Preston back there?" he asked the officer behind the thick, tinted glass window.

From where Trina stood she couldn't see what Becker looked like.

"Yeah, they are in a meeting with the captain. But they are here, been in and out all day," a voice came from behind the glass.

"They have a special delivery. I'm gonna bring her back," the patrolman informed him.

"Come on, I will help you set up the coffee and doughnuts and let them know you are here." The door buzzed and clicked open.

He held the door open for her, and entering was like walking back in time. She had spent quite a bit of time in and out of a similar precinct as a child. Cops didn't usually have a take your kid to work day, but her father had liked to show her off from time to time. He'd also taken the opportunity to scare her enough to keep her on the straight and narrow.

Not that she'd needed the extra push. She had never been one to start trouble. However, her father had known all too well that good kids were just as likely to take a turn down a dark path as any other. He had seen it too many times, and he'd never shied away from telling her just how hard some of the kids had fallen.

Trina followed the patrol officer down the center of the station floor, past a wall of windows. Behind the first set of glass panels was a conference room. She could see the detective that had caught her eye earlier that morning. He had his arm around a woman with the blackest hair she had ever seen. In front of them, a slightly older man with a receding hairline and mustache sat at the long table. Behind him, a short woman in a suit stood with her arms crossed over her chest.

Trina didn't stare. She actually kept her eyes straight ahead, locked on the back of the officer that was leading the way, despite the flutter in the pit of her stomach. She wasn't sure if the detective had seen her walk past, but she hoped he had.

"This is our fancy coffee station. You can set your box here." He waved his hand over the space before pulling the two boxes of doughnuts out of the bag. "Do you mind if I grab one of these?"

"No, that's what they are here for." She looked at the office behind the window in front of the coffee station. She didn't need to read the sign on the door to know it was the captain's office. Had her father made captain, he would have set the coffee up outside of his office too. Not just because he'd loved it, but also because he would have been able to keep an eye on what was going on in the station.

"I can see the detectives are in the conference room, I can walk you over to their desks, and you can wait for them there." He spoke with half the doughnut in his mouth, his lips dusted with powdered sugar.

"I don't need to stay. I just wanted to drop this off. I don't need to talk to them."

"Are you sure? You were at the diner this morning, are you one of their witnesses?" he asked.

"Witness, no. I don't think so. I don't know anything about their investigation. Just pancakes."

He started to laugh. "You're funny. I'm gonna walk you over anyways, just in case. My name is Kane, Patrolman Andrew Kane. Thanks again for the doughnuts."

Trina giggled, "Nice to meet you, my name is Trina. I guess I could stay for a few to see if I can be of any assistance."

Trina followed Kane across the room. She noticed out of the corner of her eye that the suited woman, followed by the older detective, exited the conference room. She wondered who the woman was in there with Detective Dex.

Part of her motivation in stopping by with doughnuts was to see if he was, in fact, single. She felt as if they'd had an instant chemistry at the diner. Maybe she'd read him wrong, and the woman was his girlfriend. God only knew that she was beyond ready to welcome a worthy relationship into her life. She hadn't had the best of luck with men as of late.

Dex gave his partner a hard look as he walked out behind the captain. He was not interested in being left alone with Bethany. Had the circumstances been different and had he run into her again, he might not have minded. She was hot enough that he would have like to spend some more time with her, maybe even while he was sober enough to remember it.

Instead, his one-night-stand was standing before him, crushed by news that he'd taken a part in delivering to her.

He didn't want to seem insensitive about being that guy that didn't call, because now he had to call, it just wouldn't be to court her.

"Dex, listen... About last night. It was really... It's just that I am... I'm in a relationship with someone else. It maybe shouldn't have happened on my part, but anyway, I just was hoping that we could be discreet about the nature of our relationship."

"Oh, yeah." He was slightly dumbfounded at what she said.

"I am going to need him to be with me through this, and I know you and your partner are going to come by the apartment tomorrow."

"I don't have a problem with that, but it will be documented in the case file. I don't have a choice in the matter. I don't want to make an issue of it, and will respect your privacy the best that I can." He wished he could erase the previous night, but that was a wish that could never be granted. He was good at digging ditches for himself to get stuck in.

"Let's get you out of here. Let one of the officers follow you home. It will be for the best. And call your boyfriend. Have him meet you there, if he can. You shouldn't be alone right now." Free from the burden of feeling responsible to fulfill that position, he felt his shoulders relax.

Bethany wrapped her arms around him, squeezing him

tight. "Thank you. This news couldn't have been worse, but having you here made it easier to take. I will be fine. I don't need an escort home either."

He hugged her back with one arm, not fully engaging in the embrace, but reciprocating enough to hopefully ease her suffering a tiny bit before she left.

"Thank you, Dex. I am going to call my boyfriend now, so he can meet me at home."

Her head fell on to his damp shoulder again, just long enough for him to catch a glimpse of the stunning blonde from breakfast, laughing, as she walked across his precinct with one of the younger patrolman. He felt his jaw tighten a bit.

He put his hands on Bethany's shoulders and pulled her back. "You are okay. You are going to be okay. A terrible thing happened last night, and we are going to find out who did this to your friend. You have my word on that."

He didn't want the case, but he'd just made it personal. He'd made a promise, one he wasn't going to break. He couldn't allow that to happen, not this time.

Dex walked Bethany to the lobby, where the captain had an officer waiting to take her home. He again suggested that she let the officer follow her, but she refused. He was beyond relieved that she had a boyfriend, but that didn't change their relationship and its connection to the case. He was eager to get back to his desk to tell the news to his partner.

Even though their desks were located at the rear corner, he could clearly see the blonde-haired beauty sitting at his desk. He felt his blood quicken through his veins.

He pushed his hair up and over to the side, hoping the little bit of sweat that coated his palms would be enough to tame it. At least he had showered since he'd met her that morning. He felt the tip of the left side of his upper lip rise into a bit of a smirk as he forced himself not to smile.

He welcomed the sight of her. She was fresh and wholesome looking, although he knew from their encounter earlier that day that she had enough of a snarky personality that she could handle him. Or so he hoped.

Before his feet reached his desk, she stood up to greet him. He looked around to see who was watching him, because he knew that he was already on the captain's shit list for having been with the victim's roommate on the night in question. Now he had another stunning female sitting at his desk. He wondered why she was there, if was it to see him, or if she know something about the case.

"Hi. Trina, right?" Dex walked up to her with a swagger that exuded confidence. He had never met a woman that he couldn't have. He had even met a few that he could have considered wanting forever, but he would never allow himself to invest that kind of emotion into someone. It wasn't for him. He didn't deserve that kind of life and was okay with it.

"Yea. I just stopped by to drop off coffee and doughnuts for you guys. Kind of as an apology for the spill this morning."

He watched her blue eyes trace his body.

"I see that you rectified that. Sorry you had to change your clothes."

"Ha, it's okay. I needed a shower and a change of clothes anyway. I didn't have time this morning. I had to rush over to the crime scene." He still wasn't really sure why she was still there.

She made a face he couldn't read, like maybe she wanted to say something. He wanted to stay something too.

"Doughnuts. Mickey's?" he asked working on the conversation.

"Of course, is there any other?" Her lips extended, exposing a wide smile, and her cheeks scrunched up, creating two little dimples on each of her lower cheeks.

He could see himself kissing them, and for a moment, he was lost in the idea of that fantasy. "Not in my book, but I try to limit my visits over there. It is hard to resist the smell when you drive by though. So do you know Patrolman Kane?" *They looked friendly enough,* he thought to himself.

"Oh no, I mentioned that I wasn't sure what your name was, and that I wanted to drop off the coffee for the detectives that were at Moe's Diner. He said that you would probably want to talk to me. He insisted I might be a witness. I told him the only thing I witnessed this morning was pancakes."

"Do you know a woman by the name of Tammy Larazzo?" He thought he might as well ask her. The town was small enough that there was a chance that they had been acquainted.

"I don't think so, should I?"

"I suppose not." He realized she was still standing. "You want to sit?"

"Do you want me to sit?" She tossed the ball back in his corner.

He wanted her to sit. He wanted to get to know her. He wanted to know why she kept catching him off guard. He was a smooth talker, and he prided himself on making people feel comfortable with him all the time. He always found something that made it easy to connect with people. Johnny always said he should have been in sales, because Dex could have sold a bat a pair of glasses.

He didn't think he needed to interview her. She didn't know the victim. As far as he knew, she hadn't been at the diner or in the area the night before—but he didn't know.

"Yes, I would. If you are not in a rush I would like to ask

you a few more questions." He pulled out Johnny's chair and sat at the desk in front of her, leaning in on the table. He couldn't stop looking at the way her soft pink lips shimmered when she spoke.

"Are you going to take notes?"

"Nah, I remember everything. I write my notes later. So can you tell me where you were last night between the hours of twelve am and four am?"

"In bed."

"Alone?"

"Excuse me?"

"Do you have anyone to back up your story?" he asked.

"I don't have a story. Would you like to tell me what happened or what you're investigating? Maybe I could be a more helpful, because I'm not sure where your line of questioning is going. I was alone last night and I was home from about seven pm until just before you saw me at the diner." She rubbed her lips together again before gently biting at her bottom lip as her eyes searched his face.

Dex nodded slowly and sank back in the cheap office chair. It squeaked and gave a little bounce from his weight. He debated on whether or not he should tell her about the case. It wasn't public knowledge just yet, but he was sure that they would be getting calls from the local reporters pretty soon.

"I am not really at liberty to say, but what the hell right?

A young woman was killed behind the diner very early this morning. The investigation is lacking in leads, but it has only been a few hours. Make sure you don't stay out late alone."

"I am never alone when I am with myself. Besides I'm a school teacher, early to bed early to rise." She grabbed a pencil out of the cup holder on his desk and waved it around in front of him as if to tease him in a teasing way.

He watched her eyes dart up, and at the same time, he felt a heavy hand slap him on top of his shoulder.

"Who's your friend, Preston?" Johnny's mocking tone coated his words.

"This is Trina Hayes. She just dropped by to bring us all some coffee and doughnuts. Which, I am in serious need of. Those fast-food burgers left a lot to be desired. I hate eating on the go, it's never satisfying." Dex wanted to go get a cup of coffee, and he also didn't want to let Trina walk out of there without knowing how or when he would have a chance to see her again.

"Nice to meet you, that was very kind of you. Detective Jonathan Harrington..." He reached out over the table and shook her hand. "I think I am going to grab a doughnut. From Mickeys?"

Her eyes lit up, and she nodded with a smile confirming.

"You guys want me to bring one over for you?" he asked them.

"Yeah. Bring me coffee and whatever is left over there. Thanks, man." Dex turned back to Trina and tried to size her up.

"You know you shouldn't eat fast food," she said as she put the pencil behind her ear. "You are better off eating a protein bar and waiting a little while longer to eat something fresh and healthy. I hope you take some time to have a good dinner between your interviews. You should have your girlfriend drop something off for you."

"I don't have a girlfriend. I feed myself. Always have."

"Oh, I thought that you were just talking to your girlfriend." Boy, she had a set, and he liked it.

"Oh, no. She's not my girlfriend. She's a material witness in the case." *Shit.* They probably did look like they had a more intimate relationship. Sure they had been intimate, but there was nothing intimate about how they knew each other.

Trina narrowed her eyes at him, in what looked like disbelief. He made that face often enough when he listened to criminals lie about their innocence. He looked down at his watch. The day was dragging, but they still needed to get back to Moe's and try to get with the medical examiner.

Trina followed his line of vision and looked, with him. Dex realized that he may have been a bit rude, but he had work that needed to be done. Not to mention, he needed to rest at some point. He looked up and their eyes met as she stood.

"I know you have a lot of work to do. I didn't mean to keep you. If you don't need to ask me any other questions related to your case, I am going to head out," she said as she tucked a few blonde strands behind her ear.

"No, it's okay. I think we are all set. It was really thoughtful of you to drop by with the stash from Mickey's. God knows, we always need it. And it is true what they say, cops love a good doughnut." Dex got to his feet. "I can walk you out. We need to get going anyway."

"Do you want my number?" she spoke quickly before he was able to answer. "You know, in case you need it for your investigation."

"No, I don't think so. Besides I know where you work, so I can always find you through the school." Dex stuck his thumb and pinky in his mouth and whistled across the floor. Harrington held up two white insulated cups and gave him a nod. "Looks like I'll be taking my treats to go."

Johnny came stumbling across the floor with a stack of doughnuts and three cups of coffee. Dex shook his head. "I better help him. You can walk out with us. Looks as if he might have made you a coffee too."

"Oh," she giggled "I don't need a coffee, I brought it for you guys." She followed behind him as they met his partner near the front doors.

"She doesn't want that coffee. My goodness how many

doughnuts did you take?"

"I don't mean to be rude, ma'am but the extra coffee is actually for Detective Preston. I don't want to hear him bitching about how he needs more coffee while we are trying to work. And I heard you say no thank you." He winked at her and she smiled back.

"Well, I hope you left some doughnuts for the other guys," Dex said as he relieved his partner of two of the cups. "I will help you eat one of them."

"I'll get the door for you." Trina stepped up, and opened the security door, and held it for the detectives.

"Thanks' again for the joe, it was very thoughtful of you," Dex said as they walked down the front steps of the precinct.

"What he said! Oh, how I love Mickey's doughnuts." Johnny's mouth was full and he had a smudge of pink jelly at the corner of his mouth.

"My pleasure." She waved and walked in the opposite direction to her car.

CHAPTER SEVEN

"SO WHEN IS THE BIG date?" Johnny said stacking his doughnuts on the dashboard as he started the car.

Dex reached over and grabbed the cinnamon and sugar coated pastry on the top of the pile. "No date. Dude, you know I don't do dates."

"You need to start slowing things down. One day that pretty face of yours ain't gonna be so pretty, and you are going to be alone."

"Who says I don't like being alone? With this job, I can't, I'm just not that kind of guy."

"You can be any kind of guy you want to be. Real men commit and have families. And I resent you saying that you can't have a family with this job. I am your partner dumbass, and I have a wife and two kids, so that line of shit isn't going to fly with me." Johnny was the most stand up guy that Dex knew. Maybe there was some truth in what he said, but he couldn't let anyone else down.

"I will take that under advisement. Where are we going first?" Dex looked down at his watch. "It's getting late. We should call over to Moe's and tell them that we will come by in the morning. I would rather be there when they open, rather than have to keep them any later today. We need to see if Shea has anything for us and we won't be able to talk to her during the day tomorrow if she is with patients. Unless you want to split up?" Dex sorted out their plans orally, hoping that Johnny would take the lead on things.

"First of all, we're partners, we don't split up unless we have to. I agree the medical examiner is a priority. You call Moe's on the ride over to the morgue. Do we need to stop for coffee for the old lady too?" Johnny backed out of the parking lot.

"Crap, I did give her the impression we would bring her a coffee, I don't think she is still there, and you know Shea is never without her latte.

⛧

"Moe said that we can be there any time after four thirty a.m. but he would prefer we get there before seven, because that is when the rush starts," Dex updated Johnny as they stepped into the elevator.

"And Becky?"

"She will be there. You know she works every day, except Sundays."

Johnny rolled his eyes. Dex knew he was sick of hearing that chick tell everyone the same thing. The elevator door dinged and opened up to the yellow walled basement.

Dex felt the sting of a slap on his arm, alerting him to the fact that the nice lady from earlier was still sitting behind the reception counter. Johnny gave him an annoyed look.

"What? I will go run up to the gift shop, you go ahead without me," Dex offered.

"No. You might get lost or fall asleep along the way. I will go, I want to check in with the misses and let her know I will be home late. I have to tell her to leave a plate of food out for me."

"Ok, see you in a few." Johnny turned and went back in the elevator.

"Hi honey, you boys are back again." She was still the sweetest thing. She must have been working overtime. "Where did your friend go?"

"Oh, he went to grab you a coffee. We didn't expect to see you here this late."

"I am usually gone by now, but Tim called out sick, and I have my yarn. So I told them if they didn't mind if I did me crocheting, I didn't mind covering a few extra hours. And how lucky for me, I get to see your handsome face twice in one day." She held up a scarf or blanket that she was working on.

"It's more like my lucky day getting to see you again." Dex winked at her, the charm always turned on. "Can we sign in? We are heading back to the morgue again."

She pulled out the logbook and opened it up to the page they had signed earlier. The only other person on the list was Dr. Shea Sinclair. He would recognize her signature anywhere.

"It's starting to get chilly out there. I hope you have a scarf," she said with a questioning tone as he handed her back the signed book.

"I don't need one. I don't get cold enough. I gotta run. I'm going to get in trouble with my partner if he catches me still standing here flirting with you." He offered her his winning smile. "Have a good night, and don't work too hard."

Dex took a deep breath before he slid his security badge through the scanner to get into the morgue. He hoped that it didn't take Johnny long to come back. He had not been alone with Shea since the funeral, and that had been almost seven years before.

"Hey, Shea." He slid his fingers into his front pockets as he walked into the examining room.

Tammy Larazzo's body covered the stainless steel table. Everything about the metallic room sent chills up and down Dex's spine. He was sure that the temperature had been significantly lowered, since their earlier visit. A warm room and a dead body would not make a great combination.

"Hey, Dex. You startled me. It's so quiet in here. You usually call before you come." Shea was wearing light blue scrubs and a white lab coat. She had on an oversized plastic eye shield. A mask covered the rest of her face and muffled her voice.

"Why don't you put some music on in here? Can you get a cheap speaker and stream it through your phone?" The silence would have made him jumpy too.

"Me, stream music? I don't even know what that means. I can't wait for Abigail to get a little bit older, so she will be able to help me with all of that technology stuff." He could see her eyes scrunch up giving away the smile she was hiding under the mask.

"How is Abigail? I always mean to get over to the house and see her. I hope she got my birthday card." Dex looked down at his boots. He still found it hard to look her in the eye even after all this time and he didn't want to look at Tammy's open torso either.

"She did. She would like to see you too. She always asks for you. You are her godfather Dex. For heaven sakes, you really shouldn't be such a stranger." She put down her tools, and took off her rubber gloves, and tossed them in the trash, along with the mask she had been wearing.

"Yeah. Work has been extra crazy, and I started training at the gym. I think I might enter a boxing tournament next month."

"That's great, Dex. Let me know, I would like to come support you." Her words sounded sincere, but for him, it was hard to understand how she could ever find forgiveness for him. He wondered if she was really just being sarcastic. Either way, her words cut him deep. He didn't deserve her support.

"Yeah, sure, Shea. So, you got anything for us?"

"Yes and no. I am sure that you noticed that there was not an excessive amount of blood around the body at the crime scene. The bruising on the anterior side of her body from post mortem blood pooling is indicative of a body that was moved. She was not killed at the diner. That much I can tell you for sure." She walked over to the computer and pulled up a file on the screen showing him images of the body and what she was describing.

"But the body was covered in so much blood. So what about the time of death then? Was that misread at the scene?"

"No, that has to do with the body temperature, and although depending on how the body may have been stored, which I don't think the killer took any extra time to think about that. I would still say that it was between twelve am and four am, but my guess would be closer to midnight.

"She does not have any marks on her wrists or ankles to suggest that she was restrained in any way. She does not have any foreign tissue under her nails. I don't see any signs of defensive wounds. And, by the way, you and your partner better not come in here and compromise the cadaver again until I have had time to do my full examination." She minimized the images on the screen and turned around to scold him with her narrowed eyes.

"I knew you would be pissed about that. I was following orders. The captain said for us to get over here and print the body. I don't know why it wasn't done at the scene this morning."

"Me either, and not to sound like a bitch, but that isn't my problem or fault. You are putting my reputation on the line. If you need something, and it is urgent like that, you need to contact my office. I can't promise you that I can make it here when you need me too, but you need to give me a chance." The door opened and stopped her train of thought.

"What?" Johnny walked in and threw his hands in the air. "Am I interrupting something?"

"No."

"Yes," Shea said at the same time. "I was reprimanding your partner for your lack of following procedures by coming in here and touching the corpse," she said, her hands now on her hips.

"Boss's orders," Johnny said with a shrug.

"See." Dex's lips curled up on one side as he tried not to laugh.

"I see you boys have found the time to stop by Mickey's though," she said pointing to Johnny's shirt.

Dex and Johnny looked at each other, and then realized that Johnny had a jelly stain on his button up shirt.

"Ah shit. One of his many girlfriends came into the station today and brought in doughnuts and coffee for everyone." He lifted his eyebrows.

"Don't be such a douche," Dex said. "Excuse my crude language, Shea."

"Sounds like she is a keeper. But seriously, Dex, how many girls did you have visit you at work?"

"I don't have a girlfriend, let's get that straight. Both women were there as material witnesses for the case. One I happened to have met last night, and the other I met at Moe's while I was waiting for our breakfast. She spilled her drink on me, which is why she brought in the coffee and doughnuts."

"I'm sure she wasn't hard on the eyes either. You are such a chick magnet. Hopefully one day you will let one of them stick around long enough to get stuck." Shea rubbed her hand on his back before she grabbed another pair of latex gloves.

"So what about the case? What do you have? Anything helpful?" Johnny sliced away at that conversation before it went any deeper than it needed to.

"The body was dropped. So, we still need to find the murder scene. Does she have anything on her to guide you in a direction?" Dex both explained to Johnny, and questioned Shea.

"Like I said, she was not restrained. So she either knew her attacker enough that she didn't see it coming or she was drugged. It will take at least twenty-four hours to get back the toxicology screening. It was the first thing I did, so hopefully I will know better tomorrow, but it might take two days until you have the results."

She walked back over to the body and pointed to the victim's throat. "A very sharp knife was used to slit her throat. It could have been a professional kitchen knife or hunting knife. I would almost say it could have been medical grade, but the lines were not quite clean enough, the blade would have been thicker than a scalpel. One thing I can tell you for sure is that the wounds were lacerated with a smooth edge. The blade was not serrated or jagged in any way.

"I don't know if that helps you at all, I wish it were more. I still have a lot of work to do, and my assistant is on vacation," she said, putting on a new mask to protect her face.

"Very funny, you mean permanent vacation." Johnny laughed at the idea.

Shea made a clicking sound out of the corner of her mouth and pointed at him twice.

CHAPTER EIGHT

"YOU GONNA DROP ME AT my truck?" Dex asked as he slid into the passenger seat of his partner's less than tidy car. With a grunt, he took in the half-eaten doughnut on the dash, three empty coffee cups in the holder, and a white bag in the backseat that he knew wasn't from that day.

"I think I'm just going to drop you at your place. I don't really feel like taking the ride back downtown to the diner. We have to be there again at the crack of dawn." Johnny slid the key into the ignition and turned over the engine. Dex looked his partner up and down, suspicious of his motives, but too exhausted to argue with him.

"Don't sit over there pouting, I'm doing you a favor. You need to go home and climb into bed. I know you didn't sleep last night."

"Do I ever?" Dex rubbed the box of cigarettes, pressing

them into his chest and wishing he'd thought to smoke one before they got in the car. That was probably Johnny's only cleanliness rule- no smoking in the car. At least he had one.

"I don't know what you do, but this isn't like busting guys selling dime bags behind the five-and-dime or a druggy shit-bag shoplifting something he can pawn to get his next fix. This is real life detective shit, and you need to have your head on straight, Dex."

"I am quite aware of the stakes. I will be damned if this bastard is going to kill anyone else. I will catch his ass, and there won't be any technical bullshit for him to get off on without paying for his crime.

"And another thing, I don't need anyone telling me my business, not you or Shea. I am a grown man, I do what I want and what makes me happy. When I'm not on the clock, it's my business. I have never let you down. You called me this morning, and I was there in less than twenty minutes. I am always there to do my job." Dex pulled his lighter out and rubbed the pad of his thumb over the etching on the front of the cool metal.

"I don't give a shit what you do, but you can't keep showing up to work reeking of where your lips were the night before. You know I can throw them back like the best of them, but you need to curb that shit off at some point so it works its way out of your system before you wake up. I wouldn't be surprised if you were still drunk when you woke up today. And then you drove to work in under twenty minutes, you see where this is going don't you?" Dex saw the skin on Johnny's knuckles whitening as he gripped the wheel.

Dex didn't want to hear it, but his partner and friend was right, he should not be showing up to work in dirty clothes smelling of sex and whiskey.

"So what time are you scooping me up?" Dex asked.

"What time is the meeting with Miss Larazzo's employer?"

"Eight thirty, and it's in the city." Dex extended his arm over his knee lifting and clicking the top to the lighter as he tried to keep his fingers and his mind busy with the trivial actions.

"Six should do it. That should give us enough time to do our interviews at Moe's and drive out there. We will even be there early enough to beat the rush," Johnny explained. "We can grab breakfast there again."

The ride to Dex's apartment was a short one. Before he got out of the car, he grabbed as much trash as he could. He would need somewhere to put his coffee in the morning, and he did not have confidence in Johnny's motivation to clean up the mess they had made. He tossed the stuff in the development dumpster before he walked upstairs to his apartment.

Dex took off his shoes and his flannel as soon as he walked in and put them away neatly in the hall closet. He tossed his keys and phone on the counter. He nearly tripped over his pants as he was still attempting to take them off while walking. He never kept the dirty clothes he wore at work on once he made it home. He actually kept two separate laundry baskets, one for work clothes, and one for stuff he wore at home or to the gym. He took a quick shower to wash away the filth and griminess of having made two trips to the morgue and the station house.

Dressed in a pair of basketball shorts, he went straight to the fridge. He wanted to fix himself a drink but opted for an Indian Pale ale instead taking notice of the lack of food options while he was in there. He popped the top on the glass bottle and leaned against the cabinets as he shot the cap across the room with a quick snap of his fingers. He never missed the trash. He grabbed his phone from the counter that divided his small galley kitchen from the living room in his garden apartment.

There were two pizza places and a Chinese take-out that allowed people to order using mobile apps. Dex loved the convenience of this feature on his phone. He ordered a meatball Parmesan and an Italian salad and looked into his living room knowing he needed to surrender to the call of his oversized black leather couch. If he sat down and turned on the television before the food got there, he was afraid that he might doze off.

He opened a drawer and pulled out a spiral notebook. They still didn't have any solid leads to go off of for the case, but he jotted down the information they had. They knew that Tammy had had a date with someone named Sheldon. She was murdered somewhere that couldn't have been more than three hours away, but the likelihood that the killer had moved the body that far was slim to none. She was most likely cut with a knife that was sharper than the average household variety so the killer might have access to hunting knives or professional kitchen wear. Dex was going to need to pull out his laptop and search for knives. Maybe even where to purchase them in the area.

They planned to interview Moe and Becky in the morning, but he didn't think that was going to get them any closer to the answers they needed. Unless, by some chance, they'd spotted her there dining with someone the night before. Moe probably would have mentioned something had she looked familiar to him. Becky was in everyone's business, so at least her answers would be fairly secure.

He considered telling Johnny that they should skip the diner and move on to other interviews that may have more clout. He knew that not making Moe's interview a priority was against protocol, but in his gut he knew it was a dead end. His truck was there, but they would probably spend the day riding together again anyway.

Dex closed his eyes and pictured Trina's bright blue eyes. He told himself that anyone would have remembered the unique green and orange sunburst that hugged at her pupils. She looked like a delicate flower, but she clearly had a tough interior that he'd been surprised by.

She was easy enough to talk to, but she didn't just laugh at whatever he said. She had a snarkiness to her that he was not accustomed to with the women he usually met. Dex was not super conceited and didn't want anyone's world to revolve around him, but he'd never met a girl he couldn't bed in one night. He was surprised that he hadn't tried to ask her out, and he wasn't so sure she would have said yes either.

Prospecting the diner would have its advantages. A good hot breakfast to start their day and a glimpse at the woman that kept creeping into his thoughts, those were positives.

They needed Sheldon's last name, and his contact information, as he was quite possibly the last person to have seen Tammy alive. There was a good possibility that she might have kept that in her office. He may have even been a co-worker. If they didn't have any luck at her job, the search at her apartment would be crucial.

A knock sounded at the door at the same time his cell rang, and Dex jumped. "Shit," he mumbled to himself. "Be right there!"

He picked up his phone and answered it before even looking at the number, as he went to the door. "Hang on a second."

Knowing it had to be his food, he opened the door without looking through the peephole. He never had to worry about females dropping in because he never dated anyone long enough to bring them home. The only other people he even had over were a few of the guys from work for an occasional poker game or sporting event.

He could smell his dinner as soon as he opened the door. "Thanks, man. I tipped on the app." He took the food and closed the door.

"Hello?" He asked into the phone, wondering who would be on the other end of the line.

"What's up, Dex, you having takeout again?" Johnny only called him Dex when they were off the clock, but for him to be calling him that late in the day, he knew it had to be work related.

"Meatball parm, how can I go wrong?" Dex grabbed a few paper towels and a fork and sat at the small bistro table he had tucked away in the corner of the would-be dining room.

"Well, I am having homemade meatloaf with mushroom gravy, a twice baked potato, roasted veggies, and a salad. That is the difference when you come home to a woman who loves you. But, you don't have to be jealous, Wifey wants me to invite you over for dinner Sunday night."

Dex didn't bother grabbing a plate, why wash it when all he had to do was eat over the paper bag and toss it in the trash when he was through. There wouldn't be any leftovers. There was no better hangover cure than a meatball parm.

"I can probably do that if we aren't still working on this case."

Johnny always invited Dex over for special occasions such as birthdays and holidays, and the occasional barbecue in the summer.

"Good chance we will still be working this case. But on that note, the real reason I called you is Sam, the tech guy, called me. He hasn't had any luck triangulating a signal from Tammy's phone. He said that either it is turned off or it has been smashed. Either way, not so great. He will have a printout waiting for us in the morning of her call log from the past thirty days."

"That could be like looking for a needle in a haystack depending on how many calls she makes on a daily basis. The stupid phone companies don't show who the calls are made to, only the number. Hopefully, we can get her personal or work computer. If all her contacts are backed up, we can at least cross-reference them to see who she was talking to, especially last night." Dex leaned forward, squeezed his sandwich into his mouth, and put the phone on speaker so he could keep eating. "I was also thinking starting the day at Moe's might not be the most efficient. What do you think?" Dex had a slight twinge in the center of his stomach, and it wasn't from indigestion.

"I was thinking about that too. But we can't interview anyone else that early. It might only take us a few minutes, but I want to at least show them Tammy's picture and see if either of them identify her. Besides, I was really looking forward to another breakfast sandwich. He is the only one in town that puts potatoes and peppers on his egg sandwiches."

"Mmmm. That is true," Dex agreed. "I do think we really need to hone in on investigating the potential list of weapons tomorrow as well. I am hoping that Shea can maybe narrow down more detail to the blade, but I think we need to see who is selling hunting knives in the area. Try to see if you can think of any other type of knife that would be that sharp. We need this guy, Sheldon. He is our top priority tomorrow."

"I'm with you on that. I will let you go get back to that greasy take out of yours. I have to read the little guy a book, or he won't go to sleep. See you at six."

Dex hung up the phone and finished eating his food. The couch was still calling for him.

CHAPTER NINE

"WOW, LOOK AT YOU." JOHNNY almost had Dex blushing, and that was not an easy thing to do. "You are looking extra spiffy today."

"I figured I showed up to work at maximum slob-fest yesterday. I don't need to give the captain, or you, for that matter, any extra ammo to bust my ass." He tossed a gym bag in the back seat and was glad to see that Johnny had taken a few minutes to clean out his car.

"I saw you eyeballing my mess yesterday. I figured, since I asked you to step it up and not show up for work stinking like a bar, I figured I should do the same. Looks like we both rose to the occasion."

"Feels good to shower and get ready at home. Not that I need much, but I didn't have any of my shit with me yesterday. I am starving. I almost made myself instant oatmeal."

"That shit is no good for you. You need to get the steel cut."

"Why?"

"Beats me." Johnny started to laugh. They both knew that he was just parroting something he heard his wife say. "I don't even like oatmeal."

Johnny turned on a local talk radio station that they zoned out to until they arrived at the diner, since there wasn't much they hadn't covered the day before.

There were only a few cars parked in front of the diner. The quiet atmosphere was quite a contrast to the day before when the street and parking lot had been lined with municipal vehicles and restaurant patrons. Dex wasn't sure if the sun was shining brighter and making everything look clearer, or if it was his sudden realization that he wasn't carrying the weight of a throbbing headache. Either way, he would take it, and was glad that he had on his favorite pair of shades.

"I'm gonna let you take the lead on this one, big guy," Dex said as he slapped his hand on his partner's shoulder.

"Who are you calling big?" Johnny stood up a little taller and sucked in his belly. "And I might advise you not to antagonize your superiors before their first fix of caffeine, and or in my case, food."

"Superior?"

"Well, I am older than you, and I have seniority, so yes."

"Okay, partner. Let's get you some eggs and potatoes." Dex chuckled enough that it strained his diaphragm.

"Will you stop talking about food? I'm hungry and we are actually working."

"Gotcha. You take Moe, I will talk to Becky and order our food at the same time." Johnny shot daggers with his eyes at him as they opened the door.

Dex smashed his lips together, struggling not to burst out laughing. The only thing that stopped him in his tracks was the sight of long blonde hair. His heart skipped a beat, and he almost choked on his own saliva. His breathing became shallower as they approached the counter.

Becky came storming out from behind the breakfast bar. "Hey, guys. You grabbin' breakfast?"

"You bet! We also need a moment of your time. Is Moe in the back?" Dex asked her.

"Sure is."

"Mind if I head back there?" Johnny asked her. "Then I can talk to him while he works."

"I don't mind. Moe might kick you out though. He is a bit territorial at times, so enter at your own risk," she said, snapping her gum between sentences.

"I will take my chances." Johnny nodded to Dex and walked through the single swinging door.

"You wanna grab a seat? Or do you need to talk to me in private." She smiled and pulled on the end of the ponytail hanging over her right shoulder. It gave him a chill, and not the good kind. There wasn't enough whiskey for him to want to be alone with her.

"This should be fine, Becks." He smiled and took a seat at the end of the bar. He wanted to look to see if the blonde was Trina, but he didn't want to be caught staring. "You're not too busy this morning, huh?" Dex took the opportunity to scan the small dining room, making sure to let his eyes trace over the length of the counter. The woman sitting at the other end of the counter was a lady that was at least ten years older than Trina, and sans the hair, there was no resemblance whatsoever.

He twisted his head to the right until his neck cracked. He shook his head a few times to both loosen his muscles, and in utter disapproval of him actually having had his hopes up at something so simple and silly as seeing Trina again. That's why he preferred one-night-stands. It was for the best that she wasn't there. He needed to keep his focus on the case.

Dex took out his phone and pulled up an image of Tammy Larazzo's photo from her license. There was something morbid and unsettling about making people look at a picture of a dead girl. He'd had no choice, but to show it to Bethany, and he didn't want to think about the impact that moment would have on her for the rest of her life.

"I need you to look at this photo and tell me if you recognize this woman," Dex said to Becky. He spoke slowly, his voice strong, but not so loud that anyone else could overhear what they were talking about. He turned his phone so she could see the full screen, and she picked it up to look more closely.

Becky shifted her weight back and forth a few times. She looked as if she was thinking so hard that she may have broke something in her mind. Dex had no problem with gum, but it was off-putting that she was always working her jaw like a cow. He did, however, admire how many snaps she could get in such a short amount of time.

"Gee, Dex, I don't think so. Should I recognize her? She isn't...the one? The dead one from yesterday?" She handed him back his phone and took to twirling the end of her hair again.

"So you didn't see her come in here the day before yesterday to either eat in or take out? I know how you are. You don't forget faces, but there has been a lot of commotion in here over the past twenty-four hours." Dex took his phone.

"You are right about that. I don't ever forget a face, especially not one that pretty. I'm sorry. I didn't see her in here. There wasn't no one else waitin' on tables neither. Isn't there some other way I can help you?" If he didn't know any better, he would think she was coming on to him.

"Yes, as a matter of fact, you can take my order."

"Oh, I sure can do that!" She whipped out a small pad and pen from her apron. "What can I get ya?"

"Same as yesterday, doll. Two belly busters and two coffees." The door jingled behind them, breaking her attention for a brief second. "You got it. It might take a little longer. I don't know how long your partner's gonna be in there."

"I understand. Let me get a cup of joe while I wait." His stomach growled, and while the coffee might not tame that beast, it would at least distract him from the hunger. Although he wasn't completely sure the belly buster would do the trick either.

"Is this seat taken?"

The voice was melodic in a way that made him think about ribbons of honey. He turned to face her, fighting off the waves of flutters he felt reverberating in his chest. Her eyes were like the warm inviting sea forcing waves out onto his shore. *Trina*

Her golden locks were tucked back against the back of her head, showing off a thin neck and a petite jaw line. There was a softness to her skin, perhaps it was the leftover glow from the extended summer sun. He wanted to reach up and trace every last line on her face. He told himself there was no way her skin felt as good as it looked.

"So, does that mean that someone is sitting there?" She looked at him as if he had antennas on top of his head.

"Oh, no. I'm not staying. You can sit there if you promise not to spill your drink on me." Dex pulled it together enough not to stutter, he would have to take it.

"I can't make any promises. I don't always have control of what my body does. Two left feet, or arms in my case." Her smile was genuine and had a certain air of innocence to it. "I thought you don't do breakfast?"

"I did say something like that, didn't I?" She nodded. "I don't usually. We have a few early interviews this morning, so I figured why not make the best of it and get something to munch on at the same time."

"Or maybe you just couldn't wait to see me again so you figured that you would stalk me here." She took off her coat and put it on the seat next to her. She wore a cream-colored sweater that hugged her delicate curves.

God. He couldn't stop staring at her. She didn't have any exposed skin other than her neck and he felt as if he was seeing more than he should. He felt his cheeks warm to the thought of her realizing that his eyes were all over every inch of her body.

"You found me out. That's my MO. I go around stalking pretty girls until they get up the nerve to ask me out." *What?* What on Earth did he just say to her? Becky put down a cup of coffee for him and a cup of tea for Trina, and he uttered, "Thanks, Becky."

"So you think I'm pretty then?" She pulled out all the punches, catching every word of what he said and used it to her advantage. She had spunk, and no problem speaking her mind.

He took a deep breath through his nose and stirred in a packet of fake sugar into his coffee. He watched the spoon stir the black magic and wished that it wasn't mimicking the sensation that resided in the pit of his stomach. He put the spoon on the counter and turned toward her.

"You are not exactly what I would call pretty. Wild flowers on the side of the road are pretty, the cupcakes my nana used to make my cousins on their birthdays were pretty, a schoolgirl's Sunday dress is pretty—you are stunning. When you walk into a room it is like the sunshine coming out after a stretch of long, dreary, winter days."

"Wow. I was just busting your chops. Just wow, I am beyond flattered. I guess I kind of set that up though didn't I?" She rubbed her shiny pink lips together and looked up at him through her long black lashes.

He was a bit surprised by his response as well. He wasn't one for feeding ladies cheesy lines. He never had to. Maybe it was too much. He looked toward the door to the kitchen, hoping that Johnny would come out and save him from his embarrassment.

"It's okay, I don't mind stating the facts. It's what I do, ma'am. I investigate and observe people." He sipped his coffee and scalded the tip of his tongue. He'd given up cream a few months back when he started boxing. He still hadn't adjusted to how hot coffee was without it.

"So then I guess it's only fair that, since you have worked so hard to stalk and observe me, I should ask you out. Bowling maybe? Yeah would you like to take me bowling?" she asked as she sipped her tea and watched him from the corner of her eyes.

"Bowling?" he asked. "Sure why not? Could be fun. It might be one of the only sports I have never really played."

The kitchen door swinging open caught his eye, and his partner walked out, pushing his hair back. His eyes locked in on Dex, slid right, and then back. Johnny smiled and nodded in approval. Dex waved him over.

"You all set?" Dex asked him.

"Yeah. How about you? Or am I interrupting your date here?" He might have wanted him to make more of an effort dating, but hey, it was his job to torture him along the way. What were friends for anyway?

"No chance, if we were on a date, it wouldn't be here. There is no ambiance, and it's way too quiet," Trina spoke before Dex had a chance to rebut.

"Firecracker, right?" Dex said. "I am done with Becky, but we are waiting for our breakfast."

"Speak for yourself. I ate like ten pieces of bacon while I was in there listening to Moe give me a play by play of his morning routine, including every detail of how he takes out the trash." Dex knew that bacon had most likely only whet his appetite. There was no chance they were leaving without those sandwiches.

"You're not spilling drinks on this guy again are you? We don't have time for him to take a midday shower again. We have a lot of work to do."

"Very funny. No spills yet. I can see that he made a lot more effort in his appearance today. He cleans up nice." She wagged her eyebrows up and down. He hadn't had two people attempt to make him blush that much since he'd been in high school, and that was two lifetimes ago.

"Here you go, guys. The coffee is on the house, sandwiches are nine forty-five." Becky came over and dropped a check on the counter, with a white paper bag and a couple of to-go cups.

"Here, give me that. I got it today," Johnny said. "Put the ladies breakfast on there too, it's on Dex."

Dex just chuckled and watched Johnny follow Becky over to the register to pay the tab.

"I have to run. Here is my card. Why don't you give me a call tomorrow, and we can make arrangements for this weekend. My cell is on there as well. If you need me to call you first, just shoot me a text with your number." He handed it to her before he picked up their breakfast. "It was a pleasure seeing you again."

"Ditto." She smiled and tucked the card into her purse. He could watch that woman smile at him all day long.

CHAPTER TEN

DEX SQUINTED FROM THE EARLY rays of sunshine. He wasn't happy he'd left his shades in Johnny's car. That combined with the incompetence of Tammy's employers, had his headache creeping back up on him.

"I need to have a smoke before we get back in the car." Dex pulled the box out of the pocket of his windbreaker. He turned his body away from the wind and covered his cigarette with his left hand while he lit it.

"I wish you would quit that shit. You make my car stink."

"Oh yeah, because you keep your car so clean. It usually smells like stale french fries." Dex blew the smoke away from his partner. "You should have just let me drive."

"We can go get your truck now. I don't know why we rushed over here for an eight-thirty appointment. You would think that they would have a little more respect for cops," Johnny gruffed.

"Or a sense of urgency in the matter of the fact that one of their employees was just murdered. What is wrong with people?" Dex agreed.

"At least the extended trip was worth it. We had to wait but they got us exactly what we were looking for. Of course, I would have preferred that they just let us take her computer with us." Johnny looked at his watch.

"We could obtain it with a court order, but I don't know if we need to. We got Sheldon's contact information and his last name. We should grab lunch on the way back, or order something to be delivered to the station. We need to look this guy up and pay him a visit as soon as possible."

"I wonder what kind of doctor he is. Maybe Dr. Sinclair might know him."

"You know, I hate when you call her that."

"You shouldn't worry about what she does with her name. She did what she needed to take care of herself and her daughter. Paul would be proud of her, and he would respect her choices, you should too."

Dex took one last drag and threw the butt on the ground. If he could throw the tiny weightless filter hard, then it would have hit the pavement like a ton of bricks. Instead, he smashed and pulverized it with the tip of his boot. He was about to step off the curb to get in the car, but turned back, and picked it up, and tossed it into one of the trash receptacles scattered around the oversized parking lot.

"Besides, no chance I am involving Shea in this case. She has her job and that is it. What if this guy, Sheldon, is the killer? No chance I am going to be the reason that Abigail is left an orphan." Dex felt his lips crinkle together, and he was sure that his nostrils were flaring.

In the modern world, being a godparent didn't mean what it used to. That hadn't stopped Shea and Paul from deciding that, if anything ever happened to them, he would be Abigail's next of kin and legal guardian. When he'd signed the legal documents, he'd never thought that it would ever really be a possible reality. He had done it more for their piece of mind than anything else.

Those were also the days when he'd thought he would follow his friend's footsteps and be lucky enough to meet a lady that he could make a family and a future with. Those things were no longer options in his book. He couldn't blame anyone but himself. He was by no means in any kind of state of mind to be an instant parent. He wanted more for his goddaughter than he could ever offer to Abigail.

"I hear what you are saying. It was just a thought. We will do our own digging, no worries. How about, while I drive, you order food and have it delivered, so it is there when we get back. Use one of those fancy apps on your phone, so you can pay for it ahead of time."

"Italian or Chinese?"

"Just order us salads with chicken. I want pizza, but if that gets there before us, it won't stand a chance. Someone will devour it."

"I hate when people at work steal my food. There should be a way to punish food thieves. My goodness, you would think, since they're cops, they would know better." Dex found it humorous, but the weight on his heart at the moment didn't allow it to grow into a laugh. He opened the same app that he used the night before and ordered.

"So if we don't need this guy's number anymore, does that mean that we don't have to go to search Tammy's apartment?" Dex asked casually as he placed his phone back in his lap.

Johnny had his hands at ten and two. Dex thought that it showed his age, or his nature to follow the rules all the time. The only other person he'd ever saw drive that way was his grandfather. He'd tried it a few times, to see how it felt, and didn't like it. He actually thought it restricted his control of the wheel. He wasn't one for rigidity in any aspect of his life. He was a one-handed driver most of the time. On occasion, his knee did the trick just fine.

"You mean Bethany's apartment?"

"That too. Getting Sheldon's contact information was the ultimate goal of going there right? What else would we need to look for? I don't think she was murdered there. I think that Bethany would have noticed if there was a giant pool of blood." Dex wasn't looking forward to the awkwardness of having to go there and seeing Bethany with her boyfriend. He thought of himself as a stand up guy for the most part. He never went out looking to sleep with a woman that was in a committed relationship, but he was also often too drunk to care to ask.

"Speaking of a pool of blood, we need to find that pool. There has to be trace amounts of blood somewhere that we can follow. Someone is driving around with a vehicle stained with Miss Larazzo's blood. This might sound like a crazy idea, but we should go out there with the black light and see if there is any kind of trail. There is always a chance that it leads somewhere." Johnny suggested.

"Hmm. I don't know Harrington, I guess there is a chance that would lead us to the crime scene. It has been almost two days, if there had been trace amounts of blood, I would imagine that they have been degraded by now. Even if not, where could they lead? The parking lot, maybe. Where would that get us?"

"You are probably right, but what if it happened somewhere within walking distance? There are quite a few businesses around there, they have trolleys and carts in the stores, and shit, almost everyone in this podunk town has a wheel barrel." Johnny was getting his hands going. Dex braced himself for the potential repercussions of Johnny not driving with his hands on ten and two.

"I am going to call it in. We will set up a town-wide search for wheel barrels." Dex rolled his eyes.

"I'm going to go pull this Doctor Rubio's profile up in the system. Get our food and meet me back at our desks. You can start searching the web for his practice and find out where he is located. I don't want to call him. He is getting a drop in from us." Johnny laced his fingers together in front of him and pressed them outward. "I don't want this guy getting spooked at all."

"Yes, sir. I am all over it." Dex saluted him and went in search of their lunch. He wasn't as hungry as he thought he was. He was either still bloated from their oversized breakfast sandwiches or anxious about getting a drop on this guy. He wanted this case shut and prayed that whoever had committed the murder wasn't cooking up their strategy for their next kill.

It hadn't been a crime of passion, that was for sure, and so far, there was little to no evidence. Tammy didn't seem like the kind of person that had a hit out on her. The murder was pretty clean and it seemed if some planning had gone into it. She hadn't been restrained at any point, and there was no evidence of a struggle. They needed that toxicology report back.

"Dex!"

Whenever he heard Captain Kard's voice, he felt like a child waiting to be scolded. Even though he was the black sheep in the office, he was a good cop. He knew it, and so did his captain. He spun around with a move that was as smooth as Michael Jackson's moonwalk.

"You guys are rolling in here a bit late in the day. I hope you were following a hot lead all morning." The captain always wore a suit with a skirt, and always below the knee in length. He wondered why she never wore slacks. There were not a lot of women that worked in law enforcement in general, and to have a female captain, especially in their neck of the woods, meant that she was a pretty bad-ass cop. She stood alongside the best of the best, but she always kept her little bit of femininity.

Dex suspected that she felt as if it made a statement about her being a woman. Why should she have to dress like a man to do a man's job? Society was changing, but it wasn't really all that different in its expectations of gender roles. He didn't mind having a female superior, but there were some old timers in their precinct that found it hard to swallow. He ignored their ignorance.

"We actually just stopped in here to dig up some information on the last known person to have potentially seen Miss Larazzo. Detective Harrington is pulling up his info now. We are going to stuff our faces while we prep for his interview," Dex informed her while she was leaning on the metal frame that surrounded the door to her office.

"I hope you're not calling him in here. I don't have to tell you the ramifications of you potentially tipping off your only suspect." Captain Kard stood with her arms crossed and one foot kicked out to the side.

Dex was distracted by her stance. She reminded him of the lady of the house that Tom and Jerry lived in. He was waiting for her to start chasing him with a broom or a rolling pin. He dared not laugh at the images of his once beloved childhood cartoons commingled with his current state of reality.

"Please tell me that your silence is not a confirmation of such?" her voice was stern but there was a quiver of genuine concern. She didn't get to her position by not caring about the people that they took an oath to protect. The fact that someone died at the hands of another on her watch did not sit well with her.

"Sorry, captain, I was just thinking about the case. No, we did not call him in. We are planning to go to him direct. We just want to get as much information as we can, before we show up asking him if he killed his date."

"Did you get the medical examiner's report yet?"

"No, but I know she said it would take at least twenty-four hours to get back the toxicology result. We will follow up with her before the end of the day. I know that she will call as soon as she has everything finished, or if there is something imperative to the case."

"Ok, she has been one of the most reliable and effective medical examiners we have had. Albeit, we have had very few suspicious deaths that have needed to be investigated. I prefer to keep it that way. We need this guy behind bars before he gets his hands on someone else." She walked back around behind her desk and pulled out the chair.

"I will keep you in the loop Captain. I better get back to work, Harrington is going to think I am goofing off somewhere."

"There is no option for failure. Are we clear?"

"Yes, ma'am." Dex turned the corner back out of the entryway to her office, tempted to make a coffee. It had been a few hours since his last fix. It would have to wait. He needed to grab their lunch before—

A loud fast whistle shot across the room causing him to look up. Johnny was standing next to his desk with the food and an annoyed look on his face.

"Shit," Dex mumbled to himself, trotting across the room.

""What the hell are you doing?" Johnny held his hands out in front of him, and that meant his emotions were amped up.

"The captain called me into her office when I was going

to grab the food."

"What did you do wrong this time?"

"Nothing. She wanted an update. Why you gotta say it like that?"

"Well, you don't see her calling me in there all the time. You know why? Because she doesn't have to keep checking in on me like a child. I take my job serious all the time." He sat down so fast his chair almost slipped out from under him, not helping to ease the sudden tension between them.

"I take my job very serious. What I do in my personal time has nothing to do with how well I do my job."

"You sure about that?" Johnny pointed to his head and tapped his forehead. "Think about it bro."

Dex was pissed. Johnny busted on him often, but he was flat out insulting him, and he was trying really hard not to get baited into a fight with his partner. They didn't have time to waste on trivial things like that when they had a killer to put behind bars. He sat down and pulled the metal tin filled with cheap lettuce and grilled chicken in front of him. He stabbed away at the food and took a bite that was too big to be polite, but he needed his mouth to be occupied, so he didn't say something he would later regret.

CHAPTER ELEVEN

SOMETHING WAS EATING AWAY AT Johnny. Dex knew him well enough that, as much as he might piss off his partner, he had never been that standoffish with him, and out of nowhere. They ate in silence. Johnny gave Dex some of Dr. Rubio's information, and Dex did the Internet searches while he ate his lunch.

Johnny was only a few years older, but it was enough for there to be a technology breakdown. He didn't have social media accounts, and he only just upgraded to a Smartphone because his wife had twisted his arm. Dex was on it all. Johnny might have thought it was a waste of time, but Dex knew better. It had helped them on several cases.

He would never understand why people would post things online that were illegal. Whatever they post publicly is there for the world to see, and they can't take it back. Not only did they post the pictures, but they had them tagged with their locations more often than not. It actually made his job easier a lot the time.

Dr. Sheldon Rubio was a forty-two-year-old podiatrist. He was single and signed up for three different dating sites. It was unclear whether he was on there looking for Mrs. Right, or just easy access to an ongoing stream of women to date. It didn't look as if he had listed being in a relationship with anyone over the past six months or so. Dex didn't search further back than that.

He did, however, have plenty of pictures up of him and his friends partying and of him with a variety of women. They were all dressed nice, as if they were at a bar, club, or party in most of the images. The guy definitely knew how to have a good time, or at least make it look like he was an expert. Dex could have learned a thing or two from him.

It was getting late in the day, and the doctor only had office hours until four o'clock. They were cutting it close. The ride over to his office was uncomfortably quiet. He did not live or practice in Hawk Creek, so they had a nice drive through the wooded area of Shady Cove.

His office was in a building that housed several different doctors and attorney offices. They checked the directory, and his office was on the second floor. Dex stepped up to the elevator and hit the up arrow. He was relieved when the doors opened immediately.

"You want me to take the lead on this one?" Dex hesitated asking, but he wanted to make sure that they at least decided that when they walked in. When they'd first started working together, there were several times they'd gone to interview people and had stumbled over each other's words. It made the whole process confusing, unprofessional, and less productive than it could have been.

Dex was pretty good at reading people. It was one of the characteristics that made him so easy to get along with. It also was one of the things that most women were attracted to. He noticed stuff, so he was able to respond accordingly in situations. It wasn't something that he really over thought, it just happened. Johnny was more meticulous about doing things by the books. They complimented each other's police work well in that respect.

"I got it." Johnny pulled out his small notepad and pen from the inside pocket of his coat. The muscles on his jaw were twitching from him clenching his teeth together. Dex furrowed his brows together upon inspection.

"May I help you?"

She was the kind of receptionist that Dex would have wanted for himself. She had thick dark hair, so shiny that you could almost see your reflection in it. Although she was sitting, you could tell by the length of her torso that she was tall. Her black eyelashes went on for miles and batted against her brows as she looked up at the two detectives. Her eyes darted back and forth between the two men, and then back onto Dex as her full red lips stretched apart.

"Do you have appointments? Are you together?" She sat up extra tall and lowered her shoulders back so that her full breast became the focal point. She opened an appointment book and double-checked the computer screen. "I don't actually have another appointment here on the schedule for today."

"No ma'am, we don't have an appointment." Johnny flashed her his badge. "Detectives Harrington and Preston, here to see Doctor Sheldon Rubio."

"Oh, sure. Is this foot related or official police business?" she asked pushing her chair back to get up.

"It is a police matter. If you could let him know that we are here. Please."

Dex felt bad about how short Johnny had been to her when he saw her eyes fall to the ground before she moved to walk through another doorway that probably led to the examination rooms.

Dex was right, she was tall and had on a nice pair of gray slacks that clung to her round behind. He had been to the gym enough to know that she worked hard at her squats to have that kind of definition. He was impressed. Too bad he wasn't meeting her out somewhere. The captain would kill him if he dated or slept with anyone else tied to the case.

Dex and Johnny stood there staring at each other as they waited for her to come back. Dex thanked his lucky stars that she was quick about it. She came into the waiting room and opened the door for them.

"If you would follow me, I will show you to his office, and he will be with you in a few minutes. He just needs to finish up with his patient, and then he will be with you."

They started to follow behind her. "If it is all the same to you, I am going to wait out here until he is finished," Dex announced, and Johnny gave him a look. Dex wasn't sure if it was a look telling him that he had a good idea, or if he thought he was trying to stay out there to talk with the receptionist.

"I need to make a call. If you could just let me know when he is through with his patient, I will be right back." He didn't have anyone to call, but he wasn't about to sit in the man's office while he walked out the front door. There was a chance that there was a back way out of the office, but unlikely, since they were on the second floor. He wished they were on the first floor though so he could have stepped outside for a smoke.

"Ok, no problem. I can do that." She turned and walked

his partner down the hall.

Even though Dex actually didn't have anyone to call, he pulled out his phone. Sure, there were people that he probably should call, but most of them he had let so much time lapse, he wouldn't have enough time to catch up. He wanted to call Shea and see if her report was ready. If it wasn't, then he would be stuck with having to make small talk. She was the one person that muted his easy going and charming personality everyone else got to experience.

He stayed in the corridor that led to Dr. Rubio's office. There wasn't anyone in the waiting area, so as soon as the patient exited, Dex would know that they were pretty much alone. He wouldn't complain about seeing the receptionist cart her sweet ass back down the hall either.

Dex leaned back against the wall with one foot supporting him, and the other bent behind him. He looked down at his phone and scrolled through his contacts, and then through his apps. He considered just faking a call. He heard the opening and closing of a few doors and when he looked up, he saw the dark-haired bombshell re-approaching her workstation.

Shit, he thought to himself. Just as he held the phone up to feign talking, it vibrated against his ear. The sudden and loud alert startled him. His body reacted just enough for him to lose his balance, and he needed to put both feet on the ground.

He looked down at his phone to see the alert was for a text from a number he didn't recognize, and he swiped the screen to read it.

Hi, it's Trina. Save my number. Call me when you are free so we can set up our bowling adventure. One other teacher and I are going to Kagley's for drinks and appetizers after work to celebrate her birthday. Stop by if you are in the area.

Dex realized that he'd stopped breathing while he was reading. He pressed his eyes together in an attempt to push her out of his mind. Instead, visions of her crystal clear blue eyes and giant smile plagued him. He didn't understand why he was having that kind of reaction to her.

Sure, she was incredibly attractive, obviously smart, and her snarky attitude was sexy as hell, but Dex had been with plenty of beautiful women. He didn't gloat about it, but he was a charmer and women flocked to him. Shea always told him that it was because he was so unavailable, which in turn, only attracted women not worth being available for.

It didn't completely make sense to him, and he liked the type of women that he attracted. His focus was on work and training. He was who he was, nothing more nothing less. So why did this woman have him fumbling like a teenage boy?

"Excuse me—"

The voice broke his train of thought, and Dex looked up at an older man with a wrinkled face, standing in front of him with a large bandage over his foot and some kind of walking boot. His other foot was housed in a giant Frankensteinesque shoe. "You gonna move out of the way, or do you not have any manners, son?"

"My apologies, sir, I was lost in my own thoughts. Pardon me." Dex stepped aside, so the man could pass. He was glad that he'd moved when he did, the older man looked as if he was gearing up his cane to swat him.

"You can come back now. The doctor's office is down the hall to the right, first door on the right. I have to schedule this patient for his follow up, but I think you will do okay."

"I think you're right." Dex winked at her and showed himself to the doctor's office. When he walked in, Johnny was shaking Dr. Rubio's hand introducing himself.

"And this is my partner, Detective Preston. We need to ask you a few questions regarding an ongoing investigation."

"Can I ask what this is about?" Sheldon searched the faces of the two detectives.

"I think, for now, we will be asking the questions." Dex was taken aback by Johnny's bad cop attitude. "Let's start with where you were Wednesday night between the hours of let's say six pm and four in the morning?"

"Wednesday night, well I was here for the better part of

the early evening, and then I had a date, but I was late. I was really late, so that never happened. He rubbed the back of his head as if he were trying to figure out what was going on.

Dex watched his body language, and the man seemed genuinely confused by the line of questioning. There was a chance his tense body also could have been a sign of guilt, but Dex usually could tell the difference.

"Do you have anyone that can corroborate your story?" Dex asked him. He liked shifting the doctor's focus to throw him off.

"No, not really. I live alone. It is possible that someone in the neighborhood saw me when I got home, but who really watches their neighbor's house? I left work and was on my way to meet a gal I have been dating, but my answering service called and said that I had an emergency on their way into my office."

"Wouldn't they go to the emergency room if they had an emergency? No offense, but what kind of foot or ankle emergency would bring a person to a doctor's office after hours?" Johnny continued the questioning, pushing his pencil to his small notepad. Dex saw Sheldon eyeing the pad with concern.

"You would be surprised. When my service called me and told me this, I asked them why they didn't send the patient to the ER, she said that the caller had said that they were already on their way to the office, and then the patient had hung up on them." Dr. Rubio walked around to the back of his desk. His eyes jerked from me to Johnny, constantly moving while his hand twitched. He reached into his desk, a bead of sweat moved down his forehead.

"That's enough! Hands where we can see them!" Johnny yelled and put his hand on his weapon. Dex didn't know where this was going, but he followed Johnny's lead.

Dr. Rubio lifted his hands in the air. "I'm sorry. I...I was going to get you the card with the number for the answering service."

"Step away from the desk. We need you to remain seated as we talk. When we are ready we will let you know when you can retrieve something you think we need."

"Okay, shit, I'm sorry. I am a bit flustered I don't understand why you are here asking me all of these things. Did I do something wrong? Or is one of my patients in trouble?"

"How about you finish telling us about your emergency and what happened after that." Dex stepped up closer, trying to let Johnny know that he was there for him.

"I came back to the office, and no one showed up. I called the answering service twice, to see if they'd called back in. I also asked for the patient's information. The name that was given is not one of my current patients. I checked my files several times. I was so caught up in trying to figure out what was going on with the emergency that I forgot to call Tammy, my date and let her know I would be late.

"By the time I called Tammy, she didn't answer her phone. After about a half an hour of waiting, I decided to just drive out to the restaurant and see if she was there." He stopped rubbing his hands together long enough to point at Dex. "You can call there too, the hostess will tell you I came in looking for her. She said that she sat at the bar and had one drink before leaving. She must have been really pissed because she still has not returned any of my calls. Honestly, I really liked her. I actually was considering canceling my subscription to my dating site."

"You mean dating sites." His cheeks flushed as he turned in surprise at Dex's question. "We do our homework buddy."

"Ok, I am on a few different dating sites. I have dated many women. Most of them are just flakes. What is going on? Did something happen to Tammy?"

"So what happens when these women flake out on you? Or when they surprise you by not flaking out?" Johnny hammered him.

"What do you mean? I don't know. I move on to the next one."

"Does it make you angry?"

"No, should it?" his answers were as quick as Johnny's

questions. Dex would have expected more of a hesitation from him, he seemed nervous as hell.

"Tammy was found murdered early Wednesday morning. You were the last person that was supposed to have seen her alive." Dex explained.

"You think I had something to do with it?" His eyes widened at the accusation. "No way, no how. That is not my style. Like I said, I date a lot, I liked her, but there are plenty of fish in the sea."

Johnny tilted his head.

"How? This can't be." Sheldon shook his head and his brows furrowed together, so tightly they almost merged into one. "This is awful. However I can help, just let me know. I can't believe this, and you think I had something to do with it? Do I need a lawyer?"

"Do you want a lawyer?" Johnny pointed his pen at him. "We can bring you down to the station and make this more official. Just say the word."

"I guess that would be a no then. I don't have anything to hide."

"So then, I guess we will be taking that phone number then." Johnny walked over to Sheldon's desk waiting for the doctor to get up and retrieve that card with the phone number he'd promised them. "Nice and slow."

Johnny hovered over him, his pistol already unlocked from his holster. He rested his hand on the top of the gun's handle. Sheldon opened the desk drawer and sorted through some papers and junk until he pulled out a small brochure with a business card attached.

"This is the contact info for the answering service company. They not only keep record of the calls in their database, they also record all of their calls for quality assurance and to make sure that if someone calls in with an emergency, they have a record of it." He extended the pamphlet to Johnny.

"How about you give me the name of the restaurant that you went to as well. We will be following up on your story."

"It was called the Salty Peach. I don't know who the hostess was, but I am sure they can tell you. Are you sure that Tammy is dead? I really wish I hadn't been late for dinner, maybe things would have turned out different." He stood there, waiting. Dex and Johnny continued to glare at him and watch his every move.

"We are getting back the toxicology report and the final medical examiner's report later today. Are you willing to give a sample for DNA to compare if need be?"

"Of course, whatever will help your investigation. I can assure you, I would never harm another person, let alone kill someone. I seriously hope that I am not a suspect."

"Let's just say that you are the closest thing we have to a suspect right now. The more information you can provide us with, the faster you get yourself off that list." Johnny slid his notepad and pen back in the inner pocket of his coat. "We will be in touch with you tomorrow to set up a time for you to come in and provide your DNA."

"I will make myself available whenever you need. Are we through here then?" Dr. Rubio came back out from behind his desk making his way toward the door. He put his hand out in front of him, suggesting that he was showing the detectives out.

"After you," Dex said. He never turned his back on a potential suspect, even if he got the feeling that the person was innocent.

"Very well." Sheldon Rubio huffed and slumped his shoulders as he walked past Dex, and Johnny took up the far rear.

CHAPTER TWELVE

"WHAT'S GOING ON, JOHNNY?" DEX couldn't let things slide any more. He knew something was wrong, and it wasn't anything he'd done. No way would Johnny still be mad at him because he didn't get their lunches fast enough. His partner wasn't that kind of a guy. He was, however, the kind of guy that wore his heart on his sleeve.

Dex put his hand on Johnny's shoulder and gave it a manly enough squeeze to try to encourage him to ease down his tension. It had built up throughout the afternoon, and Dex knew it was getting close to a breaking point.

Dex felt the muscles that ran across the top of Johnny's back tighten at his touch. He watched as his partner and good friend sucked in a shallow breath and held it. Dex was actually getting nervous about what was going on. Johnny was typically a solid and stable guy, and it was hard to shake that man. Something had him way off balance.

"It's my mother," his voice now hoarse. "Betty called me when you were in the captain's office."

They stood outside of the car. Johnny opened his door, but instead of getting in, he rested his arms over the top. He lifted one of his hands into a fist and pressed it against his mouth.

"Dude, she passed." He pressed his eyes together and shook his head fighting back the potential stream of tears. "She's just gone."

"What? When, how?" Dex was not equipped to deal with this kind of emotional situation. He was all too familiar with loss and his way of coping with it was less than mature. If he could have banged the back of his head against something he would have.

"They aren't sure. Natural causes. She went in her sleep. Her visiting nurse found her. Betty is handling everything for me right now." He pushed open the door to get in. "She knows how important this case is."

"Maybe you should go home and be with your family." Dex didn't know what to say, or how to comfort his friend, but working was probably not the best thing for him to be doing. He needed some time to grieve. At least that's what everyone had told him when Paul had died.

"No man, we have a case to work. I can't sit at home,

that will make me go crazy. I will probably have to take a day for the services, but other than that, I need to stay busy. I am not going to rest while there is a murderer walking around the streets of Hawk Creek."

"Well, I think that we should take a break, I thought that you were going to break that guy in two in there." Dex got in the car wishing he had taken the time to smoke. He really needed it.

"Break? What time is it?" While Johnny put the keys in the ignition, Dex pulled out his phone. Johnny might have had the only car with a broken clock.

"Almost five. We need to put a call into Shea and regroup. Let's get dinner and a drink. You need a drink." Dex felt a funny unfamiliar twinge in his stomach. "Where do you want to go, my treat?"

"I don't care as long as they have beer and buffalo wings. I need to OD on hot sauce right now." He chuckled without smiling. "There are too many things I just don't want to face right now."

"Kagley's it is." Dex said it, and he couldn't believe he had. He'd just decided, really without thinking.

It wasn't like him to go out of his way to go see the first woman that had captivated his attention for more than a twenty-four-hour period and it scared the shit out of him. "I could use a drink too. We might need to take a cab home tonight."

"You ain't shittin' me." Johnny put the car in drive. "So what do you think about this Doctor Sheldon guy?"

"For the most part, I believed what he was saying. You shook him up a bit in there, but he didn't really hesitate on any part of his story. I could be wrong, so we should keep our eyes on him. There is a part of me that wants him to be responsible so we can lay this to bed, and because if he isn't our guy we have much bigger problems."

"Yeah, like no real leads."

"Exactly. He did give us a slight direction. We will need to call his answering service to confirm his story, and we can check out the Salty Peach, maybe an employee saw her leave with someone. We might even find her phone around there. Would you mind checking in with Dr. Sinclair for me when we get there? I will call Betty and tell her that I am taking you out. I don't want her to worry about you."

"That sounds like a plan. Just don't let me get too drunk, she will be pissed at me."

The guys made their calls before they went into the restaurant. There was nothing worse than trying to hear someone on the phone with that amount of background noise. Dex also didn't want Betty to be pissed because they were calling her from the bar already. "Hey, Betty. How are you holding up?"

"Just keeping busy. How is Johnny? I'm worried about him." She wasn't always so soft spoken.

"On edge. But now that I know what is wrong, his behavior makes sense. I told him he should go home." Dex looked in on Johnny, still sitting in the car making his own call. He pulled out a cigarette and his lighter.

"That would be nice, but you know Johnny. If he were home, it would be worse for him. At work, he has something else to focus on. He needs to channel that energy somewhere. There is not a lot for him to do here."

Dex put his index and middle fingers on top of his brass lighter with his thumb on the base, and with a hard fast motion, he squeezed it open to light his beyond needed cigarette. He flicked the lighter outward causing it to snap shut. He loved hearing the crisp swooshing sound echoed back at him in the phone. Clearly Betty heard it too.

"You really should stop smoking, Dex. You are way too handsome for such an ugly habit. I have a program that one of my girlfriends did, and she has been smoke-free for six months. I can send in the info with Johnny if you want?"

"I don't know if I am ready for that, Betty, but sure, send it. It can't hurt to at least give it a look." Dex had no intention of quitting smoking. It was one of his favorite ways to kill time. He knew that people didn't like it, and it had become fairly taboo. He didn't like people telling him what to do, or how to live his life.

"Great. I think it could really help you."

"Listen, Betty, we have had a rough day. We still got work to do, but I am forcing a break on your husband. I am taking him for wings and a beer. Please don't be upset with him, I will make sure he gets home safe. I just wanted to let you know."

"Ok, don't let him get too drunk or eat more than two orders of wings. He's been on a diet, ya know?"

"Really, I didn't know that." Dex quietly snickered to himself but was glad to hear that. Although, he wasn't sure how the doughnuts fit into his diet. Now maybe he could persuade Johnny to come down to the gym and spar with him.

"And why isn't he calling me to tell me this?" Betty didn't sound mad about it, but Dex suddenly realized that it might have been odd for him to be calling her.

"Eh, I don't know. Honestly, I was avoiding calling Shea, so I told him I would check in with you, if he would call her for me."

"Dex, she cares a great deal for you. You really don't need to keep avoiding her. I know it's none of my business, but we have all known each other a long time."

"I know, Betty, I know. I'm going to get going before Johnny thinks I'm on the phone flirting with you." Dex took a final drag off his cigarette. Betty giggled.

"Cute, Dex. I needed that laugh. Thanks for calling. Tell Johnny I love him and to call me later."

Dex slid his phone into his back pocket and bent down to look into the car. Johnny was still on the phone, so he lightly banged on the hood of the car twice to get Johnny's attention. When he looked up, Dex swirled his finger around in the air, signaling him to wrap it up.

"I called Betty and let her know that you would be home later, and most likely intoxicated." Johnny frowned and rutted his brow. "But that I would make sure that you get home safe and don't eat too many wings. She wasn't thrilled but understood."

His friend moaned and nodded, shoulders uncharacteristically slumped forward. He looked too defeated to protest anything Dex might have said to his wife

"That was easier than I would have expected. I'm thinking a wing eating challenge might be in our future, what you say, buddy?"

"Thanks. Sounds perfect. I am starving. That weak ass salad only got my appetite started. All I have been thinking about is what I was going to eat for dinner." His shoulders were uncharacteristically slumped forward. He looked too defeated to protest anything he might have said to his wife.

"So what did Miss Shea say? You were on the phone

awhile."

"Dr. Sinclair said she was still waiting for the toxicology report, but she had all of her other findings ready for us. She'll send over what she has. It should be there when we get back to the station, and, if we need to meet with her she has time in the morning."

"I don't know if we will be heading back to the station tonight. I think we would be better off calling it an early night so we can get started first thing tomorrow morning.

"I told her about my mom too. I figured she would hear it through the grapevine anyway." Dex patted Johnny on the back.

They walked into Kagley's and happy hour was in full effect. The parking lot was fairly full, but Dex wasn't expecting the bar to be quite so crowded. He nonchalantly scanned the faces of the people at the bar, looking for Trina.

"What are you looking for?" Johnny asked, with a confused look when he took pause by the entryway.

"Oh, I was looking for a seat at the bar. I hate sitting at tables. The service always sucks." Dex was disappointed that he didn't see Trina and also relieved. He didn't want to seem like a stalker. He wasn't one to chase a girl.

"There are a few seats down there. Now, *you* are acting strange." Johnny looked at him sideways.

"Let's just get a seat before someone takes them." Dex

wasn't thrilled with having to rub elbows with so many people to get to the bar.

Dex might have promised Betty that he wouldn't let Johnny eat more than two orders of wings, but they were on their third. He figured that if he ate half of them then Johnny really didn't eat more than two orders.

The beers were knocking back too easy. Dex was fighting off having to look at what the case was stirring up for him, and facing Johnny's loss. He needed more than a few light beers to help stuff the swirl of emotions that were threatening to break free.

An older guy with way too much facial hair and a girl in her twenties, with curly red hair and tight body stood behind the bar. Dex waited for her attention, and waved her over.

"Hey, darling, can you get us two shots of Jameson's, please?" He waved his fingers back and forth over the top of the bar.

"Sure thing. She turned to use the computer behind her to punch in the order.

Johnny caught Dex staring at the bartender's rear end. "Why don't you ask her out? Or take a picture it will last longer."

"Very funny. She is cute but I don't date kids." Dex

laughed and licked his fingers clean so he could take a swig of his beer. "Besides, right now, I don't have time to invest in dating. Maybe after we close this case I will think about it. How does that sound? Make you happy?"

"Yes very." The bartender poured out two shots of Jameson's without interrupting them. "To Myrtle Harrington, may she rest in peace with my pops."

Dex raised his glass and clinked shots. "Cheers to that, she was a great woman."

Just as he felt the familiar burn sliding down his throat, the gentle pressure of two delicate hands squeezed on his shoulders. He felt his heart drop into the pit of his belly and almost choked on the shot.

"Sorry, did I startle you?" He was mad that he recognized her voice. He could have picked it out of a thousand voices. It was dripping in sweetness. He turned to face Trina.

"No, well, maybe a little bit. How are you?" The muscles on his cheeks started to hurt from smiling so hard. He wiped his face with a napkin and stood up to be polite.

"This is my girlfriend, Gladys. We work together." She gestured to the woman standing behind her.

Gladys was a few years older than Trina, and had stunning chestnut colored eyes that swept up in the corners. Dex couldn't help but notice how smooth and tight her skin was. Her dark hair and creamy brown skin cued him in to the assumption that she was of Filipino heritage. She reminded him of Rochelle Pangilinan, and he wondered if she had the same exceptional dance moves, mainly because he needed to get his mind off whether or not she had a bubble butt.

"Nice to meet you." Dex shook her hand. "Ladies, please take our seats. The bar is full, unless you were planning on sitting at a table?"

"We prefer the bar. I hate waiting for the waitress to come out of the kitchen when I need something. I guess I am a little impatient like that."

"I am the same way. Please sit." Dex pulled out the chair he had been sitting on, offering it to either lady, and Johnny got up to do the same.

"Thanks, we are actually going to run to the little girls room first. We will be back in a few to steal your seats. Make sure you keep them warm, it was pretty chilly outside." Trina bounced her shoulders up and down in a flirtatious fashion before they walked off.

Johnny's knuckles smashed into Dex's bicep, giving him a charlie horse.

"What the heck?" As if he didn't know.

"Don't play coy with me. She seems to not be unsurprised by your presence here. Did you make plans with her?" It was the first time his sullen friend had cracked a smile all day.

"Not exactly, she texted me that she was going to be here. I kind of suggested we come here before I realized. I think it was a subconscious decision."

"Yeah right. So when did you two exchange phone numbers?" Johnny stood behind his chair wagging his eyebrows.

"Ok, she actually asked me out on a date. She asked if we could go bowling. I gave her my card and told her to text me with her number. She did and happened to mention her and her friend would be here, but that wasn't my intention when I suggested we come here. I know that this place has your favorite wings." His backpedaling was getting him nowhere fast. He took a swig of his beer trying to force down the lump in his throat.

Dex felt his palms moistening at the idea of her coming back from the bathroom. He really had not thought out the repercussions of showing up when she'd texted him. Johnny already rode him about needing a steady woman would for sure bust on the fact that the gal he finally agreed to go out with, actually had asked *him* out on a date.

Could Johnny blame him? She was breathtaking in every way. There was a gentle elegance about her, but she seemed to have a concrete footing that impressed Dex. She would be able to give him a run for his money with her spirited attitude. Perhaps most of the women he had been with were "yes-ers" and he needed someone who didn't have a problem saying no.

Or what he needed to do was to slam a few more shots of whiskey and have his way with her so that he had every reason not to commit to another date. How could a woman want to date a man that would treat himself and others with such lack of regard?

"Two more!" He directed the bartender to serve them up another round.

CHAPTER THIRTEEN

"SO HOW LONG HAVE YOU ladies been teaching at the HCE?" Johnny asked. "Both my kids went there."

"This is only my second school year there," Trina answered. "Last year, I was only there for a few months, substituting."

"I am actually the Librarian as well as a teacher. I have been there for eleven years. What is your last name?" Gladys asked sipping on her Bloody Mary.

"Harrington, Jonathan, and Lilith are my kids' first names. They are both in the middle school now, you must have had them."

"I am sure I did, Lilith sounds familiar. That is not a common name, but Jonathan, I have a handful of them every year."

Dex was less than interested in the conversation between Gladys and Johnny. He was too busy memorizing the contours of Trina's profile. Her nose fit her face perfectly and pointed up ever so slightly at the tip. It was like an open invitation to kiss her pouty upper lip, the only thing that didn't look fragile on her face.

He was starting to feel the whiskey coursing through his veins and it made him feel more human. There was less to distract him. Watching Trina was like looking at a picture where the only thing that was in focus was the primary subject. Everything else around her blurred just enough that he forgot to notice they were there.

"So, Trina, what did you do before you started teaching at the elementary school?" Dex asked. He knew he was looking at her with the appetite of a deprived tiger.

"I was a curriculum coordinator for the Portland public primary schools. I loved what I did. I worked with some amazing educators, but I needed a change. My grandfather left me a property here in Hawk Creek that I'd considered selling for years. Instead, I decided to move here and see if the old house was worth fixing up."

"So you are on your second year here, I take it you like living here so far?" Dex waved over the bartender. "Do you want a drink? Or do you want me to order you some food?"

"I am good with my tonic water, I have a feeling I will need to drive a few people home tonight. Food sounds good." Trina tapped Gladys on the arm. "What do you want to eat?"

"Let's just get a sampler or some appetizers. Keep it easy, I can't stay out too late. I have to get home before my husband leaves for work." She went back to her conversation with Johnny. Dex assumed they had probably moved on to comparing stories about their kids. It was the only thing other than sports that he spoke passionately about.

"Can we get a sampler platter, some fried clams strips, and another round of drinks. Extra lime for this one over here." He pointed to Trina and winked at her. Hanging out with a sober woman was a new experience for Dex, at least it felt like a first.

"I hope you guys are going to eat some of that food." For some reason, Trina had never taken the seat Dex had offered. Instead, she stood there, slightly swaying to the faint sound of music and sipping through her straw. Her head was pointed down, but her eyes gazed up at Dex, and he felt them melting away his reservations.

"We are always hungry, and Johnny has what seems like a bottomless hole at the pit of his stomach. I've never met anyone that could eat like him and stay in such good shape." He was stretching the fact that Johnny was in good shape, but he certainly was not fat. Sure, he had some excess belly fat, but who didn't at his age? It just meant he was content with his life. "We had a few wings before you got here, but some more food would be a good idea. I told the misses that I wouldn't let him get too drunk. It might be time to cut him off."

"Other than the fact that you just ordered another round of drinks." Trina put her soda on the bar and a hand on her dainty little hip. "I know you guys are cops, and all, but from my own experiences, I have known a few that thought they were above the law. I hope that you don't intend on driving him home."

"I am deeply offended." Dex pressed his index fingers into his chest. "I take road safety very seriously. I am a one and done kind of guy."

Trina nodded her head slowly. "Mmm hmm. That's what I'm afraid of."

Dex heard what she said. Knowing there was a double meaning to the comment, he pretended to let it go over his head. However, he knew darn well that was the kind of guy he was when it came to the ladies, and he wasn't planning on having it any other way.

"We cab it after one drink, or for me, if I can't drive, I grab a hotel room and get home in the morning after I sleep it off."

"I'm sure you have an unlimited supply of travel sized toiletries and extra toothbrushes. It's good to know. So, how long have you been a cop?"

"Me, I've been a cop since I was twenty-three. I started in

a uniform and worked the beat in Portland. I grew up here in Hawk Creek. I moved back about seven years ago and took a detective position. I have been stuck with this guy ever since."

"I heard that," Johnny chimed in. "Hey, Dex order me a coffee when that gal comes back over here."

"You got it." Dex realized that Johnny had already had three shots too many and that was on top of a few beers. He might be able to throw down the beers when he was watching the game, but he normally didn't drink liquor. Dex was the opposite. He usually didn't drink beer. He was more of a whiskey kind of guy — straight up, on the rocks, or with coke. They all worked.

He'd first gotten the taste for whiskey when was just a boy. His grandmother had always had a whiskey sour with dinner. At first, he would just steal the cherries out of her drink, but the sweet and sour mix was a much better treat than the blah milk his mother made him drink. His grandmother was a bit senile so she never noticed the missing sips. When he'd become old enough, he'd offered to make them for her. He'd always made sure there was a little extra for himself. His love affair with the amber liquor had only grown from there.

The bartender came over and put down another Bloody Mary, two shots of Jameson's, and a tonic water with extra lime. "The food will be out in a minute. Do you need anything else?"

"Can you get the big guy over there a coffee, please? And a round of waters," Trina spoke up.

"Thanks. I kind of forgot." He pushed the shots over to the right away and out of reach of his partner. He debated on not drinking either of them, but he didn't like to waste things. He lifted one of the small glasses to his lips and tilted the smooth elixir.

"How do you drink that stuff?" Trina asked him.

"It's delicious, and it makes me happy."

"It doesn't burn at your stomach drinking shots of whiskey?"

"Not this kind. It has a clean light finish. You don't get the burn whiskeys leave behind. My grandmother drank it, how bad can it be?"

"I guess, for now, I will have to take your word for it. Maybe one night, when I don't have to drive my friend home, I will have to give it a try." Trina lifted the extra shot and took a whiff. "Doesn't really smell too strong."

"See that. I am an expert at making whiskey sours if you like things a little sweeter."

"Are you offering to make me drinks? Sweet is good sometimes, other times, I prefer it a bit more spicy." Trina put the drink back on the bar. The food had arrived, so she hopped up onto the bar stool and grabbed a plate.

Dex bit his lip behind her. He liked the sound of sweet

and spicy. He could definitely do spicy. He wondered just how hot she liked it. He leaned forward and whispered over her shoulder. "Yes, that was an invitation. I would like to make you cocktails, maybe dinner too, if you like."

Her hair smelled like a sunny spring day. He inhaled the sweet cherry blossom aroma. God, how he wanted to sweep the curtain of long blonde hair away and expose her neck. He could almost taste her essence. He was entranced by her scent.

Trina turned her face toward him and he could feel her breath on his cheek. Her eyelashes seemed to go on for miles as they fluttered to life.

"I would really like that, but I think we should leave the whiskey drinking to me. I don't care for burnt food." She reached up and pushed a loose strand of hair that had fallen down into his face back in place. He felt as if she was looking so far into him that he was afraid of what she might see.

"Perfect. Maybe we can order in." He leaned back and took a breath. The whiskey may have been amplifying everything he was feeling. There was such intensity already between them that he felt as if he could have sliced through it with a knife, but he didn't want it to end.

"Who ordered the clam strips?" Johnny asked reaching in front of Dex to grab a potato skin. "Those things are nasty."

"I love clam strips," Dex and Trina said in unison and started to laugh.

"I ordered them. Don't eat them if you don't like them. There is plenty of food. How about you Gladys, do you like them?" Dex asked.

"Sure, I love all seafood. They wouldn't be my first choice, but I like them just the same. I am kind of more of a fried cheeseburger kind of gal." She bit down on a piece of celery and grabbed a bar napkin to catch the drips of tomato juice.

"See that. They are not so bad. I bet you never even tried them," Dex prodded at Johnny.

"Well, today is not the day either." Johnny started working on their fifth order of wings.

The girls picked at the appetizers, but Dex was pretty sure that he and Johnny downed most of the greasy food. He didn't feel guilty about the calories either. He figured the more he ate, the more he could drink, and he still had another whiskey sitting calling his name on the bar.

"Excuse us for a minute." Gladys pulled gently on Trina's arm. "We need to powder our noses."

Trina smiled at Dex and shrugged her shoulders.

"Are you ladies done eating?" Dex asked.

"Yes…" her voice trailed off as they pushed through the happy hour crowd.

"I am stuffed. How about you, buddy?" Dex raised his

arms up to squeeze Johnny's shoulders.

"If I eat another wing, I might fly away. Betty will have to send out a search party. I am going to call a cab in a few. I don't want to get home too late, and we have a lot to catch up on in the morning." He put his napkin on top of the plate of empty wings and pushed the plates to the edge of the bar, so the bartender knew they were finished.

"You want another—"

Dex was interrupted mid-sentence by some guy in a suit, pushing past him to take the seat at the bar where Trina had been sitting.

"Excuse me, someone is sitting there."

"Seat looks empty to me. You two chums look like you are leaving anyway." He was tall with a slender frame, with black hair slicked back to the side. Besides his smug attitude, his sparse mustache agitated Dex, and could feel his face flushing.

"Right now, me and my friend are here, and our friends that are sitting there are in the restroom. Perhaps next time, you will get here earlier if you want a seat at the bar. Or you can wait like everyone else until we leave before you try to take our seats." Dex tried his best not to be too brash. He knew that Johnny didn't need the extra stress.

"Whatever man, you don't have to be such a dick."

Dex's teeth clenched as his jaw tightened and every muscle in his body flexed to attention. He took a half-step in the direction of the suit. It didn't take much to set him off. Dex's nostrils flared and his fist tightened. His anger wasn't well reined in making him a ticking time bomb.

He felt Jonny's hand cup his left bicep, stopping him in his tracks. The shift in attention was enough to diffuse the situation, only because the suit turned his back to them and didn't continue to engage him.

Dex looked into his partner's eyes. Johnny's drooping lids and distant stare were full of bereavement. Darts of sorrow replaced Dex's anger, and he lifted his hand to his partners shoulder.

The exchange was thick with feeling and understanding. Words weren't needed, nor would they have quite the right meaning. Dex leaned over the empty bar stool, grabbed his fifth shot, and slammed it before waving over the bartender.

"We are going to get out of here, can you please grab us our check." Dex was letting her know that they were finished eating but was interrupted by the sound of Trina yelling.

"Get your hands off of me," Trina's voice soured behind him.

He spun around, so fast he almost lost his balance. He wasn't happy with what he saw either.

"You are disgusting! What is your problem?" Gladys pushed the suit.

He stumbled back a half step before he lunged forward, and pushed her back using both hands. Lucky for Gladys, there was someone walking behind her to break her fall. Not so lucky for the suit.

Dex had heard and seen enough. His eyes darted to Trina as she helped Gladys to her feet, making sure neither of the women was in danger. Seeing they were safe, his feet took him to where he needed to be, without giving them direction.

A rush of adrenaline flooded his body. He felt the surge expand down his arm as his fist cocked back close to his body. His first shot made contact with the suit's chin, dropping him to the ground like a wilted flower.

Most of the crowd around them took a step back. One man, with a darker complexion and a light grey suit, stepped up to Dex. "What the fuck, bro! You want a piece of this?"

Johnny moved in between the two of them and flashed his badge. "Take a step back, son. HCPD."

The gray suit lifted his hands surrendering his intentions. "Alright. You're going to arrest this guy, right?"

Dex stood behind Johnny with his fists clenched at his waist. His hands were so tightly wound that his nails were cutting through his thick palms. He huffed as he tried to focus on the pain.

"Let me get this straight. You want me to arrest a guy for

knocking out a man that just hit a woman?" Johnny was always cool under pressure even with his elevated level of stress and intoxication.

The gray suit gave Johnny a dirty look and went over to check on his friend. "Dude, you alright? You need to get up."

"Gladys, are you okay?" Johnny asked. "You can press charges if you like. We have a bar full of witnesses here to back up your story."

Gladys and Trina stood off to the side of the action, holding each other, and Gladys looked to her friend for some kind of assurance. Without a word, Trina rubbed her back. "I should, but honestly, I think I just want to get home and forget this even happened."

"You sure? I will call a patrol car to come pick him up." Johnny walked over to the two ladies and assessed Gladys with his eyes to make sure she didn't have any injuries.

"Yeah, I'm okay, I didn't get hurt. Just shaken up. He is just a low-life pig." Gladys spit on the floor at the suits feet turned to Trina, and they walked toward the exit.

"I suggest the two of you pay your tab, tip your bartender, and get the fuck out of here. I don't want to see you two rude bottom feeders in here again." Johnny put his badge away and stood with his arms crossed, watching as the gray suit helped his friend up off the ground.

Gray suit pulled out a wad of cash and tossed it on the

bar. The people that were standing nearby just backed out of his way and whispered.

Dex stepped aside to stand in front of Trina and Gladys. He didn't want any reason for the two assholes to start any more trouble with them. He was fired up and ready to go. It would only take one wrong look in their direction, and someone was getting a beat down.

They all watched as the two guys walked out of the bar. Dex took a deep breath through his nose because his jaw was still so tightly clenched that he wasn't sure if he could open it.

Johnny walked over and asked, "Everyone here okay?"

Trina looked over at Dex, and her eyes were like two tiny radars as she gasped at the blood dripping off the peaks of Dex's knuckles.

"Oh, my goodness. You need to get that washed and put some ice on it." Trina lifted his fist to examine it more closely.

Gladys scurried the short distance back to the bar where they had been seated and grabbed a wad of napkins to put on his hand. She brought them over and handed them to Trina.

"I just need to pay our tab so we can get out of here. I think the party's over," Dex said, using his left hand to reach his back pocket for his wallet. He handed it to Trina. "Can you help me out?"

"Sure, let's go get this taken care of." They walked over to the bar. The tab was sitting in a pint glass in front of the two empty seats, no one else had dared to move in on where they'd been sitting. Happy hour was winding down, and after the altercation, much of the crowd had thinned out.

Trina went to open her purse to take out her wallet.

"I got it. Don't even think about offering money." Trina closed her purse and took heed to the stoic look on his face.

"You have sixty dollars in here. How do you want to pay it?" Trina asked him.

"Toss one of those credit cards up there and leave the sixty cash for the bartenders. I can stop at the five-and-dime next door to get cash from the ATM for the ride home." Dex put pressure on the napkins while Trina took care of paying the check. She also asked the bartender for a bag of ice to put on his hand.

"Sorry about everything," Dex hollered over to the bartender.

She waved her hand at him. "That guy is always an asshole, and he is a shitty tipper. Hopefully, they won't be back. Nobody needs to deal with guys like that."

Dex nodded and waved to her.

"I can drive you guys home if you want. It is still early and I have to drop Gladys off anyway," Trina offered, "No need to go to the ATM."

"You don't have to drive us both home. We don't mind taking cabs."

"I won't have it. I just have to drop Gladys off first." She smiled at him and slid her arm around his waist, guiding him out of the bar. His blood was still thick with anger, but her touch brought it down to enough of a simmer that he almost smiled.

CHAPTER FOURTEEN

"TRINA, THANK YOU FOR YOUR consideration in securing us a ride home," Johnny said slowly, hovering just outside of the open rear door of Trina's yellow hatchback. "Dex, I have so much to say to you, but since I am intoxicated, it may not all make sense, so I will see you first thing tomorrow morning. I will pick you up at seven."

Dex laughed to himself. He wanted to call out to his partner to remind him that his vehicle was back at Kagley's, so unless he used Betty's car, someone would be calling for a car service in the morning.

"It really was very sweet of you to take the time to drive all of us home." Dex rubbed at the breast pocket of his jacket, wishing he could smoke a cigarette. He looked around her car, and there were no signs of her being a smoker. He would normally have just lit up, but didn't want to be rude by asking her if it was okay. "Take a left at the light and the fourth right hand turn."

"Sure, it's no big deal. I don't mind at all. I don't see any reason for you guys to spend money on cabs and hotels. It's not like you are an hour away." Trina glanced over at him. He was leaning against the corner of the seat and the door. His eyes mostly focused on her.

"I am only a few minutes away. What part of town do you live in?" he continued to make small talk.

"Oh, I live off of Beauport Road, by the old saw mill. You know, I normally don't go around driving strange men home or telling them where I live before we have even gone out on a date."

"That's good to know. You should never do either of those things."

"Well, I figure that I know you enough and you are a stand-up cop. As for where I live, I haven't really told you, but you could easily run my plates or look up my license to find out that information." Dex could see her lips curl up even with the limited amount of light.

She took the fourth right as instructed. She turned to him for guidance on what her next move would be.

"Oh, turn up here, on the left." Dex pointed. "I live in that apartment complex. Once you turn in, it is the third building to the right."

Dex was inebriated, but not really drunk, at least not by his standards. No one had ever complained about the way he acted when he was drinking, but he hoped that he wasn't talking with slurred speech or anything that could potentially be a turn off to her.

She pulled into a spot in front of his building, and put the car in park but kept the engine running. He watched as she pulled the edge of her thick bottom lip into her mouth, slightly biting on it and wished he was the one doing the biting. Her eyes hung low staring at her hands.

"I had fun tonight, minus the jerky guy in the suit." Her voice was gentle even when she cursed. "I am looking forward to you making me that whiskey sour."

"I am looking forward to making it for you. I would offer to make you one now, but I'm sure you have to get home," Dex said, kind of testing the waters. He wanted to invite her up, but he didn't want her to get the wrong idea.

"I don't sleep much, but I told you I don't drink and drive. I could come up and have that drink and stay." The pitch in her voice was a mix of a statement and a question, and she didn't look at him when she spoke. "I could drive you to your car tomorrow morning. If we get up early enough, I will have time to go home and get ready for work."

"Really? That is what you want to do?"

"Sure, why not?"

"Sounds good to me. Come on then." Dex felt a small burst of energy. "Make sure you lock your doors. You can have my bed, I will take the couch."

"Ok. As long as you set the alarm." Trina turned off the car and they met up on the sidewalk. She hit the lock button on her key fob and the horn made a small beep.

Dex held out his bent elbow and she slid her arm into the hole holding on as he guided her toward the stairs.

"I'm on the third floor. Sometimes it is a pain, but I like the little bit of extra exercise I get from it, especially when I forget something in my truck."

"You have a truck?"

"Sure do, a black F150."

"I have my grandfather's F250 from the seventies. I don't drive it, but I keep it insured. I used it when I moved from Portland. I just keep it in the old barn."

"That is pretty bad ass. Is it in good condition?" He asked as he opened the door.

"I guess. It has some rust spots, but other than that, it is in decent shape. I guess that's why I kept it. And there is only like forty-thousand miles on it. Not sure it is really worth much though."

"It might be if it is in good enough shape. I know some guys that restore them and customize them with fancy upgrades. If you ever decide you want to get rid of it, I can take a look at it for you." Dex tossed the contents of his pockets on the counter. He took his boots and coat off and put them in the closet.

"Do you want me to take my shoes off?" Trina asked as she shut the door behind her.

"Well, you surely are not wearing those shoes in my bed. They may look sexy as hell on you, but they will come off eventually. Your preference really."

"You're funny. I guess you're right, I just wasn't sure if you have a shoes off kind of home," Trina said as she held onto the back of the couch and removed her amber colored pumps.

"I don't ever wear my shoes in the house, but I am often in some pretty gross places, and I am a bit compulsive about things being in order here. It is just habit to put my stuff away as soon as I walk in. Please, make yourself at home. Do you want me to grab you something to change into?" Dex asked, looking into his fridge.

"You should clean your hand off. Do you want me to help you?" Trina suggested.

"Oh, you're right." He stopped what he was doing, went over to the sink, and washed his hands. "This is nothing, I am used to it. Maybe I will throw some more ice on it later. That is if there is any left after I make you this drink."

"It's actually kind of early, I am good like this. For some reason, I thought it was later. I hate when it starts getting dark so early, it really throws me off." Trina stood on the opposite side of the counter that divided the kitchen from the living room watching him.

"Sorry, I need to get stools for over there, but I don't usually have company." He pulled out two plastic bottles shaped like lemons and limes, an egg, and a tray of ice. He set it on the counter and proceeded to search for more ingredients in the cabinets.

"I don't mind standing I was just sitting in the car for the past half hour. Why don't you have company?" she asked. You seem like a guy that would be the life of a party."

"Me? I guess I was at one point in my life, now I actually keep to myself, for the most part. I go out a few times a month, and other than work, the only other thing I do is go to the gym."

"Hmm." Trina's reply was not full of belief, but what could she say? "What are you doing with the egg? Didn't you eat enough at Kagley's?"

"You don't know?" he asked.

Trina just shook her head.

"This is my grandmother's secret recipe. It will not disappoint you. That is one of the few promises I can actually make. Feel free to make yourself at home. You can relax on the couch and turn the TV on, if you like."

"I am way too intrigued by what you're doing to watch TV. The view over here is much better than over there."

He wasn't sure if she meant to wag her brow at him, but he liked it. Dex squeezed some lemon and lime juice into the shaker, then added agave nectar and water. He cracked the egg over the garbage only saving some of the white, which he added to the large metal canister. He measured the Jameson and popped half of the ice cubes into the shaker, the rest went into a tall glass, followed by a single cherry with a nice long stem.

After he put the top on the shaker and shook it hard into the air and wiggled his hips for effect and tossed the shaker in the air before catching it behind his back. Snapping off the lid of the shaker, he strained the frothy contents into the glass.

Trina clapped.

"Here you go. Enjoy."

"If the drink tastes half as good as your moves, this will be excellent." Trina took the glass and giggled a little. She licked her lips and rubbed them together before pressing the rim against her wanting mouth.

Dex leaned back against the refrigerator, watching her. His buzz was starting to fade, so he decided to make himself one too. Stepping forward, he almost lost his footing on an ice chip on the floor. He caught a hold of the counter in front of him, hoping that Trina did not notice his clumsiness. His eyes never wavered away from her mouth.

Her eyes were closed as she tilted the glass, taking a slow lingering sip. "Mmm," was all she said. With her eyes still closed, she took another taste.

"So what do you think? Was it worth coming up for?"

Dex asked as he worked on his own cocktail.

"Who says the drink is all I came up here for?" She batted her eyelashes at him from behind the rim of her glass. "It is really tasty. I never had a whiskey sour with Irish whiskey. It is slightly less sweet than with bourbon, but it does have a smoother finish. I like it, and might want another. I have a feeling this one is going to go down too fast."

"I take it you're not hungry? If you are, I might be able to scrounge something up. I eat mostly take-out though."

"I am good, and this drink is perfect. I really wanted one at Kagley's, you guys all looked as if you were having so much fun. At least until that jerk grabbed my ass."

"Excuse me!" Dex's eyes shot up at her with the speed and precision of an expert archer.

Trina looked startled probably wondering what she had said wrong that had suddenly changed the mood in the room from playful to stark.

Dex put his drink on the counter beside hers and walked the small distance into the living room to stand toe to toe with her.

"I was not aware that he had violated you like that." Dex stood at least ten inches above Trina. Looking down on her and thinking about another man putting his hands on her without her permission, had his blood reaching an all time high temperature.

"I thought that is why... I'm sorry," she whispered looking down.

Dex lifted her chin so she would look at him. "No one should put their hands on you, or anyone else for that matter, without permission. I thought he was just being rude to you ladies, which I have no tolerance for. Women deserve respect and should be talked to in a courteous manner."

Trina nodded her head.

"He is lucky that I didn't know that. Your friend should have pressed charges."

"She didn't want any trouble. I'm sure she didn't want to have to go home and tell her husband what had transpired either," Trina said.

"I can assure you, that no one will disrespect you again, not in my presence anyway." He pushed her golden locks away from her face. He wanted to lean in and kiss her and it took everything inside of him to take a step back.

Trina cleared her throat and reached for her drink.

"I probably shouldn't have lost my cool that fast. I don't usually let my emotions get the better of me like that. Something just snapped when I heard you yelling." Dex grabbed his glass and held it up to hers to clink glasses. "Here is to us relaxing for what is left of tonight."

"I can drink to that." Trina smiled and sipped on the cocktail. Dex grabbed her free hand.

"Let's sit. If you don't want to watch TV I can put some music on if you like. Do you have a preference?" He asked sitting down on the black leather sofa.

"Anything is fine; I listen to everything, but nothing too extreme. I want to hear you tell me more about yourself." She sat on the couch beside him. Her posture was tall and she rotated her torso stretching her back causing her breasts to become more pronounced. He tried not to stare.

Dex watched as she crossed her legs so that her right foot tickled the front of his leg. It sent shivers up the center of his back. He hoped that it wasn't obvious. She was having quite an effect on him, and he didn't want her to feel uncomfortable thinking he was looking for a fast night.

"Are you okay? You didn't get hurt in the shuffle did you?" he asked continuing to watch her every move.

"No, I am just tight. I might have tensed up enough to have pulled something, I don't know. I have become a very jumpy person. I think that is why I don't sleep much. I always feel like I hear something at my house. I don't much like being alone at night."

"Oh, I see, so that is why you offered to stay, it's not my drink or my dance moves," Dex said playfully.

"I don't know about that. Maybe a little, how could anyone resist you and this homemade drink?"

"That might be true, but I don't usually offer. You are

actually the first female to ever come to my apartment."

"How long did you say you have lived here?" She looked at him again in disbelief again.

"I don't know, maybe seven years."

"So, you are telling me you haven't dated any women in the past seven years?" She shook her head.

"I didn't say I haven't dated anyone, just not anyone that I ever brought home," Dex admitted.

"Oh. Hmm, that's interesting."

"Not really, I work a lot. I could rub your back if you like." He wanted to touch her body so bad it hurt.

"What about your hand?"

"This? It's barely a scrape. My knuckles have been through much worse. A small scuffle isn't enough to stop me from being able to caress a beautiful woman. That is for damn sure."

Trina took a swig of her drink, she had been right it was disappearing quickly. Dex had barely sipped on his. Of course, he was several drinks ahead of her.

"I have a better idea, how about you fix me another drink, and then I will rub you, and you can tell me about why your day was so rough, besides what happened at the bar."

Dex stood up and lifted both of their drinks. "I have some extra in the shaker already, and you are welcome to drink mine. I probably had enough at the bar anyway. I have to get up early and be functional for work tomorrow. We have to crack this case before it becomes high profile." He reached over the counter and grabbed the shaker.

"We can do a rub for a rub. Come with me, I will get you something more comfortable to wear. Don't worry. I am not luring you to my bed to take advantage of you." They didn't really know each other that well for them to wind up sleeping together, which was not Dex's normal train of thought. He also had not had a woman in his home in a very long time, especially not one that he intended to take to his bed without actually bedding her.

"I don't think I will fit into your clothes." Trina waved her hand over her much more delicate frame. "And I am not worried about you trying to sleep with me. I can tell you're not that way, and I know enough self-defense that even this little thing would give you a run for your money if I needed too. I am actually quite strong."

"I love that fiery spark you have. You probably won't fit into any of my bottoms, but one of my tees will cover you like a nightgown. You can try a pair of my drawstring sweats if you like." Dex put the drinks on his empty nightstand.

"Here is a tee and a pair of basketball shorts, I think you will have better luck with these sweats. It's kind of warm in here anyways, isn't it?" he asked, laying the clothes on the edge of the bed beside where she stood.

Trina sucked in a breath and agreed, "It is."

"I am going to use the bathroom unless you need it first?" he offered. "I think I will be quicker than you. Women have a tendency to get lost when they use the restroom."

"Very funny, I can wait," she said.

Dex went into the bathroom adjoining both his bedroom and the hallway. He brushed his teeth and relieved himself in record time. He left a new toothbrush on the counter for Trina. He didn't think about the fact that she may have started to get changed until it was too late.

He opened the door just as she was lifting her sweater over her head. Her creamy pink skin glowed in the dim light. He felt himself stiffen at the sight of the protruding pink buds beneath the sheer lace that covered her breasts. She may or may not have heard him open the door, but it didn't stop her from undressing.

He considered closing the door and giving her another minute of privacy, but instead he cleared his throat and stepped back into his room. "Sorry, I thought you were going to wait for me to..." He turned and pointed to the bathroom door.

"That's okay, I don't have to go. I went right before we left Kagley's. How about you make yourself more comfortable and lie down. I will rub you first." Trina put his white tee on over her bra and then removed her pants.

The sight of her flat stomach and curvaceous breasts were branded onto his eyes. He had no problem with the idea of closing his eyes and reliving the view while she gave him a massage.

CHAPTER FIFTEEN

DEX LIFTED HIS SHIRT OVER his head. He wasn't shy about his body either. He had little to no body fat. Ninety percent of the time, he ate three things, chicken, broccoli, and egg whites. The rest of the time, he cheated.

Hours at the gym demolishing the leather bags with his fists burned off more calories than he could consume in a week. His body never disappointed the ladies, and they didn't have to tell him to take his clothes off twice.

He saw Trina watching him out of the corner of his eye. There was no real need to, but he flexed his muscles as he unbuttoned his jeans. A wave of relief, that he wasn't going commando, washed over him. Free balling it might have made things a bit awkward at that point in their relationship. The zipper came down with ease, as did his jeans.

He had on a pair of light blue trunks that cut away just

beneath his muscular ass. They were a low-rise cut, exposing the tops of his hips and accentuating his core muscles. He picked up his shirt and jeans and tossed them in one of the laundry baskets in his closet and went to grab a pair of shorts from the drawer.

"What are you waiting for? You can put shorts on later. If it makes you feel better, I will put mine on later too." She was torturing him with her relaxed attitude toward clothes. He couldn't quite read if she was completely coming on to him or just cool about everything. Either way, he liked it and didn't want to fuck it up by making any assumptions.

He climbed onto his bed grabbed a pillow, and pulled it under his head, so he could still see her. He watched as she joined him, her moves resembling that of a cat, and he pictured her purring and nuzzling up on him.

Instead, she spread her legs and straddled him sitting on his butt. Her soft skin was cool against his hot body, which was still flushed from the alcohol. Her thighs felt like pieces of pure silk.

"Do you want your drink? Can you reach it?" he asked her.

"I think I can reach it. I'm okay right now, though." Her hands engaged in slowly rolling the taut flesh of his back from the lower center, and up around the edges of his spine. Her thumbs worked the tight muscles over his shoulders.

"You are really tense. I can even feel the tension in your lower back between my legs. Try to let go."

He took a deep breath and forced it out in an attempt to follow her command.

"Tell me what you and Johnny were so upset about. Then take a deep breath and let it go."

Dex could feel the full palms of her hands engaging their battle with his muscles. He preferred to think of them as being tight from all of his hard work at the gym because he tried to keep stressful elements to a minimum in his life.

"Besides the case we are working on, Johnny found out that his mother passed away today." Dex let the air out of his lungs trying to let it go.

"Oh, I am so sorry to hear that. Did you know her well?" she asked.

"I knew her. We have been partners for seven years. Although he is older than me, we grew up in the same neighborhood, so we all kind of knew each other and our families. She was a good woman, but she has been fading in health over the past few years." He paused for a minute. "I don't do well with death."

Trina's hands stretched across his traps and over his deltoid muscles until her arms were wrapped around him, her soft breast pressing against his back.

Her voice, barely a whisper in his ear, she asked, "Is it

okay if I hug you?" He nodded in agreement.

Either her soft breath or her hair stimulated the tiny hairs on his neck, and he felt a million tiny prickles along his neck, causing his shoulders to shudder.

He pressed his eyes together as his emotions rose to the surface. He didn't want them to come spilling out into an ugly mess in front of her. Dex also didn't pull his usual move of stuffing them as far down as possible. He let them just sit there.

Trina kept her torso pressed against the middle of his back but continued to glide her fingertips over the outsides of his arms. He knew a lot of guys that shaved their arms, but he did not. He was glad that he had a small amount of fine blonde hair that did not restrict the fluid motion of her touch.

"It's okay to get upset when someone you know or care about passes on. Just remember that it is you who is experiencing the loss. They are going home and experiencing the true bliss of the love of the universe." Her head was nestled between his two shoulder blades. "It's okay to let the physical aspect of them go and keep the spirit of them alive in your heart."

Dex felt as if there was an angel telling him that everything would be okay, and he didn't have to blame himself for the suffering of others. But was that really what she was saying, or was it just that way if someone passed from natural causes? He felt all of what he was letting go start to build back up as his muscles tightened beneath her.

"Whatever it is, or who it is, it's okay. I know you see some messed up stuff in your line of work, you can't control everything, and you can't save everyone. Being open to grief does not mean that you have to be consumed by it. It takes courage to face it. If you ever need to talk about it, I am a very empathetic listener."

Dex rolled over and held on to her, keeping her on top of him. He lifted a hand to uncover her face, tucking her hair behind her ears. He wanted to be angry with her for trying to talk to him as if she knew anything about him. How dare she tell him how to cope with what he had lost?

What did she know about loss? Certainly she didn't know what it was like, to feel as if you were the cause behind your best friend being gone. No one could bear that existence. It was why he chose to spend much of his free nights in a whiskey haze. Women made him feel as if he were alive. They stimulated his senses, and what he thought were his feelings.

The sudden surges of emotions he thought he felt with those random partners had kept him single for many years, but staring into the eyes of the angelic creature in his arms had him rethinking everything.

The depth of compassion in her gaze made it hard for him to keep eye contact with her, and he felt his entire world unraveling around them. He desperately wanted to reach out and grab a hold of the last bit of thread and reel it back in.

Trina's fingers weaved into Dex's hair, and he leaned into the palm of her hand as she stroked his head, combing his hair. He felt as if there was so much he wanted to say to her, but he continued to hide behind the silence of the intense moment.

"You didn't let me finish rubbing your back." He watched her pouty lips move as she talked, they hardly opened when she spoke. If he could have tasted her voice on his tongue, it would have been like eating cotton candy on a sunny summer afternoon.

"No, but I feel better already. How could I not take the opportunity to stare into your breathtaking eyes?" his voice was hoarse and came out raspy.

"Are you saying that I take your breath away?" she asked.

"I suppose I am."

"I know mouth to mouth if you think you can't breathe." She giggled, but he didn't think it was because she didn't mean what she said. She joked, but the look in her eyes burned with desire.

"Is that so?" He grabbed her and rolled her under him. She let her legs spread apart, so his broad frame would fit between them. He pushed her hair back and stroked along the edges of her cheeks, contouring every curve of her oval face. "God I want to kiss you so bad."

Dex felt Trina's legs wrap around him and she pulled him in closer to her. He couldn't stop himself from hardening against her. He really didn't want things to go that way. He didn't want to continue to use sex as an escape, not with her.

He tried to picture Johnny in his softball uniform to distract his mind from the almost uncontrollably enticing specimen that lay beneath him. He had to keep control.

"So what's stopping you?" She reached up and took his face in her hands, and pulling herself up, so that her lips could meet his.

Dex watched her face as it got closer. How he wanted to devour her, instead, he knew would savor every last drop of her. He could almost taste her sweet breath. Her lips hovered just below his. If either of them moved a millimeter, they would be touching. He was plenty strong, but his arms began to shake, threatening to crumble beneath him. His heart pounded, so loud, he was sure she was going to ask him if he was okay.

He had never been so close to someone, so close to engaging in a kiss, with his eyes open. How could he close them? How could he ever stop looking at her? Her skin was so smooth it disguised her age. He wanted to learn and memorize every inch of her face, her body, and her soul.

Her soft velvety lips ever so slightly brushed against his and their breath became one. The intense heat building between them was dangerously close to igniting into flames.

The warmth of her mouth sent shivers down into his legs. *All three of them,* he thought trying not to laugh at the notion. His hands were pulsing with need to reach down and touch more of her.

The longing became unbearable. He had to taste her. His nose filled with cherry blossoms and strawberry lip balm as he sucked in a quick breath. He was starting to feel as if he might pass out from the sheer suspense of this kiss that he could no longer avoid.

Dex closed his eyes and eased in closer feeling her tiny nose as it brushed against his. There was so much need in him, but he used every ounce of restraint he could to enjoy and memorize every second of her mouth.

Their lips glided against each other with a sweetness he had never known. He took his time tasting her; kissing and lapping up every last drop of her lips. She may have initiated the kiss, but he would be the one to control it.

He felt as if his insides were going to burst into the most extraordinary display of fireworks, and he had not even slipped his tongue in her mouth yet. The exchange between them was in their breath. They had become one, existing on a single cycle of air.

Trina had found a way into a part of Dex's heart, that he'd kept locked up tight for so many years that he wasn't sure he could remember where he'd put the key. It didn't matter, though, because she'd picked the lock and found a way to merge their hearts into one rhythmic song.

It may have been the longest first kiss in history, and it wasn't about to end any time soon. He felt so much, so deeply, that his extremities numbed enough to give him the sensation that he could fly away.

Trina's hips rocked up against him and he about lost it. The sweet innocence of the kiss shifted. Her lips parted and his mouth dove deep. The whiskey sour lingered on her tongue, and if he could have drunk her up, he would have.

His breathing became strained and was replaced with soft moans of desire. Her body responded to his and she too moaned into his seductive mouth causing his lips to vibrate.

Her soft breasts pressed against his chest. Passion and need drove his hands to her aroused body. He couldn't suspend his desire to touch her any longer.

Before he realized what he was doing his rough hands found the soft skin of the back of her thighs. He explored her flesh until he found the sweet spot where her leg and her round ass met. He pressed his thumb into the crease of skin and palmed her hips.

He wanted to slide his fingers beneath her panties. He knew that her body was responding to his touch in a way that she would not deny him. As much as he craved to dive into her, what he really wanted most wasn't beneath the thin strip of fabric that divided them.

He, instead, let his hands search the outer edges of her body. Her skin was silky and smooth. Her lips were like a drug he had never consumed. He was addicted, and it had only taken one kiss.

There was a sense of euphoria that he couldn't remember ever experiencing with a woman. Sure sex was one of his addictions, but this was different, it wasn't about the climax, it was about the ride to get there. For once, he really didn't care if he got there or not. He just wanted more of her. He wanted every touch, every caress, every swipe of the tongue to last just a little longer than the last.

Her delicate fingers explored every inch of his back. The pressure switched back and forth from gentle strokes to forceful pulls of the skin, bringing their bodies closer and closer together.

Dex could feel her arousal dampening the front of his trunks. He reveled in it, breaking their kiss, so he could look down at her body beneath him. His oversized shirt had inched its way up, exposing her flat belly. He sucked in a breath and grunted as he let the air hiss out of his nose.

He wanted his lips grazing over her tiny belly button. He imagined sliding his tongue across her soft skin from hip to hip. He also knew he wouldn't be able to stop there.

"Shit, you are beyond exquisite, Trina." Dex blurted out. His head started to hurt. A sudden fear washed over him. He didn't want to fall in love. He didn't even know this woman, and he was in deeper than he had ever been. What the hell was going on with him?

Trina smiled up at him like a fox. She bit the corner of her swollen bottom lip. He wished she would stop looking at him as if he was a steak dinner because all he wanted to do was hand feed her every morsel of his existence.

"You're not so shabby there, detective. I really like the way you feel in my hands."

"I'm really enjoying touching you. It is hard to keep my hands to myself." He laughed, but he knew the situation was far from funny. He scooted off to the side of the bed and grabbed one of the whiskey sours. "You want one?"

He could see the confusion in Trina's eyes as she pushed herself back in the bed to sit up and lean against the headboard. "Um, sure."

Dex handed her one of the drinks. She took it and slammed the rest of it. He felt the shift in the energy in the room. He'd probably just fucked everything up. He'd known if he found himself in a situation like this, no matter his actions, they would be destructive.

"Hey, you want me to make you another?" Dex asked her, trying to find anything to say to diffuse the awkward moment he created.

"No, I'm good. I was just thirsty and it hit the spot." She looked over at his alarm clock. "I can't believe how late it is."

"Shit, it is. I'm sorry you have to get up so early to drive me back to my truck."

"No worries. That's what I do. I go out of my way for people." She stood up and grabbed the pair of shorts off the end of the bed. "I'm going to get ready for bed, do you happen to have one of those spare toothbrushes in there for me?"

"Yeah, I left one on the counter for you. Help yourself to anything else you might need in there." He watched her walk into the bathroom, and she didn't bother looking at him as she passed by.

"Fuck!" he whispered to himself. She was pissed. He'd probably insulted her. He worried that she thought he was turned off by her or something weird. He felt an awful tightening in his chest, thinking about the way her eyes had darkened and seemed to go hollow after he'd stopped their make-out session.

He got up, grabbed a pair of basketball shorts for himself, and grabbed a pillow off the bed. He'd told her he would take the couch, and he didn't want her to think that he couldn't keep his word. Too bad he didn't have any extra sheets or blankets. He never had or expected to have company.

As Dex was about to walk out of his room the door to the bathroom opened, and he was face to face with Trina. He felt his heart skip a beat at the mere sight of her.

"Are you sure you're okay?" she asked, rubbing her hands over his chest. "I don't mean to come off as a crazy girl, but I thought that we were in the middle of a moment, and then you just got up as if it never happened."

"I think I just had too much to drink, and..." *Shit.* He really didn't know how to backpedal out of the situation. "It's just late, and I..."

Dex looked down at his pillow, searching for that smoothness that he normally had. It was a rare thing that he found himself at a loss for words. He didn't want to talk, he wanted to grab her by the back of the hair and kiss her so hard that he would have to hold her up so he didn't knock her over.

"It's been a really long day. I'm sorry if I made you feel uncomfortable. I am going to go sleep on the couch. My alarm is already set for five thirty. Is that early enough for you, or too early?" He asked.

"It is pretty early, but will probably give me the perfect amount of time to get you where you need to go and get myself home to get ready for work." She pulled on the pillow. "What's this all about?"

"I told you, you could sleep in my bed, I got the couch."

"You must be kidding me. We were just half-naked in your bed making out. You don't have to sleep on the couch. I know you are not going to take advantage of me. That is pretty clear at this point." The edge to her voice cut him like a knife.

"So what you are saying is, that you want me to stay in here with you?" he asked because he felt like her signals were mixed between wanting him and being utterly pissed at him.

"If you don't want to, I understand. I don't want to force you to sleep with me." She stopped herself, probably realizing that her choice of words could have been better. "That came out wrong."

Dex stepped closer to her and lifted her chin. He looked into her eyes, searching her soul. He wanted nothing more than to sleep beside her, and to sleep with her, but he didn't want to make a big thing of it.

"Let's just get some sleep." He leaned forward and kissed her forehead, turned her around and marched her to his bed. He climbed in behind her, and she pulled his arm around her.

CHAPTER SIXTEEN

FIVE THIRTY CAME QUICKLY, MAYBE because Dex had spent most of the night staring at the ceiling. He had been exhausted and buzzed enough that he'd expected to knock out pretty fast, but his mind had had other plans for him.

He sifted through his night with Trina in his mind several times, dissecting everything he'd said and done. His replays didn't end there. He watched the string of events that had been his life for the past seven years.

They were empty. There were no feelings of regret or satisfaction for that matter. He considered the possibility that he needed to make some new choices. Was drifting away, riding the whiskey wave, a future that he wanted? It was the only way he knew, and he wasn't sure he deserved anything more.

Before Trina was even awake, he texted Johnny and let him know that he would pick him up and bring coffee.

Dex would have plenty of time to hit up Mickey's, and he was sure that Johnny could more than use a doughnut.

He stretched across the bed and watched the rise and fall of Trina's breath. He couldn't help but steal the opportunity to study her delicate features. Her lips were slightly pursed as if they were asking to be kissed, and he was tempted to answer them.

Dex felt a connection to Trina, and he hated himself for it. He climbed back off the bed and got up to get dressed. He didn't really make much of an effort to be quiet. Trina needed to wake up, and he wasn't sure how to make that happen. He didn't want to poke her, and he couldn't allow himself to caress her with the softness she reflected.

He tossed his gym bag on the bed. The impact must have been enough to stir her from sleep because she rolled toward him.

"Good morning," her voice raspy enough to seduce him into a good mood. "How late is it?"

"Morning. It's not late. It's a quarter of. I was just about to wake you. I just have to finish packing my gym bag, and then we can head out. Unless you want me to make you some instant oatmeal and a coffee?" He resisted looking at her by continuing to pack his bag.

"I'm not really an oatmeal kind of girl, but thank you for the offer," she said as she kicked her feet off the bed.

"Pancakes right?"

"You remember. Color me impressed." She grabbed her clothes off the edge of the dresser where she had stacked them the night before. "I'm going to brush my teeth and get dressed."

"Cool." Dex zipped his bag and tossed on the floor, so he could make the bed after he harnessed his gun and badge onto his belt. He could smell her sweet essence as he fluffed the sheets. She smelled so good, he would never look at a cherry blossom tree the same way again.

By the time she came out of the bathroom, dressed in her own clothes, Dex was already waiting by the front door with his bag. "I hope it's okay, I tossed your clothes into the laundry basket in the closet. I saw you put yours in there last night."

"That's perfect, thank you. Are you all set?" Dex asked picking up his bag. He already had his flannel and boots on. His emotional switch was off, and he was ready to get to work.

"Yeah, I guess so. I don't really have anything to get ready." She shrugged and grabbed her keys off the counter. "I just have to put my boots back on. I guess you don't have time to make me those pancakes."

Trina smirked at him while she zipped her boots.

"I'm not so sure that you would want me making you pancakes, even if we had all the time in the world. I would be happy to buy some of Moe's pancakes though." Dex laughed as he opened the door.

"I am going to hold you to that." She gently tapped her finger into his chest as she walked past him. She stopped briefly, pushed up onto the balls of her feet, and rested her lips on his for the sweetest second before continuing past him.

He rubbed his lips together and sucked them into his mouth to taste her kiss. The palms of his hands moistened from the flutter in his chest, as he whispered, "Shit," under his breath and closed the door.

As Dex pulled out of Mickey's parking lot, his phone buzzed. He pulled it out of his pocket and looked down to see a text from Captain Kard. It was a rare occasion that she did that.

I hope you guys are on your way in here. We have a problem and you need to see this.

His brows pressed firmly at the center of his forehead. What the hell could she be talking about? She was a hard worker, but it wasn't even seven in the morning, and she was already at the precinct. That couldn't be a good sign.

He texted her back.

Picking Johnny up now. Be there in less than twenty.

Throwing a light on the roof was tempting, but luckily there were not a lot of cars on the road yet. He was able to speed over to Johnny's without any problem. It's not as if he was going to get pulled over for speeding.

Before he put the truck in park, he started honking the horn as he pulled up in front of Johnny's house. He knew that Betty would be pissed about it, but she was far less scary than a pissed off captain.

Johnny came running out of the house with an annoyed look on his face and waving a fist as he approached the truck.

"What the hell, Dex!" Johnny said as he climbed in the cab. "You know that shit pisses Betty off. Why are you honking like a crazy person at the butt crack of dawn?"

"First of all, it's not that early, and I don't usually honk. I'm sorry, but some shit is going down. The captain is already texting me. Did she call or text you too?" Dex asked, squealing the tires as he peeled out away from the curb.

"Oh, that's cute." Johnny shook his head. "No, I haven't gotten any calls from her. What's going on?"

"I don't know yet, but she said there was a problem, and I needed to see something. We need to do a quick recap of what we know and what our next step is in this investigation. I don't want to be blindsided when we go into her office. I am not at the top of her most favorite people list." Dex said as he pulled out his pack of cigarettes.

"Eh, maybe not, but she has some kind of soft spot for you. I don't think she would tolerate half the shit you pull from anyone else. But as per the case... we don't have a lot.

"We know that Tammy showed up for her dinner with the doctor on Wednesday night. He was a no-show with a false alarm call at the office. We need to stop into the Salty Peach today and ask them if they saw Tammy leave with anyone, or if she had any strange phone calls while she was there. Maybe they have some kind of surveillance system we can check.

"That is the closest thing to a lead we have. We were supposed to go search Tammy's apartment to see if we found anything suspicious or helpful. We found the doctor without needing to go through her things, but I do still think there could be something there that could help us."

Dex used his knee to hold the steering wheel straight, so he could light his cigarette.

"I wish you wouldn't do that. I am pretty sure it's against the law to drive without your hands."

"So arrest me, smart ass." Dex clicked closed the lighter and tossed it into one of the dashboard compartments. "We should get over to Bethany and Tammy's place first thing this morning then. The restaurant probably doesn't open until after ten at best, even then, we really need to talk to the night staff from Wednesday night, not sure they would be the same people on a day shift.

"I will try to call over and see if there is a manager on duty that can help us get in touch with Wednesday's staff. We might have to do some door knocking I don't want to wait until they work again."

"Ok, I will call over to Bethany while you do that. Shea's report should be waiting for us when we get there too, maybe that is what Captain Kard wants us to see."

"Yeah maybe. Drink your coffee before it gets cold. I don't want to walk in there with coffee and doughnuts. Captain Kard already thinks that I spend more time making coffee than I do working."

"She said that to you?" Johnny laughed.

"No, dumbass, but I can see it in her eyes. I can't help it if I drink a lot of coffee. There are worse things I could be doing."

"Yeah like smoking those damn cancer sticks?" Johnny pointed at the cigarette.

"About that, I am actually considering quitting."

"Really? Why the sudden change in attitude?"

"My trainer wants me to stop. He said that I can improve my stamina, and I will be a better fighter if I can lay off the smokes."

"So it doesn't have anything to do with the pretty little lady at Kagley's last night?"

"You can't be serious?" Dex said flicking the butt out the window.

"So you got up early and grabbed a cab to your truck?" Johnny nodded his head in disbelief.

Dex tipped his head to the left and looked at his partner sideways. Johnny knew him well enough to expect that he had easily spent the night with Trina. Only this was different.

"Nope. I didn't take a cab, but I guess you already knew that."

"When you texted me this morning, I knew that you had a ride. No chance you were getting up and grabbing your truck when you knew I was planning to come get you."

"You and what car? Speaking of which, how are you feeling? I hope Betty wasn't too upset about the condition you came home in last night." Dex tried to change the subject.

"Betty is my rock. She wasn't mad at me at all. She just hugged me; she really didn't say anything. I am lucky to have her. She allows me the opportunity not to worry or think about so many things in life. I honestly don't know how I would be able to deal with my mother's passing yesterday and try to stay focused on our case without her." Johnny let out a sigh.

"My heart is breaking, but if I sit around and think about it right now, I won't be able to make sure that we don't lose another woman to this case."

"I get it, Betty is amazing. I totally understand if you

need to take time off, but I can't imagine working this case without you. We are going to need to hit the pavement pretty hard today. God only knows what the captain has waiting for us." Dex eased back into his seat, trying not to let her text stress him out...yet.

"So spill it, Dex. Did you sleep with her?" Johnny asked. "I know it's not my business, but you know I don't usually ask."

"Fair enough, but when you say sleep with, I assume that you mean did I have sex with her?"

Johnny's eyes answered for him.

"She offered to stay over to drive me to my truck in the morning. Yes, we slept together. No, I did not have sex with her. Happy?"

"Holy shit! You like her. I fucking knew it. You have been acting all kinds of weird. She is a sweetheart so far, and she is stunning. I think you should go for it! Bring her Sunday." Johnny slapped him on the arm.

"Sunday? You still want to have people over?"

"Shit yeah, we can put one out for my mom. She wouldn't want me sitting around feeling sorry for myself. She would want me living my life to the fullest, which is what I have been telling you, you need to do."

"I just might give it a try." Dex pulled into the rear lot at the precinct. He preferred to go in through the back door. It was closer to the locker room, and he wanted to drop off his gym bag before heading into the lion's den.

CHAPTER SEVENTEEN

"WHAT DO YOU THINK? SHOULD we grab the medical examiner's report on Tammy Larazzo before we walk into this potential shit storm?" Johnny asked.

"Honestly, I don't know. I got the impression it was borderline urgent, or she wouldn't have been texting me at six o'clock in the morning. Either way, the heat is about to get cranked up for sure." Dex tossed his bag into a locker. "Let's just see what she wants. We can go over the report after. Even if we pick it up, it's not like we can review it before we go in to talk to her."

"I guess you're right. I wish I had another coffee. I am definitely going to hit that bottle of aspirin in my desk. I don't usually drink like that on a weeknight, let alone a work night." Johnny rubbed at his temples.

"Don't be such a wuss. You only had a few beers."

"The beer isn't the problem, I don't usually drink liquor.

That shit kills me, had my head spinning last night. I had to sleep with one foot off the side of the bed."

"You are cracking me up. You better stop. Kard is going to be pissed if I roll into her office laughing." Dex couldn't remember the last time he'd been so drunk that he had the spins.

The precinct was still on the overnight skeleton crew. The other detectives were not in yet, and Dex was glad he didn't have to see Linder's smug face on his way out of the captain's office. There was an eerie silence that haunted them as they walked the path to her office.

As soon as they came into sight of her doorway, she stood up. She usually wore a suit with a long skirt, but instead she had on a navy blazer and khaki slacks. Although she had a certain level of femininity to her, there was something more intimidating about her in a pair of pants.

"I'm glad you boys are here early. We have a lot that we need to go over. Detective Harrington, would you mind giving us a few minutes?" she said approaching them.

Dex looked at Johnny with a plea for him not to leave him alone. If only the effort wasn't in vain. Johnny would never even hint at disobeying an order from his superior.

"No problem, I need to get the M.E.'S report. Dr. Sinclair said it would be here waiting for us in the morning." He turned and walked off to the mailboxes in the back without turning to wait for a response.

"Close the door, Dex." She never called him by his first name. It was rare that anyone was called by their first name around the station.

Dex felt a tightening in his chest as he closed the door. He looked out of her window to see who was watching, but no one paid them any mind.

"You are going to want sit down." She walked behind her desk, moved around a few things, pulled out a file, and dropped in on his side of the desk.

Shit, was all he could think. Was he about to get fired or something? He had been in her office plenty of times, but this didn't feel right. He didn't feel as if he was getting scolded for some minor indiscretion or tardiness.

He rubbed the palms of his hands over his knees. He wanted to let his eyes scan his surroundings, but he was afraid that would show weakness, so he kept his gaze in direct line with Captain Kard's.

She walked around to stand in front of her desk. He was used to her taking that approach, but her closeness rattled him for the first time.

"First of all, I think you know that I think you are a good cop. I also truly believe that you are a good person. I know I ride you pretty hard sometimes, but I think you need it.

"I don't know what kind of fucked up human being is walking our streets, but we now are going to have a problem; the possibility of you becoming a suspect."

Dex felt all the blood drain out of his head. He must have heard her wrong. There was no possible way that she'd just said that he could be considered a suspect.

"Excuse me? Captain, I think I misheard you." Dex couldn't believe his ears.

"Open the folder, Dex." She pushed it closer to him.

Dex watched his hand shake as his fingers approached the manila folder. He knew that there was going to be something devastating behind the flimsy card stock. He knew that there would be the face of someone from his personal life. He wasn't prepared for it, but he had no choice but to open it.

He wasn't guilty of anything, other than maybe knocking the guy out in the bar the night before. That he was sure of, but he didn't want to look as if he was hesitating out of guilt.

Dex felt tiny droplets of sweat forming on the back of his neck. There were only mere seconds between her moving the folder and him actually opening it, but each second felt like an eternity.

Dex's hand covered his mouth instantly, pinching and squeezing his face together. His brow furrowed as he looked up from the woman's face staring up at him, and he met eyes with the captain.

He was taken aback by the concern smeared all over her

face. Her eyes looked darker and more hollow than normal. The skin around her mouth hung into jowls he'd never noticed she had.

"When?" He asked.

"They found her a few hours ago."

"Why weren't Johnny and I called? This has to be connected to our case." Dex stood up and started to pace behind the chair where he'd been sitting.

"It wasn't our guys that found her. Her body was near the perimeter of the city, the body is getting transferred here today. I have already contacted Dr. Sinclair, and she has cleared her schedule for the day. Thing is, Dex, you are most likely one of the last people to have seen her alive."

"Me?" He stopped walking and pointed to his chest. "I wasn't the only one that watched Bethany walk out of here. How do you know that no one else has seen her?" He clenched the back of the chair holding on to stable his legs.

"Last night we got a missing persons report from her boyfriend. I decided not to call you guys because it hadn't been twenty-four hours and I knew that you were taking some time with Detective Harrington to deal with his loss." She sighed.

"You should have called. So what was her cause of death?" He picked up the folder.

"They didn't do an autopsy, they are sending her here for us to do it. They will also be delivering a copy of any forensics that they collected on scene. She was gutted, same as Miss Larazzo."

"I didn't know the first victim, and I only met Bethany the night that her roommate was murdered. I wouldn't have any reason to see either of these women harmed."

"Please don't take this the wrong way, but I am assuming that you were a little bit more than friendly with this victim. Is your DNA going to turn up on the body?"

"My God, are you seriously asking me this? I don't know, maybe. Sure we had sex, and she hugged me when she was here, so it is possible. This is beyond fucked up." Dex held his head. "Am I off the case? Is that why we are having this discussion in private?" Dex had to ask.

"No, you probably should be, but you and Johnny are my best detectives, and I know that you won't rest until you find this psychopath. But now we have more eyes on this case. We need to catch this guy and do it quickly!" She went back behind her desk and sat down.

"So, Brown is just handing over the case? Doesn't sound like them."

"Not exactly. I told them that we were closing in on a lead, and we would really appreciate any support that they can offer us.

"I took a passive approach with the captain. Instead of insisting that the case was ours, I let him take the opportunity to try to sweep in and save us. You guys are going to need to work double time to get this case closed. We can't keep having bodies piling up."

"Johnny is probably talking to the Medical Examiner right now. I know that he was going to get the report on Miss Larazzo, but if she is sitting there waiting for Bethany's body to come in, she has probably brought Harrington into the loop on this."

"You are going to have to tell her that you were involved with the victim. You can't let your DNA turn up as a surprise in this case. Damn it, Dex. I wish you hadn't crossed paths with this one."

"Captain—"

"Save it, Preston. It doesn't matter at this point. What's done is done. You couldn't have known. It just complicates things, and you damn well know that I don't like complicated.

"You will document your connection in the file, but we will not be making a public issue of it here in the station. Fix this, and close this case before eyes are on you." She pushed her chair in and flipped open her laptop. She looked up at him. "I think you have work to do."

"Yes, ma'am." Dex stood up and grabbed the file off her desk.

"You will check in with me around dinner time. I suspect that you will be working a double today." She nodded at him both telling him that was, in fact, what he would be doing and also to excuse him from her office.

Dex walked out of the captain's office and made eye contact with Johnny, who was sitting at his desk. He imagined that his partner had had eyes on the captain's door the entire time he'd been in there. At least, since he'd spoken to Shea.

He watched his partner's eyes searching his face for a sign of what was going on. Concern and compassion leaked from his fatigued eyes as he stood before Dex at his desk.

"You okay?" Johnny asked simply.

"Yup. We have a lot of work to do, you ready to catch this bastard?" Dex was both freaked out and pissed off.

"You bet. I just got off the phone with Dr. Sinclair. We are going to head over there around three o'clock. She said she would try to have the bulk of the autopsy done on Bethany. She won't be able to have the toxicology report done to compare, but she said she will have a good idea if it looks like the perpetrator is the same."

"So what about the report on Tammy Larazzo? Do we have her tox report?"

"Yes, she was drugged, or she was being treated for an extreme case of anxiety. Dr. Sinclair said that she had a cocktail of benzodiazepines in her system. The list is in the report," Johnny explained, opening a file on his desk to find the list.

"Did she say how the drugs were administered? I didn't get the impression from Bethany or Tammy's boss that she was suffering from anxiety. I suppose that if she was that heavily medicated that maybe she was being well treated. We need to find out if she was seeing a physician and also finding her pharmacy for a list of her medications."

"We are going to need to get a warrant for that." Harrington popped down at his desk.

"Well, we better get on it. Email the captain. She can get us the warrant. We need to get the details in order. We need to go to the girl's apartment. The captain said that Bethany's boyfriend called in a missing persons report on her last night."

"What the fuck, seriously? Why weren't we called?" Johnny slammed his hand on his desk.

Dex just made a face and rolled his eyes. "Doesn't matter at this point. We need to pull the call, listen to it, and we need to go over there. He is going to have to ID her body at some point as well. I can't believe we are doing this again, twice in one week."

"We still need to hit that restaurant as well today. Ok, listen let's take a few minutes, we need a list. I talk, you write." Dex instructed his partner.

"Shoot."

"Email Captain for warrant, pull call from boyfriend, pull his records, visit boyfriend, search Bethany and Tammy's apartment, visit the restaurant where Tammy was supposed to meet the doctor, three o'clock with Shea, and possible physician slash pharmacy for Tammy. Does that cover it? Am I missing something?"

"I think that is a lot for us to do in one day, but that is what we have. Not to be a dick or anything, but what we have is shit. We have a bunch of questions and speculations and no clue as to who or why these women were targeted." Johnny pinched at the bridge of his nose.

"There has to be a connection between them. They must have lots of people in common. There has to be a connection there. The fact that they are roommates can't be a coincidence.

"Whoever murdered these women had some major self-control. We're not looking at a crime of passion here, or even uncontrolled rage. The women were not beaten or tortured in any way that we have seen. They were drugged. At least we are assuming that, since Tammy was. Which, to me, means that the killer either didn't want to see them suffer or didn't want them to fight back. So either we have a compassionate murderer or one that can't stomach brutality. The stabbing and cutting was precise, meticulous. There were not a lot of stab wounds suggesting uncertainty or inexperience. This killer has either killed before or has experience as a medical professional or as a hunter.

"They were able to wield a knife in such a way to cause a quick death. That's another thing, we were going to look into, check the ME's report. We might need to see what she has in there so we can stop by the hunting store and see if they can help us match up a weapon to look for."

Dex rubbed at the stubble on his chin. He had been in such a rush to get out of his apartment that he hadn't bothered to think about shaving. At least he'd dressed nice and combed his hair.

"I am thinking that the killer was more than likely between the height of five-foot-five and five-foot–eight because of the location and angle of the wound on Tammy's abdomen. Of course we will need to see if the blade marks are consistent with Bethany's wounds," Johnny added.

"So you think it was a short guy or a young man, maybe a teenager?"

"Shit, Preston, I wish I knew, but we will find out for sure! Do you think we should try to get Linder and Hart to assist us on some of these tasks? I don't know what their case load is, but we need this information as fast as we can," Johnny's face cringed as he said it. He looked as if he smelled something rotten.

"I'm not sure the stress of dealing with their childish

attitudes will help us in the long run. I think we can do this, the captain thinks we can too. Whoever is doing this will slip up, and we will catch them." Dex shuffled through the file he was holding. "That, I am sure of!"

CHAPTER EIGHTEEN

DEX WANTED TO SMOKE A cigarette more than anything in the world. The tension in his body was building, and the anxious seed planted during his meeting with Captain Kard had found a nice spot to sprout.

On the way out of the station house, he pulled the small red box out of his pocket. He fumbled with it in his hands as they walked out to the back parking lot where he had parked his truck. He stopped just before walking off the sidewalk, opened the box, and gave them a good sniff.

He loved the sweetness of tobacco, even if the manufactured cigarettes didn't have quite the same sweetness as the tobacco he remembered his grandfather smoking from a pipe. Nonetheless, there was something comforting about the mix of raisins and fresh ground coffee. How could you go wrong with that?

He didn't think he could, until he lit them and the

smoke settled into everything around him. Dex saw the way people looked at him when he smoked in public. It was amazing the difference in public opinion since he'd been a kid. He also knew that the dependency was slowing him down. He wanted and needed the crutch, but there had to come a day when he would be strong enough to kick the dirty habit.

He was pissed, had been for years. He was pissed at himself. He was pissed that his friend was dead. He was pissed that there was another meaningless murder on his turf. All he could think about was hitting the heavy bag at the gym. Good thing he had a keycard that allowed him twenty-four-hour access. He preferred to work out alone anyway.

"You coming, or are you going to make out with that box of crap?" Johnny asked him.

"That's cute." He looked down at the pack, blew out all the air in his lungs, crushed the box between his fingers, and tossed it in the dumpster behind the station.

Johnny gave him a look but didn't say anything. Dex was glad because he didn't feel like having to explain himself. If nothing else, not smoking would carve off a few minutes of wasted time throughout the day that he could be spending working or training.

"So the boyfriend is still at Bethany and Tammy's apartment?" Dex asked.

"Yes, his name is Jeremy Glover. Keaton took the call last night. He said that Jeremy sounded legitimately concerned. Jeremy said that he wasn't sure if he should call or not, but she said she was going to be home in twenty minutes, and that was the last he heard from her."

Dex and Johnny knew that would have been when she left the station house. Dex cursed himself for not being more adamant about having a patrol car escort her home.

"Are you getting a vibe about this guy? He did know both women, assumingly fairly well."

"I don't know what to make of any of this yet. One thing is for sure, I will handle the questioning. I think maybe there is a bit of a conflict of interest if you directly interact with him. Do you mind?" Johnny rubbed at his temples.

"Sure, do I ever mind?"

"No, but I mean like one-hundred percent. Don't even talk to the guy. What did the captain say about this? I can only assume that is what she had you in her office about."

"She did. She wants me to keep my discretion about my involvement with Bethany, but to make sure that it is noted in the case file. This should be fun telling Shea that I was intimate with the victim less than seventy-two hours ago."

Johnny just made a noise. It was a cross between a laugh and a painful grunt. He knew it would be an awkward moment to say the least.

"Exactly, but I don't need her finding out by some

random DNA test."

"You were using protection? Please tell me that you always protect yourself when you are on these suicide drinking binges of yours."

"Always, but I don't know if any kind of DNA trail could remain. *Shit*, she was hugging me at the precinct before she left. I was, presumably, the last person to have seen her alive. Probably not a good thing, since I am one of the detectives on the case. I wouldn't want it to cause a problem in court."

"True, but you were with me when she disappeared. And I say, disappeared because there is no trace of where she went after she left the precinct and no cell phone to track. We were able to get her phone records faster this time, and her last call was to Jeremy just after she left the station, as he stated when he called her in missing."

"It also doesn't mean that she didn't make it home." Dex put it out there. They couldn't rule anyone or anything out at that point. "We haven't even found her vehicle."

"I have to say, though, that if Bethany and Tammy were both murdered by the same person the likelihood of it being Dr. Rubio has gone down. If he only went out on a few dates with Tammy, I can't imagine what kind of motivation he would have to go after Bethany."

"That's true, and Bethany said that she hadn't met him either." He pulled into a visitor's parking space in front of the girls' apartment. He tried to hide the fact that there was a part of him shaken as he hesitated getting out of the truck.

"Are you okay?" Johnny asked.

"Of course. Why wouldn't I be?"

"Oh, I don't know because we are going to interview a guy about his dead girlfriend who you had sex with a few nights ago."

"It sounds so awful when you say it like that." He shook his head. "It isn't like Jeremy knows."

"Or does he?" Johnny gave him a look implying that the fact could be a possible motivation for Bethany's demise.

"I guess we will find out when we get in there."

It was surreal knocking on the apartment door of a woman that he had been romping in the sheets with just a few nights before. He had no problem rapping his knuckles against the solid metal door. He wanted his knuckles to smash against anything.

"Hawk Creek Police."

"Coming."

The door opened. "Jeremy Glover?" Johnny asked.

"Yes, please come in." He stood just under six feet tall and in good shape. Beneath the dark circles under his eyes and the more than five o'clock shadow was a handsome guy.

Dex wondered what it was about him that hadn't satisfied Bethany. They looked as if they would make a nice looking couple. He clearly looked as if he cared for her, since it appeared that he had not showered or slept since she'd been a no show.

"Forgive my appearance." He waved his hand in front of his body. "It's been a rough two days. I am glad that you are here. Is there any news?"

Dex looked over at Johnny, his eyeballs nearly leaping out across the room. He did a terrible job disguising the alarm on his face.

He wanted to ask his partner what the heck was going on. He'd thought that Jeremy had been informed of Bethany's death. The state of awkward had just reached a whole new level.

"Son, I think it is best that you take a seat," Johnny suggested as they entered the apartment.

"Are you shitting me?" Jeremy backed up toward the living room and tripped over one of the legs on the coffee table, stumbling back. He managed to catch himself and sat down on the couch. He lowered his head into the palms of his hands, and his head rocked from side to side. Being told to sit down for news didn't usually equate to the expectation of hearing something good.

Dex took a step back and leaned against the wall closest

to the entryway. He wanted to make sure that any questions or comments made were directed to his partner. He'd promised Johnny that he would take a step back, and decided to approach it literally.

He looked around the apartment. It was tastefully decorated and surprisingly not in an over feminine way, considering that two women had shared the space. Their furniture was rich with dark colored fabric and wood. There was a large painting of a leopard behind the couch. Based on what little he knew about the two victims he was sure that Bethany had been the one that picked out that piece of art.

He wanted to focus his thoughts and energy on anything but Jeremy, unfortunately, that was not an option. He needed to have the volume on his intuitions turned up all the way. The man was the only person or bit of evidence tying the two women together.

"Bethany told you what happened to Tammy?"

"Yes, she called me when she left the police station. She was crying and told me that Tammy was gone. She said that she was going to sit in the car until she calmed down enough to drive home. We didn't get into the details, but she said that she was found murdered.

"Who would want to do that to her? She was one of the nicest people in the whole world. She worked hard and had a big heart. Where is Bethany? Did something happen to her on the way home?" Jeremy's facial features were straining and he began to start to bite at the corner of his thumbnail.

"I called the local hospitals to see if she'd been into an accident. I don't understand, she said she was on her way home. Where else could she have gone?" Jeremy was talking fast. He clearly wasn't taking the time to breathe. The color was dropping out of his skin, making him look faint.

"I don't know who would want to cause harm to another human being, ever. That is the hardest part of my job. We don't always get those answers. The other hardest part of the job is having to inform people that their loved ones are gone."

Before Johnny could finish what he was saying Jeremy's eyes flashed up to him and instantly filled with tears. "Bethany was found by a trucker on the city line early this morning. I wish I didn't have to tell you this, but she met the same fate as her roommate and friend."

"No!" He just kept shaking his head. "It can't, she can't. Are you sure it's her? You must have made a mistake."

"I'm really sorry for your loss Jeremy."

"Please tell me I don't have to identify the body! Should I? Is it better for me to see her for myself?" his voice shook.

"That won't be necessary. She was identified by her prints, and we were able to recognize her and her clothing from our interview. Jeremy, we need your help."

Dex knew that Johnny could see the agony that Jeremy was in, but the reality was they were there because they needed information. He was the closest thing they had to a suspect. The questions needed to come.

"What can I do for you? How can I help? I will do whatever you need," he offered, blinking back the tears from his eyes.

Johnny took out his notebook. "How long have you known Tammy and Bethany?"

"I have known them both for about a year and a half. I met Tammy just after Bethany. They have lived together since they were in college. They were a package deal, but I was hoping that Bethany and I were going to look for our own place after their lease was up."

"What do you mean by 'they were a package deal', were you intimate with both women?"

"Oh, hell no! Tammy didn't have the best luck with dating, so she was around a lot. If we stayed here and had dinner or watched a movie, we were with Tammy too. Bethany didn't like to leave her alone all the time, so we invited her out with us from time to time.

"I didn't mind. Like I said, she was a great person. We were really hoping that she'd hit things off with the new guy she was dating."

"Did you meet him or know him?"

"Nope, I am not even sure what his name was. I think they only went on one or two dates."

"Did Tammy know that you and Bethany had plans to move out on your own?"

"I'm not sure if Bethany had discussed it with her yet. It wasn't my place to bring it up. I would never want to come between their friendship. God, I can't believe they are gone. This can't be real."

"What about your relationship with Bethany? What about other partners, did you and she have a falling out about anything recently?"

"Other partners? I don't understand, we were in a committed relationship. After we moved out, I was going to propose to her. I have a deposit on a ring. We were solid, at least as far as I knew, we were." He looked up at Johnny and over to Dex.

His eyes felt like hot pokers. Dex had to look down at his scuffed up boots. Keeping eye contact with Jeremy was too difficult. He found himself in a fucked up situation. It was wrong that he was there, for heaven's sake, he'd slept with the victim the day before she was murdered.

Dex felt bad that the shmuck didn't know that Bethany was out there being promiscuous while he was planning their future. Or at least, that was the story he was feeding them.

"Would you mind if my partner here takes a look around

to see if there are any clues that can help our investigation?" Johnny asked, shifting the course of the interrogation and giving Jeremy back a sense of control. At the same time, the tactic would test him, to see if he hesitated.

"No, not at all. I don't know what you could possibly be looking for, or find, but take all the time you need." Jeremy didn't get up, he just pointed down the hallway. "Their bedrooms are down the hall."

Dex nodded and spun on his heel, glad to remove himself from the conversation. Maybe having one less set of eyes on Jeremy would make the line of questioning more productive for his partner.

CHAPTER NINETEEN

"THAT GUY IS OBLIVIOUS. HE doesn't stand a chance at a happy ending." Johnny's uncharacteristic negativity hung over them like a dark cloud "What do you mean?" Dex asked as he started the engine.

"First of all, my impression of Bethany is that she was a lot more of a free spirit than he realized. She wasn't in love with that man, that is one thing I am sure of."

"How is that?"

"The way her eyes lit up when she saw you at the station. She may not have had any intentions past one night of fun with you, but there was a certain level of excitement and interest when she saw you. Women that are in love don't look at other men that way."

"I suppose you have something there." Dex rubbed at his empty breast pocket.

"In general, I don't see him as our possible perp, but we

can't rule anything out. I don't know about the whole moving out situation. If he had motivation, my imagination would tend to think that maybe he wasn't so thrilled with Tammy always being around. Clearly, the women had a strong bond, one that Bethany probably wasn't as eager to break as Jeremy would have liked to think."

"You don't think that he took out Tammy to be with Bethany?"

"I don't know, but let's just say that he did, and he thought that the loss would bring them closer together."

"But then why would he kill Bethany?" Dex was following his train of thought, but not sure that it was completely logical.

"Maybe he knew that she wasn't so faithful. It is possible that he found out that she was with you. Well, not necessarily *you*, but with another man that night. She certainly didn't go home. Was he willing to give up everything for her, even take a life for them to be together?" Johnny tipped his head at him. "Honestly I don't think that she was the settling down type, at least not at this point or with that guy. If he knew that, maybe he felt if he couldn't have her no one would."

"It is hard to imagine that people could be that sick in the head. I think we should bring him in for a more formal interrogation. We need to know where he was the night that Tammy was murdered."

"I feel like a shmuck that I didn't ask him. I'm sorry I am trying not to let my grief get in the way of this case."

"We know one thing for sure, that he wasn't with Bethany."

"You can testify to that. Johnny wagged his eyebrows at him.

"That's just not cool, and I really hope that I don't have to testify to that at any point in this investigation. There is a certain level of embarrassment that goes along with it."

"What are you embarrassed about? She was hot, and this case was not a case when you met her." Johnny made a good point,

"There is truth in that, but it was all very close, and I am one of the detectives on her case, it just feels off."

"You couldn't have saved her. It isn't your fault, Dex. You didn't know what had been set in motion that night. You were two adults that met and made a choice to spend the night together. It's not that big of a deal. "

"Jeremy might beg to differ. I wonder, if he knew, would I become his next victim? I could be bait."

"Let's not get ahead of ourselves. The guy has lost enough, and although we have some suspicion there, it is nothing really pointing to him as our guy. Let's keep that as a backup plan." Johnny cracked his window. "So did you find anything in the apartment to help us?"

"No, both women were very neat and organized. Looking through their rooms was easy. There was nothing suspicious anywhere. There were no signs of a struggle either, although I don't know what things looked like in there a week ago.

"I don't think either woman went missing from their apartment. They were taken while they were out. That means that someone knew where they were going to be."

"I would say that, if we have one killer on our hands, we can absolutely rule out Dr. Rubio. He wouldn't have known Bethany, or had any reason to care where she was or what she was doing."

"Not to mention, I am pretty sure that we were at his office when Bethany disappeared. Jeremy would have been the only one that knew she was at the precinct."

"Unless she had someone stalking her. There has to be another connection between them that we are missing. I think we need to search the database to see if there are any similar crimes in the area that have gone cold." Johnny's stomach growled loud enough that Dex looked over at him. "Mickey's?"

"I sure could use some caffeine, the lack of nicotine is starting to get to me. No doughnuts for me. We need to grab something for lunch before we go the morgue. I want to make sure my food settles before we get there."

"Maybe we should grab lunch at the Salty Peach, we do need to interview them about Tammy's date anyway. Do you have her license photo saved on your phone still?" Johnny asked his partner.

"Now, you're thinking. Kill two birds with one stone. Maybe we skip Mickey's for now and grab coffee after lunch. I am sure that Shea and the old lady would love for us to bring them some."

"That's what makes you such a ladies' man. Always thinking about their needs. I still don't understand how you are still single." Johnny never missed an opportunity to bring up Dex's love life, or lack thereof.

"About that, I was actually thinking I would bring a date to your house on Sunday."

"Real-lee?" Johnny leaned back against the window sizing his partner up.

"Take it easy."

"You're going to bring Trina aren't you? That's really cool. Betty will be ecstatic. I forgot to tell you, we are going to have a small service Sunday morning for my mom. It's only going to be family. We didn't put it in the paper or anything. She is going to be cremated, so there won't be a funeral."

"I will be there. Just tell me where."

"Lind's Funeral home, down on Mulberry. Please don't send flowers or anything. We are just going to celebrate her and enjoy our dinner on Sunday in her memory." Johnny's shoulders sunk down some. "It's easier and less painful if we keep it intimate with loved ones."

"Whatever works for you, I will be there to support you. I loved your mom. She was a great woman, and she will truly be missed."

⛤

Dex and Johnny were the first patrons to show up for lunch at The Salty Peach. Dex was glad that it wasn't crowded yet because it would make talking about a murder victim less awkward.

A young girl, probably not even old enough to drink, greeted them when they walked in. She wore all black, along with everyone else that seemed to work there. "Gentleman, can I get you a table?"

"You know, I think we are going to eat at the bar, but is your manager in?" Dex asked her.

She nervously batted her eyelashes at him. "Yes, is there a problem with something?"

"Not at all." Dex flashed his badge. "Detective Preston and Detective Harrington. We just need his help with something. Could you have him come chat with us at the bar, please?"

"Of course. I will get Bryan. Andi will give you menus when you get to the bar. I hope you enjoy your lunch," she said, leading them toward the bar. She didn't walk them the whole way, instead, she took a turn for the kitchen.

"You made her crazy nervous." Johnny laughed.

"Really? I didn't mean to. I hope she doesn't think that her manager is any kind of trouble. That is kind of funny, I may have just started a crazy rumor."

"Maybe, but I don't think that is why she was so nervous. Her eyelashes were fluttering fast enough that she could have undressed you with them."

"Don't hate me because I'm beautiful..." His laughter rumbled in his chest and echoed in the empty restaurant.

They took a seat at the bar. Dex expected the bartender to be a guy with the name Andi, but the voluptuous redhead wiping the top of the bar pleasantly surprised him.

"Hey, guys! Welcome to the Salty Peach. What can I get you to drink?" she asked, placing two cardboard coasters with the restaurant's logo in front of each man.

"I will have a water and a diet coke for my partner here," Dex ordered. "We are going to have lunch too, if you have a menu for us."

"Yup, sure do. Here is our lunch menu."

"What is the difference between that and the dinner menu?" Johnny asked.

"There are some sandwiches and salads that we only serve at lunchtime and a limited number of dinner items on there, and the portions are smaller than at dinnertime." She put two menus up on the edge of the bar. "If you have any questions just let me know."

She turned around to grab glasses and packed them full of ice before grabbing the soda gun to fix their drinks.

The detectives looked at the menus in silence while they waited for their drinks and the manager to grace them with his presence.

Dex assumed that the guy was watching them on the security camera, trying to decide what they could possibly want. He wasn't coming out either because he had no clue or he had a guilty conscience about something. One way or the other, they were about to find out.

"Are you guys ready to order?" Andi placed their drinks in front of them and gave each of them a place mat and a set of silverware and napkins.

"I am going to have the grilled chicken sandwich and side salad," Dex ordered first.

"I will have the same, but with a side of sweet potato fries."

Dex gave Johnny a look.

"Forget the fries. I will have the salad too."

"The salad is really good, our signature dressing is out of this world. I haven't met anyone that doesn't like it."

"Can't wait."

Johnny's enthusiasm was comical, causing both Dex and

Andi to laugh. "After you put the order in, I have a question for you, if you don't mind?"

"Sure. Be back in a jiffy."

Her smile wasn't nearly as big as other parts of her, but Dex couldn't help noticing how nice her teeth were.

They watched her walk to the backend of the bar to put their orders into the computer. At the same time, they saw the hostess heading in their direction with a man following her. She pointed to them and walked out to the foyer to take her place back at the hostess stand.

The man approaching them was of short stature. He couldn't have been more than five foot seven. His short orange hair was curly and receding exposing a large amount of his forehead. He was the only one in the building that wasn't wearing all black.

"Good afternoon, gentleman. I'm the general manager, Bryan Russell." He extended his hand to Johnny. "How can I help you?"

"Detective Harrington, and this is my partner Detective Preston. Were you working Wednesday night?" they both flipped open their badges for the manager to see.

"Yes, I am here at least five nights a week, today is actually the only day I am in early. Was there a problem?" He pulled at the hem of his sweater.

"Not with your restaurant, but we are looking for information about a patron that we think may have either had drinks or dined here," Dex explained, squeezing the lime into his soda water.

"I can try to help, Wednesday is not one of our busiest nights, but there are a lot of people that come through here. Are they a regular?" Bryan asked.

"Honestly, we don't know. I will show you a picture, and if you could tell me if you saw this woman in here. I would appreciate it. I can email a copy to you, perhaps someone that worked on Wednesday night might remember seeing her." Dex pulled his phone from his back pocket.

"I am always running around and half of the night I am in my office or the kitchen so I am not sure if I will remember. Andi worked Wednesday night, I can ask her to look at the picture now, if you like," he offered, sticking his hands in his pockets.

"I think that is a great idea. How about the gal at the hostess stand? She would have greeted anyone who came in if she was working, right?"

"Most likely." He took one hand out of his pocket and waved a hand in the air. "Andi! Come down here for a minute please."

"Everything okay?" she asked.

"These men are detectives with the Hawk Creek Police Department. They want to see if you recognize a patron from Wednesday night."

"Sure, I am usually pretty good with faces."

"This is her license photo, so I'm not sure if it is the best picture. If you remember seeing her in here, we would really appreciate anything you can tell us," Dex explained, sliding his phone across the bar.

Andi picked up the phone and looked at the picture for a minute. She tipped her head side to side before nodding. "I do think I remember her."

"Can you tell us anything about her, how long she was here, and if she was with anyone or left with anyone?" Johnny asked her, pulling out his notepad.

"I remember her because she was upset. She told me that she had a date, but he was a no show. She sat at the end of the bar and had a glass of Chardonnay. She didn't eat anything. She was here for about an hour."

"Did she talk to anyone else? Did she have any kind of a confrontation with anyone?" Johnny asked.

"No, actually the opposite. She and the woman next to her started to chat it up. I don't think they knew each other, but they were laughing about something. I was glad that her night wasn't a total flop. I asked her if she was going to stay for dinner, and she said she was just going to grab fast food on her way home."

"Can you tell me anything about the woman that was sitting with her at the bar?" Dex took a sip of his soda after he put the straw on the bar.

"Not really, she came in by herself too. She was pretty,

blonde hair, thin to average build. She had a warm smile and ordered a glass of Red Zinfandel. The bar was fairly busy for a Wednesday night, otherwise I probably would have hung out and talked with them more."

"Did she leave with anyone?"

"I don't know, I don't think I saw anyone else come in and talk to her. I didn't really notice her leave, sorry."

"Thank you Andi."

"Sure, I am going to go check on your food, it should be ready." She walked out the far end of the bar and went into the kitchen.

"Bryan, do you have a surveillance system that records the restaurant by any chance?" Dex asked the manager.

"We do, but it only keeps images for forty-eight hours and then the film recycles. If we don't have any emergencies or thefts, we really don't have any need to keep a backlog of security images. If you had gotten in touch with me earlier in the week we could have watched to see her come and go. Should we be keeping a look out for her to return?" Bryan took his hands out of his pockets and rubbed his hands together nervously.

"That won't be necessary. She was murdered Wednesday night. We are looking for suspects. This is the last known location that she might have been seen."

"Oh, crap! That is crazy, I am so sorry to hear that. If there is anything I can do to help, please let me know.

Once I get your email, I will ask the staff from Wednesday if anyone has any information about your victim. I hate to think that this was the last place she was." He pressed his fist to his lip and shook his head.

"We appreciate your cooperation. If you could send over your hostess to talk to us before we leave, that would be great. Here is my card, if you or your staff remembers anything. Even if it is the smallest detail, don't hesitate to give us a call." Johnny handed him his card and shook his hand.

Bryan stepped up closer to shake Dex's hand as well. "I will call the security company too, and just double check to make sure that there isn't anything they can do to retrieve the footage from Wednesday. I wish I could have been more helpful. Lunch is on me, fellas. I hope you enjoy your food."

Bryan waved a hand toward Andi carrying two plates of food. He turned and walked to the hostess stand. Dex could barely overhear him talking to the girl greeting lunch patrons. He asked her to go over and talk to them before they left. He got the feeling that he suggested that she wait until after they finished their lunch.

Andi delivered their chicken sandwiches and refreshed their sodas. She kept herself busy at the other end of the bar, tending to some cleaning and stocking. Dex debated on whether or not she and the rest of the staff should know. He didn't think that the restaurant had anything to do with Tammy being targeted.

CHAPTER TWENTY

THE HOSTESS DIDN'T HAVE ANY useful information either. She did remember seeing Tammy. The only reason she'd stood out in her mind was because she'd asked if her date had called a few times. And when he showed up at least an hour later, she was long gone.

"I don't know if it is a good thing or not that no one from the restaurant saw anything suspicious. I was hoping that maybe Tammy left the bar with someone that we could ID," Dex said as they pulled into Mickey's parking lot.

"No, but if we can find the blonde she was talking to she might know something. Perhaps Tammy mentioned to her where she was going, or maybe if she had someone else she was planning to see, maybe a booty call or ex-boyfriend." Johnny unbuckled his belt before Dex even put the truck in park.

"What are you doing, jumping out before I stop?" Dex

taunted him.

"You promised me coffee and a doughnut almost three hours ago."

"I thought you would be full enough from lunch that you would be over the doughnut thing."

"Don't get all high and mighty on me, it hasn't even been a full day since you stopped smoking. And for your information, I was going to just get one doughnut hole instead of the whole thing. That is progress, isn't it?"

"Sure. Are you grabbing them to go, or do you want to sit in there and review some of our notes?"

"Since you want to bring everyone at the morgue coffee we should probably get it to go. It is creeping up on three o'clock anyway. I know Shea usually drinks those fancy coffees, what am I getting her?"

"I think they have flavored syrup in there. Get her a large vanilla coffee light and sweet and get my girlfriend a small coffee with cream and sugar on the side. You know how finicky those old ladies can be."

"Trust me, it's not just the old ones." They both laughed.

Dex pulled out his phone. He was lying to himself about needing to check his email. When in reality, he knew that Trina was close to the end of her day at school. He was a fool for starting to fall for someone. He had done just fine on his own so far, and Dex knew too well what kind of destruction was left behind when an officer fell. He didn't want to be the reason anyone else out there would suffer such a loss.

He wasn't going to message her, but he was eager to see her name flash across the screen of his cell phone. He was planning to invite her to Johnny and Betty's for Sunday dinner. His stomach turned at the idea of it all. He wasn't sure if it was excitement, fear, or just indigestion from that special house made salad dressing. Either way, the coffee would hopefully burn through it.

Dex put his phone in the dashboard compartment and pulled out his lighter. He might not have any smokes, but that didn't mean he couldn't use his nervous energy to practice his lighter techniques. There was a time when a person could still smoke in the bars, and he'd impressed a woman or two with his smooth lighter skills.

He watched his partner walk out of Mickey's with his hands full of coffee trays. Dex counted five, he wasn't sure who the fifth coffee was for, and a white bag, surely filled with doughnuts.

Dex leaned over the passenger's seat and opened the door for Johnny. He didn't want to see him have an accident with such precious cargo.

"Thanks," Johnny said as he stepped up into the cab. He put the cardboard carrying case on the floor in front of him between his feet and the bag beside him.

"Looks like a pretty big bag for a doughnut hole." Dex

smirked at him.

"Would you shut the hell up already? I didn't even get a stupid doughnut. It is a bag full of creamers, sugars, and this fake sweetener crap you put in your body, thinking you're being healthy."

"I just don't want the extra calories. Who is the extra coffee for?" Dex asked. He could smell the sweet vanilla coffee that Johnny had ordered for Shea. It reminded him of a really good air freshener. Something he had been meaning to get for the truck, and one for Johnny's car too.

"I don't know, she poured it by accident, so she said it was on the house. Have you ever known a cop to turn down a free cup of coffee? I think not. Besides, it's not like we won't drink it. It's black, and I have this bag of condiments, so we can split it, or whoever needs it more can have it." He handed him a large coffee that had the diet tab pushed down on the top.

"Thanks. And I'm proud of you for not going for the doughnut."

"What are you doing with that lighter?"

"Just keeping myself occupied. I think I need to invest in some gum or something. Maybe one of those worry stones to rub when I feel like I need a smoke. Where would you even buy something like that?"

"I haven't the faintest idea. I can ask Betty, she knows where to buy everything."

"I bet." Dex took a slow sip of his coffee, careful not to burn his tongue. "We better get to the morgue before Shea's coffee gets cold."

"That old lady would marry you if she could," Johnny teased as they made their way down the long corridor leading to the Morgue.

Dex carried his and Shae's coffees as he tried to chug what was left of his. He knew once the smell from the morgue assaulted his senses, he wouldn't be able to ingest his coffee without risking it coming back up.

"Maybe if she was fifty years younger I would consider asking her." Dex couldn't help but smirk at the thought. "That is, if I were the marrying type."

"You will be. We all are, we just don't know it until someone comes into to our life that we realize we can't ever live without. It's funny how they say for better or worse. It really means that, even when they are at their worst you know that it's better than anyone else's best."

"How are you such bad ass cop and a mush at the same time?"

"Behind every good man..." He tipped his head at Dex. He didn't need to finish the statement. It had been said enough times by enough people.

"You should finish that coffee before we go in there," Dex

suggested.

"I will just toss it. I've had enough. We still have that other cup in the truck if I need it. Are you ready for this?"

"Why wouldn't I be? Not like I have never seen a dead body before," he snapped. Although he had seen dead people that he knew before, it was a first to have slept with the deceased less than a week before. There was something about it that made his skin crawl.

Johnny just gave him a hard look, pulled his ID card out of his pocket, and held it up to the scanner to unlock the door. As soon as they opened the door, their ears were pummeled with the crushing sound of girly pop music. They looked at each other and shook their heads.

"Hey, how about we put some music on that people actually want to listen to," Dex called out over the girl's voice moaning about how much she loved someone.

"This is my morgue, my music. Deal with it tough guy." Shea had never been one to back down from Dex, not in high school, or even in college when she had dated his very best friend. She had no problem speaking up for herself or taking a stand on her opinion.

"But...we have some things to talk about, so I will just turn it off." She winked at Johnny eliciting a slight smile.

"Brought you a coffee. Sorry, it isn't a latte, but it is vanilla." He went to hand it to her, not taking into account that she had on gloves covered in blood.

Shea gave him a, *"You must be kidding me?"* look.

"Thank you. You can put it in the corner over there on my desk. I am almost finished with your girl's autopsy."

"Why is she my girl?" Dex jumped back.

"What? She is your victim, for your case right?" She looked at him sideways. "What is wrong with you?"

"You might as well tell her now."

Johnny wasn't trying to throw him under the bus, but if he didn't say something right away, it would make it twice as awkward.

"What's up, Dex?" She asked, kicking her hip to the side.

"This victim, Bethany Kingston, and I were intimate." Dex wasn't really sure how the best way to explain to his friend and Medical Examiner.

"You were dating the victim? Are you involved with this case? Are you in trouble?" Her face lost all expression.

"We were not dating. I only met her two days before she disappeared. I was actually with her the night that Tammy Larazzo was murdered. Turns out, they were roommates. We were possibly the last people at the station house to see Bethany alive."

"This is, wow. Are you a suspect? Does Captain Kard know all this?"

"No, I am not a suspect. I was with Bethany when Tammy was killed, and I was with Johnny when we suspect that Bethany was murdered." Dex shuffled his feet back and forth and slid the tips of his fingers into his front pockets.

"The captain knows everything. She met Bethany when she came in to identify Tammy's body. This case is getting more fucked up by the day, and we don't have a solid lead. I really hope that you have something new for us."

Shea walked around to the other side of Bethany's cadaver. It was hard for Dex to see her lying there split open, and a chill ran down his back.

The underlying stench in the room was comprised of years of death and harsh chemicals. They made their presence known to him in a way he had never experienced before.

"The same murder weapon was definitely used, I would hypothesize that it was used by the hands of the same killer. I assume that is already what you guys think, especially since the victims were roommates."

"What kind of weapon are we talking about here? Anything out of the ordinary that we can use to help narrow down our search?" Johnny asked still gripping his coffee cup.

"Yes actually." She looked at Dex. "You know my dad and my brother are big hunters. Which makes me somewhat of a hunter by default from having to go with them so many times. I have seen my father gut many deer. The only thing that opens a body like this is a gut hook."

"Is that a common hunting knife? How can you tell?"

"It is somewhat common. It is a preference thing. My dad likes it, my brother doesn't, because it is only really good for opening up the large belly of a deer, but it's not good for much else, and he can't sharpen it."

"Was the blade used sharp or dull?" Dex asked.

"It was sharp enough to cut clean through her skin. It opened both women like a zipper. There were no other stab wounds on their bodies. This also leads me to lean toward the gut hook.

"We know that Miss Larazzo was incapacitated by the Benzo concoction. I found a small puncture mark at the crease of Miss Kingston's underarm. It will take us at least twenty-four hours to get back the toxicology report, but I think it is safe to say she was drugged the same way."

"Did she try to fight back?"

"I haven't found any defensive wounds on her. There are no markings on her arms or legs to indicate that she was restrained. This leads me to believe that she was either unconscious or close to it when she was killed. They both died almost instantly.

"The murderer knew how to use the blade with precision. And as much as they wanted to kill these women, they didn't go out of their way to cause suffering. The women were so fucked up that they most likely didn't even know death was coming for them."

"Geez, I don't know, I guess that is as close to a silver lining as you can get in a case like this. At least we can tell the families that they did not suffer. I know that is sometimes harder to get over than the fact that they lost someone." Johnny took a step closer to the body, looking at the opening.

"This incision is one that you made or the killer?"

"That is not me. I haven't gotten that far yet. I have to still open her chest cavity, but cause of death is pretty clear. I hope you don't have a serial killer on your hands."

"You and us both. I really don't want you to be alone at any point until we catch this person!" Dex stood up and puffed his chest. "I want you calling security when you leave here to walk you to your car. Can you and Abigail stay with your parents for a few days?"

"Seriously? I know how to protect myself, I was married to a cop for God's sake. If you are so worried about us, you should try making some time to see us."

Shea's words cut through him like shards of glass. She was right, and he knew it. He hadn't been there for them as he should have been. In his mind, the best way to take care of them was to not expose them to his toxicity.

"Don't give me crap. Call your parents and stay with them. I didn't know Tammy, but I did know Bethany. I don't know what the connection is between the two women, other than that they are roommates. I don't know if or how this killer is choosing their victims."

"Whatever, Dex. I will get security to walk me out."

Johnny broke the tension by bringing the focus back to the dead woman lying on the metal slab in front of them. "Did you happen to pull anything else from the body that ties them together? Both women were killed and dumped. We know that, what we don't know is where they were killed."

"They both had dirt on their bodies. Not the kind of loose sandy dirt, like from laying in the street either. It was darker more like a richer soil or compost. I know that might not help much, being we live in such a rural community, but there is a chance if you found a potential murder location we could match the particulates.

"There is a good chance that the soil will be saturated with blood residue as well. I also found chips of rusted paint on the exterior of their clothes. I have to send the paint chips to a lab to see if we can identify the paint, but that could take a few days."

"Send it, send anything you have. I really fucking hope we catch this sick fuck before you get the results back, but if we don't, we'll need everything we can to find this person. What about the hook cut knife, are they hard to find?"

"Gut hook, and any hunting store would have them, and they sell them online. Shit, they might even sell them at the local department store for all I know. Just because it was a sharp blade, that doesn't mean that it is a new blade. It could be an older knife that someone has had for years and just hasn't used much. I didn't find any traces of animal blood on, or in, the wounds, so my guess would be that it wasn't used on an animal prior."

"So what you are saying is that it would not serve us well to look into a location where one of these knives may have been purchased?" Johnny looked down at his coffee cup with his brow knotted together. "You got a trash can I can toss this in?"

"Sure, over there, the black one." She pointed across the room. "I wouldn't look further into where they may have purchased the blade, not if you have other leads you can work. If you have nothing, I guess you could look down that avenue, but a lot of people around here probably have similar blades. I know my dad has one, and even my brother who doesn't like them might."

"Ok, I get it," Dex said.

"There are signs of recent sexual activity, but I guess you already know that." Her eyes pierced at Dex's humility. "The info and DNA test will still be in my report."

Dex nodded. He knew it would be. He felt the tightness in his chest and his hands had coiled into fists. There was a piece of him that was angry with himself. His careless attitude toward sex and one-night stands had finally come back to bite him in the ass.

It would not look good on his record, and it could pose a potential issue in court. He was a private person and didn't talk about his business or about the way he spent his free time. Now everyone would know where he had been and what he had been doing.

"There wasn't any sign of fresh trauma, so there was no sexual assault. None with the first victim either, but if you read the report I sent over this morning, you know that." She looked at the blank looks on both detectives' faces.

"That would be my fault. There was an early meeting with the captain on this case, and we have been on the go since. We have the file in the truck, so we will be going over everything after we leave here." Johnny walked back from the trashcan but didn't get too close to the cadaver. He took a position closer to the exit. He wasn't the only one ready to get out of there.

"I don't know if you boys are on the case tomorrow, but I will get this report finished tonight and faxed over to you for tomorrow morning. The toxicology might not come back until Monday. It takes twenty-four hours, but it is late Saturday afternoon, I'm not sure how late they work, or how much they do on a Saturday."

"Well, either way, we will see you on Sunday, right?" Johnny asked.

"I wouldn't miss it. Abigail will be with me."

"You are going to bring her to the wake?" Dex snapped.

"Why wouldn't I?"

"Because she is a little girl and doesn't need to be exposed to death like that." Dex may have been out of line, but Abigail was his goddaughter after all.

"Death is a natural part of life. I deal with death every day, and she is no stranger to it. I don't hide what I do from her. Besides, she knows firsthand about losing someone." Shea took off her gloves and tossed them in the trash. She walked over to her desk in the corner and picked up her coffee that they'd brought her. "Thanks again for the coffee."

Dex had a lot more to say, but he felt Johnny's daggers threatening him to leave it alone. His emotions were running hot, and he needed to get out of there. They had too much to do to linger any longer.

"You ready? We have work to do," Dex said to his partner.

"See you Sunday, Shea. Thanks for all your hard work on the case." Johnny followed Dex toward the exit. "Don't mind him, he just cares and doesn't know how to show it."

"Mm hmm." She nodded to him before the door shut behind him.

CHAPTER TWENTY-ONE

"DO YOU WANT TO GRAB dinner?" Johnny asked Dex as soon as they got in the truck.

"Not really. My stomach is in no shape for food right now. How can you think about eating after looking at that?"

"Eh, I am always hungry. I skipped the doughnuts remember." His attempt to bring a little humor to the moment was a failed attempt.

"I think I am going to drive you to Kagley's now so you can grab your car. I need to hit the gym tonight after we are done working. This case is messing with my routine, and my head." He rubbed his eyes before backing out of the parking spot.

He looked down at his hands and noticed the whites of his knuckles showing through. His grip on the steering wheel was about the only thing that felt secure.

"I'm going to call and order take out from Kagley's then, bring it back to the precinct. You sure you don't want anything?"

"I don't know, I guess grab me a half a chicken with whatever vegetable they have. If I don't eat it, I can always bring it home.

"We need to catch this person, Johnny. I can't let anyone else die, not by the hands of this sick-o. How does someone live with themselves after they open another human being's body like that? Stealing their life from them with one flick of the wrist. It makes me sick."

"Me too, Dex. I am frustrated as hell. It has been a long time since we have had so few concrete leads to work with. I don't want this case to go cold, and at the same time, I don't want it to stay hot with more bodies piling up."

"It has been seven years since I had a case I couldn't solve." A twitch started to shake Dex's bottom left eyelid. It had also been a while since he had the eye twitch.

"Don't take yourself there. We will close them all. You and me. We won't stop until they are closed."

"The Portland PD has had Paul's case as a cold case for five years now."

"You don't think I don't know you are still working on it? I always have my ears open. I have gone through the file a few times over the years."

"You have?"

"Come on, you think I am going to let someone get away with killing one of our own?"

"I guess. I would hope not."

"No, but right now, we need to be in the here and now. We have an active killer walking the streets. If they are here in Hawk Creek, they can't be that hard to find. The population, last I checked, isn't even five-thousand people. We know almost everyone that lives here and half the people that live in these podunk towns around us.

"We know the bodies were moved, and with the times of death in relation to when the bodies were discovered, we know that the murder scene can't be that far. I don't see why someone would take the time to drive over an hour to target and kill these women. Whoever it is lives around here. People talk, and you know it always gets around."

"You say it as if that should make me feel any better. The fact that we can't narrow down this small population of people to have a solid suspect is bullshit." He hit the steering wheel and grunted out something incomprehensible.

"Why don't we call it a day? I will take home the autopsy report on Tammy Larazzo and read it over tonight. We can bring in the boyfriend tomorrow and interrogate him. We will research him in the morning. He is the only tie we have between the two women.

"We need his back history. Where he grew up, does he

have a private property that could have been used to stash and kill these women? Where was he the night that our first victim was slain?" Johnny was getting amped up.

"We can do that. My gut says it isn't him, but you are right, we need to make sure. We are missing something!" Dex's teeth were clamped so tight that he heard them grinding.

Dex pulled into the parking lot of Kagley's. His intention was just to bring his partner to his car, so they could get back to the station to work. The heavyweight bag was calling his name, but Johnny wanting to call it a day made it too easy to pull into a parking spot and take the keys out of the engine.

"If you're still hungry you want to grab that bite to eat? I'm still not hungry, but I need a drink." Dex grabbed his phone and keys and slid them into his pockets.

"I will go in and order, I am still going to take my food to go. If I go home stinking of booze and beer two nights in a row, Betty will have my ass. I think surprising them with take-out would be a better option. I know she has been doing a lot to take care of my mother's arrangements, so I don't have to."

"Suit yourself," Dex said as they walked into the bar. "Betty is really good people. It will be nice to see her again on Sunday. I sure don't want her pissed off at me, so diet coke for you."

Of course Dex would have preferred to have Johnny stick around and get blasted with him, but he was a lone drinker by nature. Sitting at the bar for a drink or two by himself was perfectly normal for him.

It was still on the early side. Happy hour had started, and there were some shift workers already at the bar, but the dinner rush was still at least another half hour or so away.

The two detectives sat at the bar. Johnny ordered enough take-out food to feed ten people. He didn't even order the diet coke, just a glass of water.

Dex slid his phone onto the bar in front of him, discreetly waking the screen up. He could easily see that he didn't have any missed calls or text messages. He was feeling a bit nostalgic from the night before and ordered a Jameson whiskey sour.

Johnny looked at him sideways. Dex knew it was a bit of a wussy drink, but it was what his lips were craving.

"What? I thought a little bit of sweet would help balance out how sour I feel."

Johnny slapped him on the back. "Do me a favor, don't spend your night here. You want to catch this guy, we need to stay sharp, and we have work to do tomorrow."

Dex's shoulders slump forward as he placed his

forearms on the bar in front of him. He held his drink with both hands and stared down at the floating cherry on top.

He knew that his friend's advice was solid and worth taking, and that the drink in front of him wouldn't taste nearly as good as his grandmother's, or the one that he'd tasted off of Trina's lips the night before.

He didn't like the feeling in the pit of his stomach, knowing that she hadn't taken the time to reach out to him yet. Just another reminder of why he didn't get involved with women past a night of pure unadulterated sex. What more did he need? Whiskey, sex, his job, and maybe a punching bag.

He'd told Johnny that he was going to bring her for dinner on Sunday, but he hadn't asked her yet. Now it seemed like the best idea not to ask her. It would probably just be close family and friends anyway. Not to mention the fact that it might be on the morbid side, considering everyone will be coming from Mrs. Harrington's service.

Dex didn't realize how long he had been lost in his thoughts until the bartender came out with a cardboard box full of to-go containers. His drink was still untouched.

"I hope you told Betty you were bringing home food."

"I texted her when we got here. She was thrilled. It worked out great because she said she forgot to defrost something for dinner." Johnny handed the bartender his credit card. "Besides, this way there won't be any dishes to do because even though I am going home early, I will be still working, reading that report."

"That reminds me, I didn't find any prescriptions for any type of sedatives or narcotics when we were at the girl's apartment earlier. Maybe we should ask Jeremy if he knew of them taking anything like that."

"Yeah, good point. We should still check in with the pharmacy too, good thing there is only one in town, makes it easy to know where they would go to fill them if they had one." He signed the credit card slip. "Not that Shea couldn't tell us, but I want to ask the pharmacist about the dosage found in Tammy Larazzo. Maybe if we can determine how much medication these women are being injected with we can find the prescription holder."

"Maybe, we are going to need that warrant for that. Don't forget that there are a handful of lowlifes in this town that sell that shit on the street too."

"We might need to pay them a visit then, and we don't need a warrant for that." Johnny fist bumped Dex.

Dex almost cracked a smile at the potential thought of getting to throw down with some shithead that didn't want to cooperate. The opportunity didn't come often, and he certainly never went out on the streets with the intention to abuse his authority. But there was something that filled him up knowing he was taking someone down that could be potentially saving someone else's life.

"Ok buddy, see you in the morning. If you need me to pick your hung over ass up, just shoot me a text before you pass out tonight." Johnny patted him on the shoulder and took off with his box of food for his family.

Dex took a sip of his drink. It didn't quite hit the spot the way he needed it to. Probably because there was too much pleasure involved in the sweetness of it. He wasn't there looking for a sweet spot. He wanted to numb out the world and let himself be consumed by his pain. It was what he knew; suffering was his norm.

He waved over the bartender.

"Let me get a shot of Jameson and an order of grilled buffalo wings."

"Is your drink okay?"

"It's fine, just a little sweeter than I expected, I really don't know why I ordered it."

"I can make you something else."

"It's okay, I will drink it."

The bartender put a rock glass in front of him and poured a heavy amount of whiskey in the glass.

"Promise there won't be a repeat of last night in here?" she teased him. "Here is a little extra if you want to add it to your drink to cut the sweetness. I will go put in your order for your chicken."

"Thanks, hun."

He didn't waste any time. After she turned to walk

away, he slammed the amber liquor in one large gulp. He probably should have put some of it in his drink, but the hot sauce on the wings would be enough of a contrast for the sweet drink.

His mind turned to the sight of Bethany alive and well on the night they had spent together. Her milky curves had looked as if someone had poured cream straight out of heaven into the bed beside him. When he had awakened that morning, he couldn't even remember what her face looked like.

All he had were brief flashes of his hands gliding over her bare breasts, and the sensation of her tiny, erect nipples grazing over his face as she leaned over, riding him.

Guilt plagued him, and he wished he could go back and remember more of that night. He hadn't even known her name until she had walked into the police station the next day. He hadn't even realized at the time how embarrassed he should have been by his insensitivity.

He took a sip of his cocktail and shook his head. He was frustrated with his inwardly placed anger. He felt guilt, but it wasn't his fault that Bethany was dead. None of the other women he had shared a bed with turned up deceased. He considered the possibility that he was maybe more of a jerk than he'd realized, since all of their names and faces were nothing more than a blur.

He was jolted from his self-wallowing by someone

brushing against his arm and sitting down on the bar stool beside him. He turned to look, his instinct was to snarl at the person for invading his space, but her face, as she greeted him with a warm smile, was just too perfect. "Sorry, I didn't mean to bump into you. I lost my balance a little. I am always so clumsy." She put her pocketbook on the bar in front of her.

"That's okay. I can take much more of a beating than that." He smiled back at her.

"Oh no, I would hate to think that anyone would want to beat on such a pretty face."

He hadn't noticed the first time she smiled that she had a deep dimple on her left cheek. He had a thing for dimples. She was not Dex's type, but there was something undeniably sexy about her. He had not seen her around before, but she looked like she just got off work. She had on a black pants suit with a blazer that hid her curves he could tell she had.

Dex had never been with a girl as curvy as she was, but he couldn't help but wonder what she looked like under all those clothes.

"Just get off of work?" he asked her.

"Sort of, I am a realtor, I am always working. I just showed a few houses to a couple here in town. I don't usually show houses this far out, but they were friends of a friend. I couldn't say no. How about you?"

"Oh, I am a cop, so I am kind of always working too."

"I hope you are technically off duty if you are drinking."

"I am a detective. My brain is always on the case, but I am done for the day, back at it first thing tomorrow morning."

"I see" The bartender came over to help her. "Can I see your menu, and I will have a Jameson and ginger."

"A girl after my own heart."

"Oh yeah? Why is that?"

"Jameson is my drink."

She looked at the floating cherry and a slice of orange on the rim of his glass and nearly burst out laughing.

"What, a man can't drink a fancy drink once and a while?" He laughed. "I was feeling nostalgic, my grandmother used to drink Jameson sours. My friend just lost his mother, and I was missing her."

"Awe, that is so sweet. Handsome and sensitive."

She was beyond forward. He was used to being out and women hitting on him, but they were usually already two sheets to the wind, so their inhibitions were down.

The bartender came back with her drink and his wings.

"Put her drinks on my tab." Dex never had a problem buying drinks for pretty women.

"Thanks. I should bump into hot guys more often." She held up her glass to salute him.

"My pleasure." And it was. He needed the distraction

more than she could ever know.

"So what's good to eat here?"

"Depends on what you are in the mood for. Mostly anything I have had here has been pretty good. I have never sent my food back, so that has to be something."

"I'm not sure what I am in the mood for is on the menu." She gave him a coy look, rolling her eyes up and to the left as her eyelashes fluttered.

"Really?" He was pretty sure that she was suggesting that he wasn't on the menu, but his intuitions felt as if they had been off, especially not making any headway in the case. "What did you have in mind exactly?"

"I am always up for anything. I just won't be in town much longer. I have to get a key back to the office before nine."

Dex looked down at his watch, it was still somewhat early, but he also wasn't sure how far she had to drive to get back to her office. He looked over at her and half her drink was gone.

"You want another drink?" He asked her.

"Maybe just one more, but I have to drive. Are you going to have one with me?"

"Sure, looks like I am taking a cab home at this point anyway. You want the same thing?"

She held the straw to her lips and slowly wrapped them around the tip, sliding the long cylinder in and out of her mouth as she sucked the rest of her drink down.

Dex smiled and waved over the bartender.

"I'm going to wrap these wings to go."

"Oh, is there something wrong with them?"

"No. I am just in the mood for something else right now. Can we get two more drinks, I will have another Jameson and she will have another Jameson and ginger." He turned to the nameless woman. "Are you ordering anything to eat?"

"I think I am going to stick with my drink for now, thank you." The bartender turned to fix their beverages. "You said you were going to take a cab home, does that mean you don't have a car?"

"I have a truck, but I don't drink and drive. This town is so small that it's not a big deal to take a quick cab ride home. My partner is planning on picking me up in the morning anyway."

"I have been thinking about buying a truck. You think you might want to show it to me?"

He ran his fingers through his hair. He had made an effort earlier that morning styling it with product, but it had been a long day. At this point it didn't really matter how tousled it was.

He lifted his rocks glass up and clinked it against the woman's drink before slamming the shot, took out a credit card, and tossed it on the bar. When the bartender brought back his to-go box she took the credit card to run his tab.

He sipped on the rest of his whiskey sour while he waited for the credit card slip. He felt something on his leg. He turned to find his companion rubbing the tip of her foot along the back of his calf.

Johnny wondered why Dex was so egocentric at times, but women just flocked to him. It wasn't often that he actually went out looking for it, but if it was there, why wouldn't he indulge in his most primal desires? He was lucky that most of the women were not looking for anything more than a good time.

"Are you ready to show me what you got out there?" her voice became more husky and seductive.

Dex was surprised that her drink was empty. He picked up his food and his receipt and put his credit card back in his wallet. She grabbed her bag off the top of the bar and followed him out to the parking lot.

He was glad that he'd left his truck in a more secluded part of the parking lot where there was minimal light. He was not a fool. He knew that this woman had no interest in his truck as anything more than somewhere that they could potentially fuck.

They made it to his truck, and he put his to-go box on the roof. As he was about to unlock the door to the passenger side, her hands wrapped around the front of his chest and trailed them down over his belly. One hand grabbed his crotch over his jeans while she used the other hand to unbuckle his pants. Once she had them unfastened she turned him around.

"All I could think about in there was how good you would feel sliding in and out of my mouth." She reached up and licked the side of his neck until her tongue reached his earlobe.

She flicked the bottom of his earlobe, and he felt her breath sending shockwaves into his ear. She sucked it into her mouth as her hand slid down into his pants. She got a handful of his hard shaft.

"Umm hmm. That is what I am talking about," she whispered against his neck.

He let his head rest back against the window. He wasn't drunk, but the whiskey was coursing through his veins, intensifying the tingling sensations that her touch was providing.

"I am going to suck your cock so hard, and then you are going to fuck me," she demanded as she pulled the front of his pants down, exposing his erection. She gazed down at it, and then back up at him through hooded eyes. The corners of her lips curved up naughtily as she moistened them with her tongue.

She lowered herself down in front of him until her lips collided with him, drawing his flesh into her hot mouth. He felt his balls tighten as his hips pushed forward to feel her throat nearly swallowing him whole.

He wrapped his hands into her wavy brown hair, helping to glide her head as it bobbed over him. She lifted her hand to stroke his balls as her cheeks hollowed out with each suck and pull of his cock.

His eyes were closed. As his body stiffened, and images of Trina and her full, soft, glossy lips flashed behind his eyes. He imagined it was her mouth on him, and in that moment, a sudden darkness filled his belly.

He pulled back away from the nameless woman, easing her head back away from him, and tucked himself back into his pants with a quick motion.

"It's okay, you can finish in my mouth." She looked up at him stunned at the abrupt pause in their encounter.

"I'm sorry. I just can't."

"What do you mean you can't?"

"I mean that I should not be here right now with you. It's complicated. I'm sorry. You are beautiful and beyond sexy, and a month ago I would have made sure that we spent the entire night together." Dex zipped his pants and held out a hand to help her stand up.

"Are you for real?"

Dex scrunched up his face in disbelief. "I'm afraid so."

"Wow, you are a jerk." She stood up with hurt and anger in her hard eyes.

"I know, that is the problem. I'm not sure I want to be

that guy anymore."

She picked her purse up from the ground. "You are a complete tool. I don't know why anyone would ever want to move to this dump of a town."

She stomped away.

He didn't even watch to see where she went. He leaned against his truck, pressed his fingers into the corners of his eyes, pinching the bridge of his nose, and banged the back of his head against the window.

"Shit."

CHAPTER TWENTY-TWO

HIS TEETH WERE CLENCHED SO tight that the only chance at oxygen was through his nose. He knew that he should be more focused on his breath when he was working out so hard, but he didn't care about the consequences.

Dex felt as if he was a fairly uncomplicated guy that stuck to a routine and worked hard at his job. He had his few pastimes that he enjoyed, but he didn't let things or people get in the way of that simplicity.

Sweat dripped down into his eyes. He did his best to blink it away because there was no way he was stopping to wipe it off. He pounded his bare fists against the black and red leather bag. There was an exactness to his technique that helped to quiet his mind if only during the execution of each punch.

Unfortunately, the other moments between the forward

thrusts of his arms were flashbacks to the past twenty-four hours.

He and Johnny had taken a hard approach with Jeremy at his interrogation earlier that morning. Dex was impressed with how much research Johnny had managed to pull up about Bethany's boyfriend before they'd began. While Dex had been fucking around at Kagley's, his partner had been hard at work.

He appreciated the effort to move the case forward, but it angered him that he wasn't the one doing the work. He should have been there, backing up his partner or working up a different angle with the same tenacity.

Although there were some aspects of Jeremy's character and the depth of the true depth of his relationship with Bethany that made him suspicious— he wasn't their guy. They wanted him to be, and of course, there was still a slight possibility it could be Jeremy.

His lack of an alibi for the times of the murder and a motive could be enough to arrest him on suspicion. However, without hard facts to back it up, the case would go nowhere, and a killer could still be on the loose.

They had expected Jeremy to attempt using Bethany as an alibi for the night Tammy was murdered. Jeremy sure didn't know that Johnny and Dex might have been the only ones that knew where she was on the night in question, and he could've easily said he was with her. As far as he knew, she couldn't say otherwise, but he didn't try it.

Truthfully, they had nothing solid to actually tie him to either crime. Johnny even emailed the manager at the Salty Peach restaurant to see if anyone recognized Jeremy as a patron from Wednesday night. They had yet to hear back from him, but Andi the bartender seemed to have a pretty good recollection of the night.

Most bartenders were good with faces. They needed to be, remembering what people's preferences are and remembering who is a good tipper is all part of how they earn their living.

Dex had confidence that once they had a worthy suspect, and if they were at that restaurant that night, Andi would be able to identify them. Sad that the bartender was the closest thing they had to a potential witness.

The bag could take the beating that Dex was administering. His blows were relentless. He thanked God that he did not find himself in a situation where he had to be physical with anyone, they might not have survived the rage inside of him.

What would Trina think about what he was doing last night? Of course he would never tell her, there would be no point to that. They weren't even dating, but he had never felt such guilt over being with a woman before.

He couldn't bring himself to respond to her text the

previous night because of it. He'd waited all day to see her name pop up on his phone, and then when he finally had, he felt like he had betrayed his feelings for her in some way.

They were supposed to make plans to go bowling that weekend, and he still had not asked her about joining him at Johnny and Betty's house on Sunday. He was being hard on himself, and there was no one that beat him down more than he did.

If only she had called him earlier. He needed someone or something to numb out his pain and his rage. Her softness would have been just what he needed to cool down the boiling waste inside of him.

He couldn't believe his audacity of putting it on her as if she pushed him to act like an ass. What kind of piece of shit gets a blowjob in a parking lot from a woman whose name he didn't even know? Was he not sitting at the bar, angry at himself for just that very same action with Bethany?

He needed to clear his mind. No matter how hard he pushed himself, the thoughts kept coming. He tried to focus on his breath, and the sound of his heart pumping his blood, it pounded against his eardrums just as his fists smacked against the bag.

He'd never let this much come to the surface before. He had stuffed and stuffed the last seven years down as far as he could. He hoped that they were pushed into an inescapable black hole.

Blackness filled his vision, and he wasn't sure if he was passing out, or if his eyes were closed. Either way he punched on. Images of his friend Paul Sinclair lying dead on the street in front of him was all he could see.

A burn started to sting his eyes as he choked back the tears between staggered breaths. The desperate, endless pain that was behind Shea's eyes that day, was too much for him to bear. It was the real reason he avoided her so much.

It was his fault that her husband was dead. Was it now his fault in some way that these women were dying in this town too? Was he not the great cop that everyone thought he was?

Even though he took his job to heart and it mattered more than anything else in the world, he never really let himself excel, he always got in his own way. What right did he have to succeed or be happy in life when it was his fault that his best friend and one-time partner no longer walked the Earth beside him?

He didn't think that the Sinclair's could ever find true forgiveness for him. How could they, when he couldn't forgive himself?

"Hey, buddy?" the faint sound of a man's voice filtered into Dex's consciousness, or rather lack thereof. He wasn't sure if he imagined it or not. Maybe he was hallucinating from dehydration. He still pounded every ounce of his soul into that bag.

"Dude! You need to stop!"

He heard the voice again, but Dex's eyes were still closed.

"Yo!"

The voice came loudly at him with a hand to his shoulder. It jolted his sense of what was going on, and before he could even open his eyes, his reflexes took over, and he turned and uppercut whoever was touching him.

Fear and reality quickly set in, forcing him to open his eyes.

"What the fuck, man? You are out of control! You are bleeding all over the bag."

Dex's chest was heaving up and down as his heart slammed against the inner walls of his rib cage.

"Shit, I am so sorry!" He could barely talk between his attempts to catch his breath. He looked down at his still clenched fists. The knuckles on both of his hands were split open and there was blood all over the bag. It was splattered all over his sweat-drenched tee shirt and on the floor beneath his feet.

"I would offer you a hand to help you up... but..." He turned his hands.

"Bro, I don't know what is going on, but you can't do

that shit here. Do I need to call the cops or someone for you?" the guy said, getting up rubbing at the side of his chin.

"I am the police. Please accept my apologies. I just, I don't know, I guess I didn't realize." Dex had really made a mess of the place. "I am going to go clean up, then I will come out and disinfect the bag."

"I will grab the first aid kit for you. You are going to need to bandage those up. I will help you. I think there are some cold packs in there too. Your shit is gonna be swollen to all hell."

"You're going to help me after I just clocked you?" Dex asked, his voice full of surprise.

"You don't think that is the first time I have been hit do you? We are in a boxing gym, you know that right?"

"Good point. I am going to take a quick shower and wash this blood off. I will be back out in a few minutes. I appreciate your help. This is a bit embarrassing."

"No worries, bro. We are all here because there is a fire burning at our core that searches for a way to extinguish. Better you hitting that bag than someone's face out there on the street."

Dex knew that was beyond the truth. If he pounded on someone like that, he would have killed them, lost his job, and been arrested. He knew that he had been in black outrage and that could never happen again.

The shower was cold and fast. He appreciated the fact that his towels were charcoal gray so they weren't stained with blood. The bleeding on his knuckles had slowed, but they were still leaking blood, nonetheless. He dressed quickly, throwing his jeans and a fresh tee on. He really wished he had brought a pair of sweats instead.

His over the top workout, if that was what you could even call it, was an explosion of stupidity on his part. He knew that he was going to suffer the repercussions of it tomorrow. The swelling was already starting to turn a bright red from the blood flooding the tissue under his skin. He wished the redness was just from stained blood, but he knew better.

He would have a blast explaining to Johnny why his hands were covered in cuts and giant purple bruises. At least it wasn't from repeated contact with some innocent, or less than innocent individual. Unfortunately, the guy that pulled him from the bag did take one blow.

Dex tossed his stuff in his bag and kept the towel out to keep pressure on the wounds, so he could get back out to the floor. When he got back out there, the guy had on a pair of rubber gloves and was spraying the bag with cleaner. Dex felt like a complete jerk that someone had to clean up after him.

"Oh, man, you should have left that. I would have cleaned that myself. No need for you to have to do that."

"It's fine. You shouldn't really be exposing those hands to the chemicals in the cleaner. I got the first aid kit. It's over there on the bench. I'll be right over to help you."

He looked as if he was just finishing up anyway. He grabbed the dirty pile of used paper towels and tossed them in the trash. There were plenty of paper towels and garbage cans in the gym. They expected everyone to clean up after themselves, and why shouldn't they?

By the time Dex sat down and opened the kit, his new friend was at his side.

"Here, let me do that. I have plenty of practice. I was an EMT for years, and I have been training here for almost three years now."

"Thanks, I don't know what I would have done if you weren't here. It's been a rough day I guess. I have never done that before. I basically blacked out."

"I've been there, bro, but you should always keep your hands and your wrists protected. We don't like to think of ourselves as fragile, but the hands and wrists can be easily damaged, not to mention you could get a nasty infection from whatever is on the bag.

"If I were you, I would have your doctor take a look at these wounds. He or she might want to give you an antibiotic. Just in case." He opened a small packet of antibiotic ointment and squeezed it over the backs of each of Dex's hands before wrapping them in gauze. "My name is Steve, by the way."

"Nice to meet you, Detective Dex Preston."

"Oh right, you're a cop. I think you might owe me one of those get out of free jail cards." Steve laughed.

"I just might. I would offer to buy you a beer, but I think it best I get home."

"Thanks, I don't drink anymore anyway. It got me into way too much trouble. That's why I spend most of my spare time in here. You, on the other hand, should think about finding another hobby that is a bit more relaxing."

Steve's face suggested that he may have been kidding, but Dex knew there was some validity to the suggestion.

Dex could hear his phone ringing in his bag, and he wasn't too excited about having to retrieve it. He was going to need to hit the Ibuprofen pretty hard when he got home.

"I better check that and hit the road. That might be my partner." Dex reached in his bag for the phone, but it stopped ringing before he pulled it out. "Thanks again for your help and sorry about your chin."

"Anytime," Steve packed the first aid kit back up.

"I will see what I can do about getting you one of those fancy freebie cards too."

CHAPTER TWENTY-THREE

DEX LOOKED DOWN AT HIS phone as he walked out of the gym. He had a missed call from Trina. He figured it was time to call her back before she thought he was either avoiding her or playing hard to get.

Surprised by how late it had gotten, he climbed into his truck. He must have been at the gym for over two hours and before he'd started in on the bag, he'd pushed his cardio beyond his limit. He was beyond exhausted, both physically and emotionally. Just as he was about to hit the button to call her back, his phone bleeped with a text. It was from her.

Hey. I'm sorry to call you again, but I really need to talk to you. I am afraid that someone has been in my house.

A rush of nausea crashed over him like a vicious ocean wave. All the sweat he had just showered off started to bead up on his skin. He couldn't call her back fast enough.

"Hello?" her voice was rougher than he remembered.

"Trina?"

"Dex, oh my God. I am so freaked out. I don't know, I might be overreacting. It's just that..." her words were coming so fast that it was difficult to understand what she was saying.

"Slow down, Trina. Where are you now?"

"I'm at home."

"I'm coming there, do I need to call for back up?" Dex was pissed. He had the truck in reverse before he even knew where she lived. "You need to text me your address, I'm coming there now. Hang up, text me, and then call me right back."

"Ok."

There was no way he was going to let anything happen to Trina. If there was even the slightest chance that she was this lunatic's next target, he would be there, and he would stay with her until he knew for sure that she was safe.

Her address came up on the screen of his phone almost instantly. He was at least seven minutes away, and that was if he pushed the pedal to the metal. Lucky for him, he was a cop, and he could get away with driving like it was life or death. He had a horrible feeling that it could be just that kind of situation. He would never forgive himself if he were too late.

When his phone rang, he didn't even let the first ring

finish before he answered through his blue tooth.

"Trina?" Why didn't he look at the screen? He couldn't afford for the line to be busy or go straight to voice mail if she was trying to call him back.

"Yea. Are you on your way here?" he could hear her voice shaking.

"I am. I will be there in less than ten minutes. Are you okay?"

"I guess so, I am just scared."

"Tell me what is going on. When did you get home?"

"I just got home like maybe thirty minutes ago. Gladys and I grabbed dinner after work, and then I went to the supermarket to do some food shopping."

"When you got home was the door open, or did it look like anyone had forced their way in the house? Are you sure that you are alone right now?"

"Yes, I mean no." There was frustration in her tone. "The door was not open to suggest that anyone had come into my house. I wouldn't have even come in if that were the case. My dad was a cop, so I know what to look for once I suspected that someone had been here. I didn't see anything suspicious at any of the doors or windows."

"Make sure that your doors and windows are locked and stay on the phone with me. If I wasn't so close, I would call a patrol car to head over there, but they won't get there before me." Dex gripped the steering wheel so hard that he could see the blood starting to seep through the bandages on his hands.

"I already did that. How far are you now?"

"Only a few more minutes. You know you live out in the middle of nowhere though?"

"That was kind of the point. I came here for solitude and to get away from the chaos of the city."

Dex knew he needed to keep her calm and her mind off of the fear until he could get there to protect her. He needed to change the subject to distract her.

"Do you have an ibuprofen or pain reliever in the house?"

"Of course, but I don't need that," she sounded confused by his question.

"No, but I do. I kind of took my workout past where it should have been. I kind of hurt myself a little. Any chance you have a nicely stocked first aid kit too?"

"Oh my gosh, Dex. Are you okay? I will go grab everything now. What kind of first aid stuff do you need, like band-aids, ace bandage?"

He could hear her shuffling around. He was glad she was doing something else. He knew he was distracting himself as well from the scenarios that had been playing in his head.

"Gauze and tape would be great if you have it, maybe some kind of antibiotic ointment. Vaseline would work for now if you don't have anything else." Dex was on her street. He had to slow down to look for a number on something. There were so few driveways and homes, he knew they lived in a rural area, but this was taking it to the extreme.

"Ok, you're in luck. I seem to be fully stocked."

"Is there any kind of landmark you can give me, so I can find you? I am on your street."

"I am about a mile up, on the right after you cross over south-east Hawk Creek Road. The number of my property is nailed onto a tree at the edge of the drive. It is kind of wooded at the street, but once you turn down the driveway it will open up."

"I will be there in two seconds then. I just crossed over. Don't open your door until you know it is me knocking."

Dex drove down the gravel driveway. He was sure that, with the amount of noise his tires were making kicking up rocks, Trina could hear his approach.

"You're here!"

"I am. I will see you in a minute. Wait at the door for me."

He couldn't believe the size of the property that she lived on. There were a few old broken down barns and sheds. Even though he'd grown up locally, he preferred to think he was a city boy at heart.

The driveway closer to the house turned into a packed dirt path. He pulled up, right in front of the porch, behind Trina's little yellow car. He could see her watching him from the parted curtains in one of the windows that faced the front yard.

He couldn't get out of the truck fast enough. The front door flew open, and Trina came running out into his arms. For a tiny little thing, her impact nearly knocked him off his feet. The fact that his legs were like gelatin from his overexertion at the gym probably didn't help. As much as he was feeling it now, he would really be paying the price when he woke up the next day.

Dex wrapped her up in his embrace, the scent of sweet cherry blossoms wafted up toward his nose. Leaning forward to kiss her on the top of her head, he breathed her in. Extending back he pulled her away from his chest. The sun was already half-set, but what was left of the light shined in her eyes, making them look as if they were made of pure magic, straight out of a fantasy movie. He stroked her hair away from her delicate face.

"You okay?"

"I am now." She half-smiled and pulled back enough to walk the rest of the way back up the porch. She grabbed his hands and held them out between them as her eyes darted up to his. "What the hell did you do? This is a gym injury?"

He wasn't sure if the terror in her eyes was from what his hands looked like, or the fact that she thought that someone had been in her house.

He dipped his head, let out the breath he was holding, and gave her a slow nod.

"Come on. Let's get you inside and get these cleaned up," she said gently, pulling him up the steps.

"I'm here to take care of you, remember."

"We can take care of each other." She looked over her shoulder giving him a smirk that looked a bit more playful than the situation called for.

He couldn't help but feel the stiffening between his legs. He just shook his head at his perverse mindset.

The house was old, not nearly as run down as the other structures on the property. A mix of modern furniture and antiques, which might have belonged to her grandparents, gave her décor an eclectic vibe. The coffee table was covered in home improvement project magazines, paint swatches, and a giant open first aid kit.

It looked like one that a paramedic would carry on a call to an emergency. He had seen enough of the red soft cases to recognize where it most likely had come from, although he did consider the fact that anything could be purchased on the internet.

"So, how about you tell me or show me what made you

think that someone had been in your home?"

"Yes, but I am safe with you here, so I think we should clean up your hands first, and then I will show you. I can tell you what is going on while I work. Sit here, on the couch. I will go grab a trash bag to dispose of your dirty bandages."

He sat down and picked up a magazine. The entire coffee table was littered with them. Just as he was about to pick up one for kitchen and bath remodels, another magazine sticking out of the pile caught his eye. He read the title, *Urban Gardening*, and wondered why she had it. It was an odd magazine to have mixed in with the lot, not to mention they were far from in an urban community. Dex rationalized that maybe it was a random convenience store purchase or a free issue.

He turned over the cover and saw that it was addressed to Lina Hayes. Either she had a sister that she'd failed to mention, or they messed up her name. He was going with the latter because he couldn't picture Trina with a sister for some reason, maybe it was because he was an only child too.

"Ok, so let's see what the hell you did to those beautiful hands of yours." She sat down beside him with a used grocery bag and began to unravel the saturated gauze from one of his hands.

"What did you do, get into a fight with a brick wall?" She

looked up for him searching his eyes for the truth.

"Not exactly. I made a careless decision to hit the heavy bag without my gloves. I know better, but I wanted to feel the impact. Unfortunately, I kind of lost control and took it too far." He looked down at the purple tint of the bruising.

"Why would you do that? You are lucky you didn't break your wrist or one of your hands."

"I know," he mumbled. "I just have so much rage inside of me. I am very frustrated with the case I am on. I can't stand knowing that there is a murderer out there, walking free, and on my turf no less. I let it get the best of me."

"There is always going to be bad people walking the streets, all you can do is your best to protect and serve as many people as you can. This kind of stuff will get you put on desk duty filing paperwork for your fellow comrades. You can't be out on the streets with broken body parts."

"You are absolutely right."

"I told you, you need to relax and let things from the past stay in the past. We can't go back and change things, all we can do is make the present and the future a better place."

Dex reached up and grazed the pad of his thumb across her cheek. He wished he could dive into her ocean blue eyes. He didn't know why, but he wanted to show her his demons. He had kept them hidden for so long. She did something to him he couldn't wrap his head around.

"You amaze me already, in a way that I have never experienced. I have never wanted to know more about another human being, ever." The darkness of the world he lived in seemed to fade away when he was with Trina.

"I am mostly an open book. Whatever you want to know, just ask." Her lips hinted at a smile. She had stopped wrapping his hand, since her eyes were locked in on his gaze. "I really need to finish wrapping your hands. Are you hungry? I can make you some food."

"You want to make me food? I am here to rescue you from a possible home intrusion. I am starving, but let's focus on you first. Tell me what happened when you got home."

"Like I said, I didn't notice any indication of a forced entry, but there have been a few things missing and moved around the house over the past week. I kept blowing it off because I tend to be forgetful.

"I actually have been known to even sleepwalk, although, as far as I know, it hasn't happened since I moved here. I wasn't sure if maybe I was sleepwalking again and doing stuff around the house and not realizing." She finished taping off his second hand and started to pack the first aid kit back up.

"Okay..."

"I have to show you the rest. When I got home from the store, I wanted to take a shower." A quiver in her voice let

Dex know that whatever *it* was, it had scared her. "I am afraid that someone had been in my bathroom."

Trina zipped up the first aid kit, tied off the plastic bag with his used bandages, took a deep breath, and stood up. "Come on, I am going to toss this in the trash. Then I will give you a quick tour of the house on the way to the bathroom."

Dex followed her into the back of the house, where there was a small, rustic kitchen. It had a colonial feel to it, although he knew it wasn't quite that outdated.

Everything might have looked like it was built at the turn of the century, but her house was spic and span. Other than the sprawl of magazines on the coffee table, everything else was in its place. Dex was a neat freak and had a slight case of OCD when it came to how he kept things in his apartment. He knew from experience, if she kept the house that meticulous, it would have been easy for her to notice if anything was out of place.

"For as big as this house is, you would think there would be more than one bathroom. I know the house isn't huge, but putting a bathroom on the first floor is something I really want to do, if I do renovate." They walked up the narrow flight of stairs; nearly each step creaked as they passed over.

Dex wondered if the bones of the house were worth renovating. He was sure that the home had sentimental value to Trina. She must have spent years of her youth running up and down the very stairs they were walking up. It was kind of cool having the opportunity to share her past, even if it was just in little bits and pieces.

"There are actually four bedrooms up here. The first bedroom, I am not even going to show you because it is still filled with boxes that I haven't unpacked yet..." She turned and smiled at him. "I know I have been here long enough, but I just haven't needed to unpack everything, and for a long time, I wasn't sure if I wanted to stay here or move back to Portland."

"I used to live in Portland too. Did you like living there?" he asked. He couldn't help but watch her butt sway from side to side as she walked in front of him. How could he resist? It was packed nicely into a pair of yoga pants. This was actually the first time he'd seen her dressed down, and it was not at all disappointing.

"I loved the city, in general. I had an apartment with a guy I was dating for almost two years, but that didn't really go anywhere."

"Did you move here because of your break-up?"

"Oh heavens no. It was a disappointing situation, but I was doing fine living on my own for a few months."

She paused and opened the door, Dex noticed her demeanor shift slightly, and her hand began to shake.

"This is my glorious bathroom."

It was in serious need of repair. Some of the white tiles were chipped, and there were even a few missing on the floor. Dex noticed a giant bottle of bleach, and a variety of cleaning products in the corner next to the toilet.

He was sure that she had made every effort to get that bathroom feeling as clean as possible, but there were not enough cleaning products that could turn back the hands of time and neglect.

She walked in and reached over into the shower and turned it on full blast with the temperature turned all the way to the left. He wasn't sure what was going on. He was starting to wonder if she was about to start taking her clothes off to seduce him into a steamy shower.

He liked that idea, but she didn't have that playful look on her face that he had become accustomed to over the short time they had known each other. She had closed the door behind him, and the room quickly started to fill up with steam. She opened the curtain on the shower letting an extra burst of haze escape.

Dex looked around the room, waiting for her to say something.

"Do you see it?" she asked and pointed above the vanity. "The mirror."

He squinted his eyes and watched as the mirror continued to fog up and words appeared. Once the entire mirror was covered, the writing was as clear as day. A chill ran down the length of his spine.

He took a step closer to Trina and put his arm around her, pulling her closer to him.

I always have my eyes on you. The words screamed at them from the mirror as it reflected their shocked faces.

"Did you take a shower this morning?" he asked her. He needed to know how long ago someone could have done this.

"I did, but I was running late, so I had the door open, and it was such a fast shower that I am not really sure if the bathroom was steamy enough to fog up the mirror. I don't know, I just can't remember. Either way, I didn't notice anything being there this morning."

He could feel her body trembling. "Ok, I am going to have to call this in. We can have the place swept for fingerprints to see if we get anything. Normally we wouldn't expend the resources for this type of situation, but given the fact that there is a murderer walking the streets of Hawk Creek I think it is imperative that we are extra cautious here. "

"Really? I don't want all those people in my house, and I know how much of a mess some of those powders can leave. Can't you just investigate what is going on, without all the fuss?" she looked up at him with puppy dog eyes.

"We need to sit down and talk about this, Trina."

CHAPTER TWENTY-FOUR

"I REALLY APPRECIATE YOU MAKING me something to eat." Dex wasn't familiar with where things went in Trina's kitchen, but that didn't stop him from helping her clean up. "I know that you were just procrastinating with this meal."

"You were clearly in need of some protein. You were starting to look gray."

"You didn't even eat anything." He gave her a look. Either way she was right that he needed to eat after the workout he'd had.

Drying the pan she used to make dinner, she said, "I ate earlier with Gladys. I thought maybe I would pick, but I'm really not hungry."

Dex put the ketchup back in the refrigerator. He was frustrated that she wasn't cooperating and didn't want to push the issue with the fingerprinting since there was a chance his captain would have thought he was prematurely requesting such an order.

"Listen, I have been thinking about this the whole time during dinner and us talking. I think that, at least for tonight, that you should come stay at my place. No one would know where to find you there, and I would feel like I can have a better bearing on a much smaller space. Not to mention, we won't be so secluded."

"I don't know, really?"

"Yes really. If I can't convince you to let me call the boys in, then I am going to keep you with me, so I can keep an eye on you until we can figure this out. Besides, I wanted to ask you to accompany me to a dinner thing tomorrow night," Dex half mumbled. He really couldn't remember the last time he'd actually asked a woman on a date.

Her eyes lit up for the first time that night. "Like a date?" she asked like a schoolgirl teasing a boy.

Dex chuckled. "Yes, I know we were supposed to go bowling, but maybe we can do that next weekend?"

He suddenly felt as if he'd just crashed into a wall. Did he just make plans, and then make plans again for the following weekend? If he wasn't careful, he was going to wind up in an actual relationship.

"Umm, yeah. That sounds like a plan. I think that dinner sounds just as good as, if not better than, bowling."

"The only thing is that I have a memorial service in the

morning." He scrunched up his lips toward his nose as if he smelled something rotten. "I can't miss it."

"Did you want me to come with you?" she hesitated getting the question out.

He wasn't sure if it was sweet or weird that she offered to go with him to such a morbid thing for someone she didn't know. Or it could be that she was just too scared to be alone.

"I don't know. I think I should probably go alone, but you will be safe at my place, and it will give you plenty of time to relax and get ready. I can call a patrol car to come sit outside, if it makes you feel better.

"I still want to ask you some more questions about who or why you think someone has been breaking into your house, but it is getting late. Why don't you go pack a bag, and we can talk about it at my place."

"Good idea. Maybe you can make me another one of your famous cocktails, I don't think I got to finish mine the other night..." her voice trailed off as she ran back up the stairs.

"If you're lucky, I will stop for a pint of ice cream on the way there." He figured every girl on television liked ice cream, especially when they were upset about something.

"Now that's what I'm talking about." He faintly heard her response.

Upon entering his apartment, he kept his usual routine of pulling his shoes off and putting them away in the closet. Keys went in their specified place on the counter. The only thing he didn't do was immediately bring his gym bag to his closet to empty his dirty clothes into the hampers.

He was carrying more than one bag, and he felt unsure as to where he should put her bag. He debated leaving it by the front door when he walked in, but he would never leave his own things there. He also thought he should bring it into his room and drop it on the bed for her, but he didn't want to seem presumptuous that she was planning to head to his bed with him.

"Where do you want me to put your things? I can make a little spot in the closet for you to hang your clothes." If he could have facepalmed his forehead he would have.

He was afraid that he'd made it sound as if he was inviting her to be a permanent guest. Chances were, that unless they figured out what was going on with her house, he would want her to stay at his apartment for a few days.

He didn't know what he was getting himself into, but his heart was open to the possibility of wanting to find out. He cared for this woman and he wouldn't let anything happen to her.

"Whatever works for you," she said clearly unsure how to answer.

"I know this is probably a little bit unsettling for you. I have never had anyone stay with me, so we can both be a little rattled together. How does that sound?"

"Oh, my God, good. I mean it's not good that we are rattled, it is good to know we are not alone."

Dex laughed. "I knew what you meant." He picked up his gym bag. "Let's go put our stuff away then. I'm just glad that you seem to be as much of a neat freak as me."

Dex took a quick turn into the kitchen first. He opened the fridge and pulled out a beer. "Want one? Or do you want to wait, and I can make you a drink?"

"No, beer sounds perfect."

Dex cracked both bottles open and handed one to Trina. She followed him down the short hallway to his bedroom. Dex showed her where she could put her things, and he unloaded his gym bag. The cold beer felt good against his lips and even better once it hit his bloodstream. He wanted to rely on the alcohol to help with the physical pain that he was trying not to acknowledge.

He went over to his nightstand, pulled out a bottle of ibuprofen, and took four. He hoped the pills would keep the swelling down, so he didn't feel like death in the morning.

Trina had done a good job of wrapping his hands

because there were no signs that they were still bleeding. He wasn't looking forward to explaining the injuries to Johnny. His partner probably wasn't going to believe his story of how it happened anyway. Dex crossed his fingers in the hope that his hands would heal enough overnight, so he wouldn't need to bandage them the next day. He certainly didn't have any gauze in his apartment.

Trina finished up hanging the few articles of clothing that she'd brought. "Do you mind if I change into my pajamas? I really need to be extra comfy right now."

"Make yourself at home. You really don't have to ask me before you do anything. If you want anything to eat or drink, feel free to help yourself. Not that I wouldn't help get something for you, I just want you to be at ease when you are here with me." Dex pounded the last of his beer. "I am going to go grab another beer. Why don't you do your thing, come out when you are finished, and then I will get changed too."

"Thanks, Dex. I am really grateful for your kindness and hospitality. Not everyone has such a big heart."

Her comment felt disconcerting. He didn't really think of himself with a big heart, nor did anyone that knew him well. Quite the contrary, he kept his heart locked up and guarded for the most part. Maybe he was changing, and maybe it wasn't such a bad thing.

He cracked open another beer for himself, and not

wanting to be rude, pulled out a second for Trina. If she didn't want it, he would have no problem drinking it. He thought she would be in there for a while and was about to crash on the couch to turn on the TV. She didn't take more than five minutes to get changed.

Dex stood at the end of the hall holding the two beers. His mouth may have fallen open at the sight of her.

She didn't come out wrapped in a tiny silk negligee or anything, but by God she was sexy. She had on a loose fitting tank top with the skinniest straps he had ever seen. The fabric, although loose and flowing, hugged her ample breasts. The shirt was a bit shorter in the front exposing just enough of her midriff to tempt him.

She had on a matching pair of short shorts, not so short that anything was hanging out, but they made her legs look as if they went on forever, even though she wasn't that tall.

"You okay?" she asked.

"Hmm…yeah. I just wasn't expecting you to come out so fast. I got you another beer, if you want it."

"Of course I do." She walked up to him, so close that they were nearly touching. "Thank you." She took the bottle of beer and took a sip.

He watched her lips as she kept her eyes on him. They were so pink and full against the rim of the dark glass. A tiny bit of beer squirted out a tiny crack on the side of her mouth.

Dex lifted a finger to wipe the droplets of liquid from her cheek. She reached up and carefully held the outside of his hand, lowering it. She closed the distance between them. Lifting up onto her tippy toes, she softly kissed the edge of his mouth. Her lips were cold from the beer, but they melted him like a flame to a candle.

He threw his caution to the wind and leaned in to kiss her, capturing her lips with a ferocity he'd been holding back. She started to stumble back from the force of the kiss, but he reached around and held onto her. There was so much hunger and need in the kiss, and it wasn't just on his part. He knew where things were about to go, and as much as he thought he should wait with her, he knew he needed her.

He grabbed her beer, and holding the two bottles the best he could between the fingers on his least damaged hand, he scooped her up and carried her to his bed.

CHAPTER TWENTY-FIVE

DEX WAS SICK OF TALKING and sick of thinking. He just wanted to feel something. Something that made him feel alive. And not just because he was drunk or that there was a thrill of conquering a new piece of ass.

Trina had intrigued him from the second he'd laid eyes on her at Moe's diner. There was something different about her, something worth getting to know. She had come into his life like a tornado, bringing up things that he had not faced in years.

He'd thought that he could deal with it by getting drunk and hooking up with the first attractive random female that threw herself at him. That turned out to be an epic fail and a wakeup call, he was ready for more than a sexual experience with a woman.

He dropped the two bottles of beer on his nightstand and laid her down on the bed. Dex dropped his knees onto the edge of the bed. His first instinct was to crawl across by resting on his knuckles, but as soon as his hands hit the bed, he flinched in pain.

"Oh shit, Dex. You need to be more careful with those hands. How about you let me help you." She moved out of his way and pulled him into the center of the bed.

"How are you going to help me?" his voice was low and raspy.

"I thought I could start by helping you get more comfortable" She kicked a leg over his lap and straddled him. He was still sitting up, which made it easier for her to lift his shirt over his head. "Now that's a start."

"It sure is." He pulled her closer to him, so she was pressed against his bare chest. He slid his hands up the back of her shirt, frustrated that he had a barrier between his touch and her flesh. He let his fingertips stroke her skin as he leaned in to lock lips with her.

Their lips overlapped in a tentative kiss. He needed to let go of his jaded thoughts and succumb to the moment and the tenderness of her touch.

Her lips parted, giving him permission to take the kiss to the next level. As their tongues slid against each other for the first time that night, he felt his heart leap. He explored the sweetness of her mouth, he couldn't get enough of the way she smelled and tasted. He planned on tasting every inch of her body.

Her hands pressed against his chest, pushing him back breaking their kiss. "Lay back," her voice was more sultry than sweet.

As he lay back, she dragged her fingernails over his chest, causing his nipples to harden. She wasted no time. Her hands went straight down until they reached the top of his jeans. She never broke eye contact with him as she unsnapped and unzipped his pants.

She crawled backward, holding the top of the denim and dragging them down over his knees. Once she tossed them off the bed, she worked her delicate little fingers back up his thighs, sliding them up to the edges of his boxer briefs. He wished for the first time that he had on a pair of regular boxers, so her fingers could have had the space to slide all the way up.

She slid her way up and over his body, like a snake approaching its prey. He could see the soft curves of her breasts as her shirt hung down in the front. He felt tingling down his legs.

Once her lips touched down on his belly, it was over for him. There was no turning back. Her tongue lapped at his taut skin, working up over his pecks to the most sensitive spot on his neck. His hips pressed up against her, and he let out a moan.

"I think you should keep your hands to yourself and let me do all the work," she whispered into his ear.

That may have been the sexiest thing any woman had ever said to him, but by God, he wanted to touch her.

"You need to let them rest and heal."

Her voice tickled at the tiny hairs on his neck, sending shivers down his limbs. He let his arms fall off to the sides. It wouldn't be easy, but he was happy to give it a try. Letting her take control of the situation more than worked for him. He wouldn't have to question his actions, just sit back and enjoy her.

"I will do my best, but I have been thinking about getting my hands on you all week."

"How about I just let the rest of your body have me all over it. We can let your hands make up for it another day." She licked her way under his chin, kissing her way back to his lips.

Her kisses felt dangerous and exciting. She may have had an air of innocence to her, but the way she took control of the situation was like a professional. Dex was lost in the moment and didn't want to be found by anyone but Trina.

"I should let you know," she said as she lowered her lips back down on to his stomach. "I don't want to give you the wrong idea here. I am not ready to have sex with you. That doesn't mean that I am not going to pleasure you though."

Her eyes, dark with desire, flashed up and down from his belly to his face. Dex watched her with eagerness and felt the blood rushing to his groin. He sensed himself growing beneath her.

Her kisses were so close to the waistband of his undershorts, he struggled for a breath as her tongue teased just under the elastic. Trina reached her hands up and skimmed them over his chest and abdomen before grabbing a hold of his last remaining article of clothing.

She looked up at him and smiled as she pulled off his boxer briefs. He felt his erection bob against his belly. Trina twisted her head, tossing her hair all to one side, so that he could see what she was about to do.

Her hands traced their way back up his thighs, stroking the sensitive skin on the inside of his lower hips. She lowered each of her hands over his shaft, stroking him with a light touch, making him crave more.

He knew that he was in trouble. She had him so aroused, he wasn't sure how long he would be able to last once her lips touched him. He reached down to touch her.

She looked up and scowled at him. "No touching for you," she whispered, just before letting her lips replace her hands. She took the tempo from slow to fast, then back to slow again. She added a hand to help with the work, pulling back to continue to make eye contact with him. He nearly exploded when she looked at him.

He sucked in a breath. "Your sexiness tops the fucking charts," he moaned between his attempts to speak to her. "So fucking hot!" He could smell her arousal, and it was taking every ounce of his restraint not to take her and roll her over.

She sat up and lifted her shirt over her head, using it to wipe the wetness from her chin. Dex had seen plenty of women with their clothes off in his life, but there was something exquisite and perfect about Trina.

He wanted desperately to reach up and cradle the soft mounds that were bobbing in front of him. He grunted in frustration and anticipation of what she might do to him next.

"I really screwed myself at the gym. My God, I am aching to touch you and caress every curve of your body." Dex squirmed under her.

"Mmm, I am looking forward to giving you that opportunity."

Her impish smile let him know she was enjoying torturing him. He couldn't think of a better way to be tormented.

Trina slithered her way up his body, dragging the tips of her breasts over his chest. They were like two tiny fuses, shooting sparks in all directions. She buried her nose into the crook of his neck. He could feel her dragging in his scent as she kept an upward movement, breathing into his ear before her breasts reached his mouth.

He extended his tongue and licked her like a melting ice pop, swirling his tongue around her tight nipples. She let him sample each of her breasts, and she tasted even better than she smelled.

"That feels really nice. Your tongue is like an extension of heaven," she hissed.

Keeping his hands off of her might have been one of the biggest challenges he had ever faced. He watched her as she leaned back enough to grab a hold of his headboard and pull up to stand over him.

She slowly wiggled her hips back and forth as she slid her tiny pair of shorts down her legs.

His mouth fell open, and he sighed. Not that he cared about whether or not the carpet matched the drapes, but he certainly wasn't going to find out because she was completely shaved. Her flesh was soft and glistening from her arousal, and he was pleased that she had become so stimulated by having him in her mouth.

He wanted his turn and he was pretty sure she was going to give it to him. She leaned forward as she lowered herself over him bracing against the headboard so that she didn't completely sit on his face.

Dex wanted to bring her pleasure that she had never known before. He had never gone down on a woman hands-free. He would have his work cut out for himself. He wanted to slide his fingers into her while he worked his tongue against her. She was wickedly delicious. He wanted more than just to devour her.

She pulled her hips back away from his mouth and wiggled her way back down to his lap. He could feel his erection throbbing under her. He wanted to slide into her wetness, but she'd made it clear that she didn't want things to go that far. He would never push her.

Trina let her body fall over him and she rocked her mound over him. He sucked in and grunted. He tried his hardest not to buck up against her, but he had little control over his pressing desires.

"I want it." Her lips brushed against his ear. "I need to feel you. I take back what I said."

He wasn't going to deny her anything. He reached into the drawer of his nightstand. The tear of foil was the only thing other that filled the air, other than their ragged breaths.

The second she settled over him, Trina's breath hitched not quite allowing herself a full inhalation.

"Yes," he hissed as she rocked against him slowly until she covered him completely.

He followed her lead and met her rhythm, plunging hard and fast up into her. He was over stimulated, and he suspected that she was too. They moaned out for each other in unison, and he filled her with everything he had. She bucked furiously, and he could feel her walls tighten around him, sending him over the edge. He pumped harder and faster until she cried out. His explosion was like an atomic bomb.

As their bodies relaxed, and they caught their breath, he was amazed that they climaxed at the same time. Trina was intoxicating. Her mix of innocence and willingness to please him made her a threat to his normal way of life.

"I think it is time for some of that ice cream. I will be right back with a spoon." Dex watched as Trina lay back on his bed with her hair spread out around her. She may not have just acted like one, but she sure did look like an angel.

He wasn't big on sweets, but it would make him feel good to see her indulging in something else for the night. Truth was, he just wanted to sweeten her up to ease back into talking about what was going on with her, and who could have been in her house.

When he got back to his room she was tucked under the covers.

"Did you get cold?"

"I wouldn't say cold, but I am cooling off," she answered.

"Two spoons!" He handed her the pint of ice cream and a small towel to wrap around the cold exterior.

Trina opened the container and placed the lid on the nightstand beside her. She took one spoon from Dex, scooped out a small taste of the creamy bliss, and lifted the spoon to his mouth first.

"You get the first bite," she said softly, feeding it to him.

He was impressed with her gesture and had a little flutter in his belly at the possibility of this woman knowing just how to treat him. Dex leaned in on his elbow next to her and scooped out a man-sized bite of ice cream. Before he put it in his mouth, he asked her, "Is there anyone that you think would want to hurt you or scare you?"

Trina swallowed hard and rubbed her lips together. "Yes and no. I don't know, maybe, but I don't know how they would know where I live."

"What makes you say they? Are there more than one?"

"Oh, no. I just don't know if the person is a male or a female. It's kind of a hard situation to talk about." Trina scraped her spoon on the top of the ice cream.

"Well, I think that it would be a good idea for you to try and explain it to me. I am here to protect you."

"I think you are doing a lot more than protecting me." Her eyebrows lifted once at him.

"Mmm, that might be true, but don't try to distract me." He cracked a smile but needed to keep things serious, people's lives were at stake, and he needed to know if her situation could be tied to the death of Tammy Larazzo and Bethany Kingston in any way.

He wanted to ask her if she knew them, or Jeremy for that matter, but he decided it best to wait and see what she had to say first.

"It goes back to Portland. I still don't really know what happened, and as far as I know, it is considered a cold case back there. I really haven't checked back with the detective that was in charge of my case, since I moved here.

"I told you that I sleepwalk sometimes. I now take medication to help me sleep because of it. The medication helps me to sleep more solidly and not have the episodes. I guess it was about a year and a half ago at this point.

"It was just after me and my ex, Vince, broke things off. I don't know if the adjustment of being alone threw my body off on an unconscious level and that caused me to sleepwalk. The doctors really were not sure and couldn't really determine if I truly did sleepwalk, it just made the most amount of sense."

"I'm not really following you. Did your ex do something to you?" Dex was confused on where she was going with her story. He didn't want to push her too hard, she was clearly having trouble getting it out.

"Sorry, I haven't talked about this to anyone. No, he didn't do anything to me. At least I don't think so." She put the ice cream on the night stand.

"I woke up in an alley at three in the morning covered in blood next to the body of a dead woman." She pulled her knees up to her chest and wrapped her arms around them.

"I still don't know how I got there. My last recollection of the night was laying on the couch in my jammies to watch television. I don't remember anything that happened that night."

"Were you hurt badly?" he asked.

"Not like the woman they found me with. She wasn't so lucky. Whoever attacked us must have knocked me out, but he cut her open. I had her blood and my blood all over me. It was hard to determine how the blood got on me because I had been crawling through it in the alley."

Dex put his spoon on his nightstand, crawled over, put his arm around her, and pulled her close against his chest. He could feel her trembling.

"So they didn't catch whoever did this?" he asked.

"No, I had to leave Portland. I always felt as if I was looking over my shoulder. I had inherited the house here in Hawk Creek and thought it would be a good place to try out. I had been avoiding selling the property, because I had so many childhood memories there."

"You're not alone anymore." He kissed the top of her head.

"I thought what happened in that alley was a random act of violence, but now with everything that has been happening in my house, I am scared that maybe there was someone after me."

Dex thought about what she was saying, and although her concern could be valid if the perpetrator had killed the other woman and not her, why would she be the target? It was possible that the other woman had been an innocent bystander that tried to intervene, unfortunately paying the ultimate price.

"We will figure it out together. I'm glad that you opened up and told me about what happened to you. I don't want to push you too much tonight, but we are going to have to talk more about this so we can catch this SOB." He pulled her in closer and hugged her tight.

"Thank you, Dex. I can't tell you how relieved I am to have someone I can trust enough to talk about this with."

"We have a long day tomorrow. I am going to put that ice cream back in the freezer and then come back and hold you until you fall asleep."

Trina looked up at him and the corners of her lips curled ever so slightly. She looked as if she had found a tiny bit of peace, but he could still see the fear in her eyes. He leaned forward and gently kissed her pouty lips.

CHAPTER TWENTY-SIX

DEX CONTEMPLATED BRINGING TRINA WITH him to Mrs. Harrington's memorial service, but decided it would be better if he went alone, since no one there would know her. Trina seemed fine with being alone at his place, and he knew that she would be safe there, considering he was the only person that knew where she was.

They had slept in fairly late, so after he got ready he showed her where everything was in the kitchen, so she could help herself to anything while he was gone. He figured it would give her some time to herself to decompress and get ready, without feeling as if she was rushed by his presence.

He was dying to talk to Johnny about what Trina had told him the night before about the attack in Portland. The memorial service just wasn't the place for it, the talk would have to wait until later in the day. It may have been

Sunday and Betty was hosting a dinner party but he and Johnny knew that with this kind of a case they didn't get a day off. Dex knew to be discrete enough not to upset Betty.

Dinner was really more of a late lunch, but who was counting. They needed to be at the Harrington house by three. From the sounds of the chatter at the service, more people would be at the house than Dex was accustomed to seeing there. The only crowds he was used to were the ones with nameless faces in a bar. The positive in that was if he and Johnny needed to talk shop or cut out, it would be less obvious with the larger crowd.

Dex got back to his apartment around two o'clock, and he was hoping that Trina was ready to go. He really had no idea if she was one of those girls that was always fashionably late to things or was the type to show up early.

He walked in to find Trina sitting on his sofa watching ESPN. He was taken back for a second, wondering to himself, *Can this woman get any more perfect?* He felt the balls of his cheeks scrunch up as his lips curled into a smile.

"Hey." She smiled at him over her shoulder. "You're back. I wasn't sure when you would return."

"I am. Have you been waiting long?"

"Not too long. I figured I would just kick back and watch a little television while I was waiting. I should have brought a book." She shrugged.

"I would have called, but I was a bit distracted last night and didn't realize that I didn't charge my phone. Sorry about that."

"I guess I can let it slide this time." She clicked off the TV and sauntered over to him. "I would like to keep you distracted like that more often."

Trina's hands slid up the front of his chest just under his blazer. He watched her like a woman on a diet watched a cupcake. If only they didn't have somewhere to be, he would have unwrapped her.

Dex leaned down and kissed her through the tiny smile she elicited. "You look stunning."

"I wasn't sure what to wear, I was hoping I wasn't over or under dressed."

She could have worn what she had on almost anywhere, and look amazing. She wore a pair of pale pink jeans that hugged her subtle curves. Her black sleeveless top was fitted to her waist but flared out a tiny bit. The top of the shirt was made of a black sheer fabric that showed the slightest bit of her cleavage, just enough to make you want to see more.

She had a matching pink blazer folded over the chair closest to the front door. It was also the first time he had seen her wearing a pair of high heels. They gave her enough lift that she was almost at eye level with him. She was even sexier than he realized.

"You look perfect. I can't wait for you to meet everyone. Well, you have already met Johnny, but you will love his wife Betty too. She is the sweetest and is totally down to Earth."

"If you love them, then I'm sure I will too."

"Just have fun and be yourself. We should get going, are you ready?" he asked.

"Yup, let me grab my purse and then we can go."

Dex pulled onto Johnny's street and couldn't believe the amount of cars lining the road. He'd thought that there were only going to be a few people there for dinner.

"I thought you said there were only going to be a few close friends here? I can't imagine what a blowout bash would be like," Trina said as they parked the truck a few houses down.

He helped her out of the truck. "That is what he told me, but quite a few more people showed up to the memorial service than he had anticipated too. There might have been some stragglers, or should I say, followers. Either way, we are together, so I'm sure we will have fun." Dex lifted her hand to his lips and kissed the back.

Once they got inside, it was obvious who had crashed the Harrington's dinner party. The living room was full of senior citizens.

"Dex, good to see you again." Johnny walked over to greet them and slapped Dex on the back. "Trina, it's a pleasure to see you as well."

"Same here. I am so sorry for your loss."

Dex could tell that her smile brought a new light to the room. She had such a warm, inviting personality, at least when she wasn't being snarky with him.

"Thank you. This is not supposed to be a continuation of the service. These old people just love this stuff. They show up with a casserole dish and push their way in. They are like wedding crashers. I guess they have nothing better to do." Johnny rolled his eyes.

"If you can't beat them, join them, right? Maybe we can get a game of pinochle going," Trina suggested in an effort to lighten the mood.

Johnny actually laughed so hard that his chest bounced up and down. Perhaps his emotions were heightened from the stress of the situation. It wasn't really that funny, but Dex and Trina followed his lead and laughed as well.

"Come to the kitchen, I will get you guys a drink. Hopefully, it is almost time for the early bird special, and they will all be heading home soon. I was hoping for a more laid back intimate dinner with friends." Johnny walked past the small crowd of people to the back of the house.

"What can I get you guys to drink? We have pretty much

everything. You want a whiskey Dex?" He stood next to a makeshift bar area on one of the kitchen counters, next to the refrigerator.

"I think I am going to skip the whiskey today. I have to drive. Maybe I will have a beer or something. How about you Trina, you don't have to drive."

"A glass of white wine would be great, thank you."

"I have one open in the fridge, hang on let me grab you a glass. Hey, Betty!" He waved over a tall and slender woman with auburn hair pulled back into a low bun at the base of her skull. She, like many of the women in the house, had on a modest black dress.

Her eyes were slightly puffy, but her makeup was still perfect. The redness around her eyes made the patch of freckles that was painted across the top of her nose pop more than normal.

Johnny put his arm around his wife. "Sweetheart, this is the woman I was telling you about. Trina, this is my wife Betty."

"Oh my goodness, I am so happy to meet you. You have no idea!" Betty said as she gently shook hands with Trina.

"It's a pleasure to meet you too. I'm sorry for your loss."

"Yeah, well. Death is just part of life. We did our mourning this morning, now it is time to celebrate life." She winked at Trina and turned to her husband. "She is even more stunning than you described her to be."

Trina's cheeks turned a shade of pink that competed with the color of her blazer.

"I'm sorry. I didn't mean to embarrass you. I have a tendency to say whatever is on my mind. You will learn that quickly about me." Betty smiled and rubbed her hand on Trina's back.

"Where are the extra wine glasses, Bets?" Johnny asked, searching the cabinet over the assortment of liquor.

"Dining room, I can get you some," she offered.

"No, you stay here with Trina. Dex can come with me. I have to ask him something about work anyway. Maybe you ladies can figure out how to get these old folks to go home."

Betty shook her head at him and turned back to get chatty with Trina. Dex looked to Trina to make sure it was okay to leave her, and she smiled, giving him a half-nod.

"What's up?" Dex asked Johnny.

"Me? You texted me last night and told me we needed to talk."

"Shit, I did, didn't I? I forgot. I wanted to wait until after your mom's service. Listen, I might have a lead for us to follow up on."

"Oh, no shit?" Johnny's eyes lit up.

"It's complicated. We should bring the ladies the glasses and head out to the garage to get ice or something," Dex suggested.

Johnny called his son over. "Here, give these to your mom, tell her we are going to get some stuff out of the garage. We will be right back."

"Okay, Dad." He took four wine glasses back to the kitchen.

"Good thing you know I keep bags of ice out there," Johnny teased. "I'm all ears, and by the way, what the hell is going on with your fucking hands?"

"About that, I went a little bit overboard at the gym last night. I pulled a thick-headed Dex move and went at the bag without protection on."

"That was dumb."

"No shit. So, when I was leaving, I missed a call from Trina, and then I got a text from her. I called her back, and she said she thought someone had been in her house."

"What? Did you call it in?"

"No, I went there to see what was going on first. I didn't even think much about it. I was closer than a patrol car would have been. She said that things have been moved around her house over the past few weeks.

"But, what made her call me was that someone had written one of those creepy hidden messages on her bathroom mirror that show up once the room gets steamed up."

"What did it say?"

"I always have my eyes on you."

Johnny opened the big chest freezer and pulled out two bags of prepackaged ice. "Why the hell didn't you call this in last night?"

"She asked me not to. She said she didn't want them to come in and get her house all dirty with print powder. I had her pack a bag and stay at my place last night." Dex took one of the bags.

"Now what? You still didn't call it in and what is she going to do tonight? Do you think this could have anything to do with our case?"

"I think it is possible. There is more to the story. I thought that I would be able to talk her into letting me have the team over there to investigate and determine if there was a home invasion or not.

"Here is the kicker, about a year and a half ago, she used to live in Portland. She said that she and another woman were attacked in an alley. They never caught the person who did it. I think we should call the detective that handled the case tomorrow and compare notes."

"I am still not clear on why you think that the cases could be connected."

"I don't know, for one, my gut is telling me. Not to mention, the fact that shit like this never happens here. Sure we have our fair share of crime and domestic violence, like any other town in America, but not gruesome murders and stalkers."

Johnny leaned back against the freezer and dropped the bag of ice on the floor next to him. "I can see why you would think that, but we have not found any evidence to suggest that either of our victims were being stalked by someone. Quite frankly, don't you think that Bethany would have mentioned something when she came in and found out her roommate and best friend had been murdered? She wasn't scared for her life, she was devastated about her loss."

"Maybe you are right, but I think we should still look into it. We don't have much else to go on, and I want to see what that case history is, then decide what to do about protecting Trina."

Johnny picked up his bag of ice and started to walk back into the house. He put a hand on Dex's back as they walked through the door.

"I am your partner, and I am here to investigate and protect with you. If this is what you think we should do, then it looks like we will be taking a trip to Portland tomorrow morning."

"I will meet you at the precinct bright and early. I have to either scoop up Trina's car or drive her to work tomorrow."

"Sounds good to me. I will be there." Johnny nodded.

"How about that beer you offered me? Something light, so I can have more than one."

Johnny opened the large cooler in the corner of his

kitchen, and pulled out a bottle of light beer and a bottle of water before dumping in his bag of ice. He handed the beer to Dex.

"Thanks. I wonder where Trina went." Dex looked around the living room.

"Knowing Betty, she is either giving her a tour or introducing her to every person in the house. She has been waiting for you to bring a woman into your life for so long. I hope she doesn't scare her away, trying to immerse her," Johnny joked.

Dex just rolled his eyes. He wasn't really afraid of Betty chasing anyone off. She was way too sweet for that. He heard the kitchen door open, and before he made a full rotation to see who was coming in, there were tiny little arms wrapped around him.

Shea walked in behind Abigail, wearing a simple black dress that hugged curves that he'd never noticed her having before. The ends of her long hair curled over her breasts. Dex was so accustomed to seeing Shea with her hair pulled back in a ponytail, wearing minimal makeup, and dressed in her work clothes that he forgot how attractive she was.

He looked down at Abigail. She looked up at him, and he saw Paul's big hazel eyes staring up at him.

"Dex! I miss you. Are you going to play dolls with me today?" she asked.

How could he say no to her puppy dog eyes? Guilt was always an underlying feeling when it came to her and Shea. He felt guilty spending time with them and guilty for not spending more time with them.

"Of course I will. That will be fun."

"Yay. Can you take me for ice cream again too?"

Dex laughed. "Not today, but we can make plans for ice cream soon."

"Ok. See you later." She ran off into the other room.

"Thanks for entertaining her requests." Shea smiled. "How are you? You doing okay?"

Dex leaned in to hug her. They both had known Mrs. Harrington for a long time.

"I am, how about you?" He pulled back away from the embrace. He could see the sadness in her eyes. She wasn't very good at hiding it.

"I'm okay. It's just nice for us to all be here together, even under these circumstances. Mrs. Harrington will be missed, but I know she has good company where she is now."

Dex pulled her in for another hug and kissed the top of her head. "I know," he whispered.

She pulled away from him. "How about you get me a drink."

"Hi." Trina was suddenly standing behind Dex. She actually startled him.

"Hey, Trina, this is Dr. Shea Sinclair. Shea this is Trina." He never thought introducing them would feel so awkward.

"It's nice to meet you. I actually just met your daughter, she is lovely. Betty told me all about you." Her full lips thinned out with her smile. It actually looked like she'd stepped on a rock.

"We are old friends. We all grew up together, and on a rare occasion, we have to work together," Dex told Trina.

"Are you a police officer as well?" Trina asked.

"Heavens no, but I work part time as the medical examiner slash coroner for Hawk Creek. It kind of happened by accident, but I have accepted my role in the town. Besides, the extra money goes into a college fund for my daughter."

"An education is a great thing to invest in." Trina sipped the last bit of wine from her glass.

"Trina is a school teacher at Hawk Creek Elementary. Can I fill up your glass?" Dex asked, taking her glass.

Trina nodded.

"Shea, what do you want?"

"I'll just have a beer, but I can get it. I should go say hi to Betty before she thinks I am avoiding her." She extended her hand out to Trina. "It was so nice to meet you. Hopefully I will see you again soon."

"Same here." Trina gave her a firm handshake.

Dex caught it out of the corner of his eye. He was always impressed with a woman with a firm grip. It hadn't occurred to him how a woman would shake another female's hand before.

"Aren't we all supposed to be having dinner together?" Trina asked Dex.

"Yes, but it looks like we might be having a buffet of casseroles instead." He laughed pointing to the kitchen table that was covered in platters and covered dishes.

"Don't you think it is a little strange to plan a dinner party the same day as a wake or memorial service?"

"Honestly, they invited me over for dinner before Johnny's mother passed. I think that they were just planning to use the time with a few close friends to celebrate her, instead of having an extended bereavement for the neighborhood." He handed her the glass of wine and finally took a sip of his beer. He was starting to think he was going to need something a bit stiffer to get through the rest of the night.

"I think I might be the only one here not dressed in black."

Dex grabbed her and pulled her in for a kiss. "You would stand out like the north star even if you were dressed in black. You are so radiant."

"You know all the right things to say, Detective Preston."

"I have all the right moves too. I think that since my

hands are feeling better, it might be my turn to pleasure you my way."

"Umm…that sounds like fun. I am much more hungry for you than I am tuna noodle casserole."

"Are you suggesting that we cut out of here early?" He wagged his eyebrows at her, eliciting an impish smile. "I actually need to talk to you about tonight."

"Yeah?"

"We still have not had anyone over to your house to investigate. I think that you should consider staying at my place again. I don't know how much stuff you packed, I can take you back to your house if you need clothes for work tomorrow."

"I always pack extra, especially since I wasn't sure what I was going to wear today. What about my car?"

"We can pick it up, or I can drop you off at the school. I am going to be riding with Johnny tomorrow. If you need my keys, I can give you my spare set in case we aren't back in time for me to drive you home."

"Awe, that is so sweet. You are going to let me drive your truck?"

He couldn't believe he was going to let her drive his truck, no one drove his truck, not even Johnny, and he was his partner and probably his closest friend.

His relationship with her had been thrown into overdrive. Knowing that she could have been in danger seemed to escalate his feelings for her, or at least his awareness of his feelings.

CHAPTER TWENTY-SEVEN

"HOUSEGUEST TWO NIGHTS IN A row?" Johnny looked at his partner out of the corner of his eye.

"Yup." Dex was in too good of a mood for him to mess with him. Forever it had been, *"Why don't you have a girl?"* Suddenly Johnny wanted to bust his ass about actually having a woman in his life.

"Sorry about dinner last night. Betty was so upset that the senior crew crashed us. She knew that they meant well, but it's been a long week for her, taking care of my mom's arrangements."

"I don't remember the last time I saw her throw back so many." There was a time, before his friends had children, that they had all gone out together, but she'd been a bit more than tipsy at the dinner.

"I know right. She speaks her mind to begin with, but with that much alcohol coursing through her blood, her mouth is like a faucet with a broken off switch."

"Speaking of which, do you know that she actually told Trina that she always thought that me and Shea would wind up together?"

"No! She didn't?"

Dex saw his cheeks start to turn red, but he wasn't sure if it was from embarrassment or anger. "I don't know why she would say that to begin with, let alone to a woman I am dating. Did you know she thought that?"

"She isn't the only one. I still can't believe that she said that out loud though. Was Trina mad?" Johnny squeezed the steering wheel with both hands.

"I don't know. She didn't seem like she was mad, but she did seem a bit taken back by the comment. I had to explain our history to her. She asked if Abigail was mine."

"What? No!" He laughed.

"It isn't funny at all. I love that girl, but me with kids..." Dex looked out the window trying not to think too hard about the implications.

"I'm sorry Betty said that. I know she will be embarrassed. She was hurting this morning getting the kids ready. It's a good thing that they had school so she can rest."

"She still needs rest? She passed out so early last night," Dex teased.

"So, did you call ahead to see whose case this was?"

"Detective Angelo Vincenza's. We used to work the beat together, but he is at the precinct now. I sent him an email and let him know that we are on our way and to have the files ready. It's a good thing you brought ours, he will want to see them."

"He's one of those, huh?"

"He wants to get his guy as bad as we want to get ours. He won't make a stink about who gets the collar, but he will want to make sure that we didn't miss anything, especially if the cases are linked."

"I hope you have somewhere good for us to grab lunch today." Johnny may have been on a diet, but he still had food on his mind all the time.

"I even have an awesome doughnut shop I can take you to, if we have time."

"That's what I am talking about. You can't tell Betty, though."

"I won't be telling her anything."

⛤

Dex's old precinct was bigger than the one in Hawk Creek, and it had more than one conference room. Angelo had one of them set up with all the information he had on Trina's case. Dex was glad, although it was nice to be back, it was also hard to be there. He didn't want to hang around longer than they needed to.

"Good to see you again, Preston."

"You too. Vincenza. My partner, Johnny Harrington." The men shook hands.

"Nice to meet you. So I hope that, since I am showing you mine, you boys brought me yours." Angelo got right down to business.

"Of course we did. I have, to be honest, I don't know if there is a connection other than the fact that one of your victims thinks that she is being stalked in our town. We have had two murders in the same week. I don't believe in coincidences like that. On the flip side, we work on hard facts, and right now, we have very few."

"Dex, you always had a good gut. Let's dissect this shit and see if we can't find a connection." Angelo rolled up his sleeves and sat down at the table. He slid his file over to Dex.

"Here is the thing, Dex, there were a lot of holes in the surviving victim's story. We considered looking at her for the crime, but there wasn't any reason or connection to think that she would have had a motive to kill this random woman in an alley. Officer O'Neil said that it was possible that the two women had scuffled with one another, but that he thought it unlikely based on the surviving victim's state at the crime scene. "

Dex felt his heart drop and his head snap back. Did he just hear him right? "So tell me where you left things with your case."

"As per Trina Hayes statements, she did not know the victim, Cynthia Strong. We could not find anything in their history to oppose that fact. Cynthia was found stabbed and cut open. Half of her guts had spilled out onto the street. When we found her, and Miss Hayes, they were both covered in blood.

"Miss Hayes was taken to the hospital, given an exam, and evidence was taken from her. The problem is that they both had each other's blood all over. It was hard to determine if they had a confrontation with each other, or if they tried to fight off an attacker together.

"They were found at three in the morning, after a neighbor heard Miss Hayes screaming for help. She said that she was looking for her purse or her phone when she found the body. She said it was so dark that she didn't realize that she was touching a body until it was too late."

"So was Miss Hayes stabbed as well? What kind of injuries did she sustain?" Johnny asked.

"She did not have any knife wounds, but she had quite a bit of bruising to suggest that she had been beaten. Miss Strong had some of the same injuries, which made us question the possibility that they had fought it out against each other."

"Wouldn't Miss Strong have had some of the other victims skin or blood under her nails?"

"She was wearing gloves. It was quite cold out that night, and like I said, there was blood everywhere. Miss Hayes said that she didn't remember the attack, or how she got into that alley. Her story never changed." Angelo's eyes pinched together.

"Murder weapon?" Dex asked.

"It was a knife, looked like it came from a restaurant, but we never identified where it came from. There were no witnesses that saw either woman that night. Miss Strong was single, so we didn't have anyone that knew where she had been that night either. Her last known location was leaving the gym that she worked at, but that was almost six hours earlier than when the two women were found."

"What about Miss Hayes? Did she have a boyfriend or roommate that was interviewed at the time?" Johnny asked.

Dex was just taking everything in.

"She was single at the time and lived alone. We did have an ex-boyfriend's name that was on her emergency contact card in her wallet, but she said that they had been estranged for a few months, so we didn't bother contacting him. What about your case?"

"We have two women, both drugged and gutted by a hunting knife. What is it called, a gut hook?" Dex looked to Johnny to correct him and his partner nodded. "There is no evidence that either woman was being stalked. They did, however, turn out to be roommates. We tried to find someone that had a connection to both of them, but other than the one girl's boyfriend, we didn't find any reason that anyone would want to hurt either of them. Again, though, you know how I feel about coincidences, so we are missing something." Dex flipped through the file and noted Trina's ex-boyfriend's name and address.

"What do you think, Angelo? You think that there is something here?"

"Shit, I don't know. It is possible, but I still don't see a hot lead to go on at all." He pressed his fingers across his brow. "I made this copy for you to take with you. Maybe you can fax me a copy of anything you add to your files. I can dig through them and see if I can catch something."

"That sounds fair enough. Listen, man, I really appreciate your cooperation on this." Dex stood up and shook his hand.

"You bet. I don't like cold cases, so if there is a chance this helps you, then by all means take it with you."

"We are going to the ex-boyfriend's, aren't we?" Johnny asked as soon as he closed his car door.

"Why wouldn't they have questioned him? Maybe it was him. Did he know Cynthia? I'd like to know if he has made any recent visits to Hawk Creek, wouldn't you?" There was an edge to his voice, and he felt the scabbed skin stretching across his knuckles.

"Those are all fair questions, good ones at that, but let's not jump to conclusions. I think we should look down any path we can find until it leads to closing this case."

"I just can't believe they didn't talk to him, they have his home and work info in the file. It is just sloppy police work. I wasn't going to say anything while we were there, but this is crap."

"It did seem as if there were a lot of unanswered questions and some level of confusion on the officer's part. They can't all be as good as us." A light chuckle erupted from Johnny's chest

CHAPTER TWENTY-EIGHT

"WE ARE SORRY TO DISTURB you at work, Mr. Santos, but we need to speak with you about a police investigation. We have reason to believe that you might have valuable information that could be imperative to our case." Johnny thought it would be best if he took the lead on the interview. Dex was way too close to the case, and he had no problem reminding Dex of that.

"Please call me Vince. If there is anything I can do to help, it would be my pleasure, but I can't imagine what this could be about."

"Do you have somewhere we can speak in private?"

"Of course. Come on back. We can go to my office. I will let reception know to hold all my calls."

Dex couldn't help but compare the differences between himself and Trina's ex-boyfriend. Vince had a professional day job and wore a suit every day. His hair was dark and cut short on the sides, and he used enough hair product to make it bulletproof.

He seemed like a nice enough guy, but Dex was skeptical about what might make him tick. Trina had never mentioned why they'd broke up, and in general, he didn't really care. However, being face to face with him, and knowing there was a possibility that he could be stalking Trina, had him on edge.

Once in his office, Vince pulled over two chairs for Dex and Johnny. Using the interoffice COM system, he notified his receptionist that he was in a meeting. Johnny sat down, but Dex decided to remain standing. He leaned against the wall behind the chair that Johnny occupied.

"So, how can I help?" Vince sat with his hands crossed on top of his desk.

Dex noticed a picture of a woman and an infant on the corner of his desk, and it dawned on him that a lot could change in roughly two years. He wasn't in the habit of checking men's ring fingers, but sure enough, Vince had on a wedding band. He was apparently married and had started a family with another woman.

Why would a married family man with a baby at home travel almost an hour to stalk his ex-girlfriend? More so, why or when would he have time to be out in the middle of the night, murdering women in the streets of Hawk Creek?

Why was what they were there to find out. They never knew what kind of situation couples had at home. Things always looked perfect on the surface from the outside.

"We are actually working on two different murder investigations and trying to determine if they are possibly connected," Johnny explained.

"Murder? And you think that I can help you?"

"When was the last time you were in Hawk Creek?"

"Hawk Creek? Shit, I have no idea. Why would I go there?"

"So, you don't know anyone that lives in Hawk Creek?"

Vince let out a breath as his shoulders slumped down. He tilted his head as if searching an invisible database. "Honestly, it is possible, but I don't think so."

"Ok. Are you aware that your ex-girlfriend, Trina Hayes, and another woman were attacked in an alley here in Portland around a year and a half ago?"

"Um, no. That is terrible, are they okay?"

"Trina survived the attack, but the other woman was not so lucky. We wanted to see if, by any chance, you knew the other victim." Johnny was very nonchalant with his questioning. He opened the file and slid a photo of Cynthia Strong across the desk.

Vince lifted his hand to cover his mouth as his jaw fell open. "Yes, I know her. Her name is Cynthia. She was my trainer at the gym for a short time."

"How well did you know Cynthia? Were you and she romantically involved?"

Dex was surprised at the angle Johnny was going with it.

"No, but Trina thought we were. Cynthia was just my friend. I paid her through the gym to train me. Sometimes we would grab a smoothie or sit at the juice bar next to the gym, but we were usually with other people."

"So, Trina thought that you were seeing Cynthia? Was that while you and she were still dating?"

"Trina and I were living together. The first year was great. The second year, things got progressively more bizarre."

Dex cut him off. "Are you referring to her sleepwalking?"

Johnny's head spun around fast to meet with Dex's gaze. He didn't look pleased with the interruption, but they never second-guessed each other in front of someone they were interviewing.

"Sleepwalking? Is that was she calls it now?" Vince smirked and shook his head as if something Dex had said had comedic value.

"Are you saying that she doesn't sleepwalk? Because in her statement on the night she was attacked, she said that she had no memory of leaving her apartment or the attack." Johnny asked.

"I don't know what she does. She thinks that she sleepwalks, but a lot of the time, she would say that she didn't do things, and I watched her do them. She certainly had blackout periods.

"There were nights when she muttered stuff about her sister being killed, but when I would ask her about it, she would tell me that she didn't have a sister. I suggested that she see a doctor or a psychiatrist about her," he used his fingers to make quotation marks in the air, "sleepwalking."

"Are you certain that she didn't have a sister?" Johnny asked.

Vince just shook his head.

"The Portland Police Department never contacted you about this investigation?"

"No, and I had no idea about Cynthia either. I can't believe she is dead. We were not friends outside of the gym, and shortly after I moved out of Trina's apartment, I switched to a different gym closer to my new apartment. I can't believe they were both attacked." He paused and looked around the room.

"I don't even understand why they would be together. Trina was not friends with Cynthia, and she did not go to the gym."

"You knew both women, did you know anyone that would have any reason to want to cause harm to either of them?"

Vince cracked his knuckles, the sound of it edged at Dex's nerves.

"No idea, and besides myself, I don't know anyone that would have known both women."

"Ok, let me ask you another question. Do you know Bethany Kingston or Tammy Larazzo?"

"I don't think so. The names don't sound familiar. Should I know them?" He looked confused.

"I guess not. I want to thank you for all your time. We might be contacting you again if we have any more questions." Johnny stood up to shake his hand.

"I have one more question. Do you know a Lina?" Dex asked pushing off the wall.

Vince's big brown eyes flashed open and up to Dex. "Do you mean Lina Hayes? Ha! Not a real person. I take it you are either dating Trina or have searched her home."

Johnny shot red-hot daggers out of his eyes in Dex's direction. Dex ignored his partner's irritation. He was more concerned with whether or not the shock showed on his face.

"Excuse me?" Dex did not like the accusation, be it true or not. How dare he speak to him with that kind of a tone? Was there a bit of jealousy left in Vince after all?

"Her mail, she says that she doesn't know why she gets mail addressed to Lina, but I have heard her refer to herself as Lina on occasion. When I confronted her, she said I must have misheard her.

"I don't mean to be rude, or out of line, but I hope you are not involved with her. She is batshit crazy. I couldn't prove it in a court of law or anything, but I know it in my gut. I got out of there as fast as I could, once I realized."

"Thanks again for your time." Johnny handed Vince one of his cards. "If you think of anything else, please don't hesitate to give us a call."

"No problem. I am here if you need anything. Good luck with your investigation." Vince walked them out of his office.

CHAPTER TWENTY-NINE

"DEX, I DON'T LIKE THE sound of anything I heard in there. What is going on?" Johnny stopped him before they got into his car.

Dex felt the sun beating down on his neck. The air was cool, but a good amount of heat radiated down when the wind wasn't blowing.

"I don't fucking know. My head is all spun around right now. I can't believe that he is talking about the same person at all." Dex rubbed at his pocket and wished he had a pack of smokes.

"What was that shit about Lina Hayes?"

"He was right, she had magazines addressed to a Lina Hayes. I wasn't sure if she had a sister or if it was a typo. The weird thing was that the magazine didn't fit in with her other selections." Dex filled his cheeks, pursed his lips together, and blew out his uncertainty about what was happening.

"We need to get someone over to her house and find out who, if anyone, has been there. If someone is stalking her, we need to know. We also need to know if she has a sister. *Maybe* an estranged one." Johnny unlocked the car doors.

"Even crazier, did she have a sister that was killed? We are going to need to search the county birth records." Dex got into the car and opened his window. "This still doesn't get us closer to who is murdering these women, and we need to set up some kind of security detail other than me, to make sure that Trina is protected."

"You are right, so what do you want to do now? Do you want to head back to Hawk Creek or Portland PD and use their systems?"

"We can head back to Hawk Creek. I am going to call ahead and get a patrol car over to the school. I need to get in touch with Trina and let her know that we are going to send a team over to her house today so we can get prints, especially in that bathroom."

"It might be hard for you to speak to her if she is teaching. I don't know if they have phones in the classrooms over there. They might be able to page her, you are going to need to notify the principal that you sending a car over there anyway."

"Good point, Harrington. I am going to email Captain Kard and see if she can help me out with the school and patrol car. I am going to call and text Trina's phone and see if I can get through.

"We still don't have a suspect, and we don't have a connection between Trina, Bethany, and Tammy."

"Dex, what about Cynthia? It sounds as if Trina could have had some motive for wanting to hurt her. I don't know if the things that Vince said about her are true, but if she is mentally unstable, anything is possible."

"Do you think she seems mentally unstable? Because aside from the magazine thing, I have not seen anything to the likes of what he said."

"I don't want to sound like a dick, but you have only known her for like a week. I met her briefly on three occasions, none of which was really long enough for me to base an opinion on. She seems like a really nice lady, and she is quite beautiful. All I am saying is keep your eyes open."

"You say that like I am some shmuck that walks around falling for every other girl I meet. You are the one that has been encouraging me to get involved with a woman, and now that I have, you haven't stopped with the comments. I thought you would be more supportive. Let's just catch this person."

"We will, Dex. I just don't want you to get blindsided. I need you to keep your focus sharp."

Dex shot an email to the captain and texted Trina to let

her know that he needed to talk to her. He even tried to call her cell phone, in case she could answer it. At least she would know that he was looking for her from the missed calls.

By the time he finished with reaching out to Trina, his phone beeped back with an email from the captain. "Captain's already got back to me. She said that she handled calling the principal of the school. She said she wanted to keep this as hush-hush as possible, the only problem is that Miss Hayes is not in school today."

"Where is she then? Didn't you drop her off this morning?" Johnny's eyes bulged slightly from the sockets.

"Yes, I did. Shit, what if she was taken?" Dex felt flustered and his breathing became shallow.

"What else did the captain say?"

"She said she would send over a car anyway, just to patrol the area. She asked that we let her know whatever we need." Dex could see his hands shaking. He wished that he were driving, so he had the wheel to hold onto. Instead, he felt as if he was slipping away.

"You should call Shea and ask her if she got back the toxicology screening on Bethany, or if she managed to come up with anything else that would clue us in to where the murders took place, so we can cut straight to the source."

Johnny had a good point. Dex wasn't so sure that Shea

would have anything new, since they had seen her the day before, but anything was worth a try.

Dex dialed her cell, and it went straight to voicemail. "Is anyone going to answer their phone today?"

"Call her at her office, she is probably seeing patients. It is Monday afternoon. I don't think she would be at the morgue, but you could try to call there too."

"I don't think she would be at the morgue either." He hit speed dial to her office. Her receptionist answered on the second ring, and Dex switched over to speaker.

"Hi. This is Detective Preston. May I please speak with Dr. Sinclair?"

"I'm sorry. She is not available to take a call right now, can I take a message?"

"No, this is a police matter. I don't want to interrupt her appointments, but it is imperative that I speak with her."

"I'm sorry, Detective. She isn't here. She left with an emergency."

"What kind of emergency?"

"Her lady friend came in and said that there was an emergency at the school and she needed to come pick up Abigail."

Dex and Johnny looked at each other, concern reflecting back in each other's eyes.

"Who is this friend?"

"I'm sorry. I don't know. I have never seen her before.

She was pretty, had blonde hair. Oh, Dr. Sinclair said that she was a teacher at the school. I thought it was weird that the teacher would come here and not call."

"Okay. How long ago was this?"

"Maybe twenty minutes. She asked me to cancel all her appointments for the day."

"Thank you. If she calls, or comes back, can you please have her call me immediately?"

"Yes, of course, Detective."

Dex hit the red, end button on his phone.

"Call the school, Dex, and find out what is going on. Find out if something is wrong with Abigail."

Dex couldn't bear the thought of anything happening to his goddaughter. He'd promised his friend that he would keep her and her mother safe. He may not have been there for them by spending time with them, but he would give his life to protect them. That wasn't something up for debate, ever.

He called the school and spoke with the principal. Dex thought it was best not to get anyone else involved. He already knew that there was a situation. The principal checked in with Abigail's teacher and said that she was fine and was in her classroom.

Dex told the principal not to let her leave the school, not even with her mother. The only two people that she was to be released to were him or Captain Kard. He wasn't going to take his chances with anyone.

It wasn't that he didn't trust Shea, but he didn't know who she was with. He had a sick feeling brewing in his stomach. A feeling that was taking his mind somewhere he didn't want it to go.

"Dex?" Johnny looked over at him.

Dex felt the car's speed increasing, and he was glad that they were getting close to Hawk Creek. He felt as if he was being propelled through a distorted tunnel.

"Dude, here." Johnny handed him his small notebook that he used to keep notes in while they worked on the case.

"Flip through, you need to find Andi's phone number, the bartender from the Salty Peach restaurant.

Dex took the pad and flipped through the pages slowly. He stopped and tilted his head at his partner. He didn't want to ask him, but he had to.

"Why do I need her number, and how do you have it?"

"She really wanted me to give it to you, but she said that if we needed to ask her anything, we could call or text her. You need to text her one of the pictures of Trina from yesterday."

"Are you shitting me?" Dex knew he wasn't.

He found the number and started to type out a message to her, but his clammy fingers were slipping across the screen of the phone. He knew he needed to get a grip. He definitely had feelings for Trina, but at the end of the day, Shea and Abigail were the closest thing to family he had.

While he waited for a response from Andi, he emailed the captain and told her that she needed to go pick up Abigail Sinclair from the elementary school. He also explained his suspicions about what was at play and requested back up to meet them.

CHAPTER THIRTY

"LISTEN, I WANT YOU TO know that I really hope that this isn't what it looks like."

Dex knew that his partner meant that from the bottom of his heart. He also knew that, although it had taken him a while for things to start to click, he was usually good about following his gut. And at the moment, as much as he didn't want his gut to be right, he feared that his darkest imagination of the situation could be a reality.

His phone beeped, and he read the text from Andi. "Fuck! You need to take South East Hawk Creek Road, off of Beauport, and you need to drive as fast as you can!"

"It's her, isn't it?"

"I can't fucking believe this. How could we not see this?"

"How could we? I can see why she would have killed Cynthia. Some kind of jealous rage. But why Tammy and Bethany?" Johnny shook his head.

"I don't know about Tammy, maybe she dated that doctor guy? When she came to the station to bring us coffee and doughnuts, she saw me hugging Bethany. Trina asked me if she was my girlfriend. They both left the station around the same time."

"Oh shit! That adds up. She must have also been the one that put in the fake call to the doctor, so he was late to his date with Tammy. But why is she targeting Shea?"

"Because your wife told her that she had always thought that I would wind up with Shae. Trina asked me if Abigail was mine. Remember? She was kind of abrasive with Shea yesterday. I thought I was just imagining it.

"I don't know how much time we have, but chances are, if she has Shea, she has already drugged her. Certainly she could have murdered these women anywhere, but she has a huge piece of property and several barns and sheds that she could be using to hide or kill these women."

"Her car is tiny as shit, have you ever been in it when we weren't hammered?" Johnny asked.

Dex knew he what he was getting at. "No, but I know she has an old F250 that belonged to her grandfather that she keeps the barn. That's way bigger than her tiny car. I better call the captain and let her know what is going on. I think we are going to need more than a patrol car."

"That's for sure, you better tell her we need a bus, and to check the toxicology report from Tammy Larazzo's case file, so that she can tell them what Trina used to drug the other victims."

Johnny was always good at staying cool under pressure. Dex got the job done, but he was a hothead, and sometimes, he let his emotions get the best of him. This was a situation where he was riding a thin line.

"We have the case files with us. Shit, let me grab them from the back seat and email screenshots to her. You seriously need to drive faster! Where is your light? I will put it on the roof."

"It's in the trunk."

Dex gave him a look.

"What? When have we ever needed to use it? Never!"

Dex flashed off some images of the files and emailed them over to the Captain just before he called her. He explained everything that was going on and told her no sirens and to keep them from bum rushing the property until they secured the site. She informed him that she was on her way to pick up Shea's daughter from the school and would bring her back to the precinct.

Dex asked her not to tell Abigail what was going on yet, he didn't want her to be any more scared than she already would be. He prayed to God that he wouldn't have to ever explain to her why he was the reason that both of her parents were dead.

He took out his gun and double-checked to make sure it

was loaded. It was always loaded, but what else could he do to prepare himself for what he was about to face.

"Don't pull all the way up the driveway, it's loose gravel. If she is here, she can't know that we are coming. We don't know what she does with these women before she actually cuts them open."

Johnny barely pulled into the driveway off the main road. Luckily, there was enough of a wooded area there to disguise his car. "We are going to need to hoof it. Where are we going?"

"We can split up, I can take the big barn, and you can check out one of the smaller structures. I don't think Trina would take her in the house. I didn't see anything when I was in there to lead me to believe there was any foul play, other than the mirror thing."

"Which, by the way, is nuts. You think she was faking that or what?"

"I don't know, but if she hurts Shea, I will fucking kill her." Dex was conflicted. He had started to develop one of the deepest connections that he had ever had with a woman in a really long time. Now, he would have her in his sights, and he really hoped he wouldn't have to pull the trigger on her.

Dex was thankful that they were the first ones to arrive

on the scene. He knew that if there was any chance of getting through to Trina, it would be by him. He was the one that she had a connection to. For some reason, she found Shea a threat to her relationship with Dex.

"Dex," Johnny whispered as they crept closer to the structures on her property. "This isn't your fault man. I need you to get that out of your head right now."

Johnny knew Dex better than anyone. How could he not, they spent the most amount of time together. Truthfully, Johnny could say that until he was blue in the face, but there wouldn't be a day that would go by that Dex wouldn't feel responsible in some way for what was happening.

"Yup," he said back quickly full of guilt.

"Is that her?" Johnny asked as he put his hand up to halt Dex from moving forward. "What is she doing?"

"I don't know. Get down, so she doesn't see us. We are still far enough out that we can't reach her if she runs into that barn."

From where they stood, they could see Trina's blonde hair blowing in the wind. She was still wearing the wispy cream-colored dress she'd had on that morning when he'd dropped her off at the school.

He felt the edge of his fingernails digging into the flesh of his palms. She was breathtaking. Her lace stockings were rolled down enough to see the tops of her thighs.

How could someone so sexy be so messed up in the head?

They watched her for a few minutes as she swung an axe at some short logs of wood. She was clearly focused on her task, and they didn't want to cause a distraction until they knew that they could secure the location and that Shea was safe.

Dex prayed to God, which pretty much never happened, that they were wrong about her. He wanted so badly for them to be wrong. If they weren't, then what did it say about him, that she was the only person he let in after being alone for so many years.

Once she went back into the barn, they continued their approach, being careful not to make too much noise. Dex kept looking behind them to see if their backup had arrived. He was concerned that they would come barging on to the property, even though he asked the captain to make sure they approached with discretion.

"At least she doesn't have any blood on her. Right?" Dex figured that she had the same dress on, and if she had cut someone, there would have been clear evidence of blood splatter on her clothes.

"Yeah, for now. I guess we are both going to the barn now. Why don't you take the same entrance that she went in through, and I will see if there is a back door."

"You think it will have a back door?"

"Seriously? Of course it will. If they housed animals in

there, they would want them to get out of either side. You act like you didn't grow up around here."

"Whatever."

Dex took out his gun and Johnny followed his lead. He was hesitant to turn off the safety, but if he needed to fire he should be prepared.

Once they reached the front of the barn, they used only eye contact and hand gestures to communicate. Dex waited until Johnny had disappeared around the side of the old wood structure, before he pushed the door open as slowly as he could. He managed to slip in through the small opening that he created without making a sound.

He was surprised at how packed full of stuff the barn was. The old F250 truck blocked his view of the rest of the barn. It also gave him something to hide behind while he tried to locate Trina and assess the situation. The uncanny level of silence both unsettled him, and allowed him to listen for her. He crept around to the front of the truck and could see her putting wood in an old, black potbelly stove.

He scanned the area looking for any signs of Shea. If she were there, she would most likely have been rendered unconscious or close to it.

Dex decided to just go for it and pretend as if he'd been worried about her and had come to make sure she was okay after she'd not been at the school when he'd called.

Slipping his gun into the back of his pants, instead of his

holster, he called out, "Trina?"

She spun around grabbing something from the shelf beside her, a small beam of light caught the small, metal blade that was in her hand.

"Hey. I have been looking everywhere for you." He was careful with the inflection in his voice.

"Please don't call me that." She snapped at him.

"Okay, what do you want me to call you?"

"Lina. You can call me by my name. What are you doing here?"

"I was worried that you were not at the school, and with everything that has been going on, I figured I would stop here on my way back from Portland to check in on you."

"On me or on Trina?" she asked him. Her eyes had a glaze over them that he had never noticed about her.

"I'm sorry, I am confused." He slowly tried to close the distance between them. The closer he came, the further she moved into the barn.

"I am here to protect Trina. She can't do it for herself, so I do what has to be done to keep her safe."

What she was saying was blowing his mind. He wasn't sure if he was talking to Trina, or if maybe she actually had a twin sister that was there to help her with something.

Things didn't add up. Vince had mentioned Trina muttering something about her sister being dead, and she'd never mentioned having a sister to Dex. Either way, he knew that he dropped the woman off in that very outfit a few hours earlier.

"That is why I am here too. I want to make sure that Trina is safe. She was scared that someone was trying to hurt her. Do you know about anyone being in the house?"

"What do you mean? I don't think anyone other than Trina and myself have been in the house. Except when you were here the other day."

"You know I was here? Were you here?" He just needed to keep her engaged until they could locate Shea or confirm that she wasn't there.

"I am always with Trina. I see everything."

"Did you write her that message on her mirror?"

"Yes. I leave her messages around the house all the time. I think they make her happy. That is all I want. To make her happy. So much has been taken from her already. I can't let anyone else take from her."

"That is a beautiful sentiment. Will you let me help you with that? I care very much for Trina." If he could gain her trust, maybe she would open up to him about what was really going on there.

"I have to make sure you don't leave her." She had a sadness that darkened her eyes.

"Is that what happened with Dr. Rubio? Was Trina dating Sheldon?"

"He was a bad man. He took advantage of Trina, he was

disgusting, and he let other women manipulate him away from her."

Holy shit, she is bat shit crazy, he thought. How is this the same woman that was so amazing about talking him through letting go of the past and things that were out of his control? Did she have a split personality, or was she pretending to be Lina?

CHAPTER THIRTY-ONE

THE SOUND OF SOMETHING CRASHING at the far end of the barn startled both Lina and Dex.

"Shit," Dex mumbled under his breath.

Lina shot a fiery look at Dex. Her eyes were full of rage and desperation. She hesitated for a minute before spinning on her heel to dash toward the noise.

Dex took off after her, carefully maneuvering around the random stuff strewn all over the place. "Don't come any closer to me, Dex," she warned him as she held the blade to her throat.

He stopped dead in his tracks. Not so much because of her threat, but because he couldn't believe what he was seeing. Dex gasped and drew his weapon from the back of his slacks, aiming it at her.

"Don't move!"

He saw something in his periphery. He looked up and

saw Shea dangling from a come-a-long attached to a ceiling joist with her head drooped down. Seeing her limp body hanging from a harness like that crushed his heart.

"What the hell is going on here?" he shouted.

Before she could answer, Johnny came out from behind a rack of old rusted oil and paint cans. He too had his gun drawn. His eyes darted around the space, taking notice of where Trina stood and how Shea hung from the rafter.

"Is she dead?" he demanded.

"Not yet. She is just resting. I gave her the opportunity to think about what she has done, and why she is a threat to Trina and Dex's future." Lina still held the blade at her throat, so closely that Dex could see tiny droplets of blood starting to drip down the side of her neck.

"What the hell is she talking about? Why is she talking in third person?" Johnny looked to Dex for answers and some kind of signal as to how they were going to proceed.

"This is Lina, not Trina. She just wants to protect Trina, isn't that right?" Dex asked her, showing her how sympathetic he could be.

She nodded.

Dex took a slow step in Shea's direction, pointing his weapon at Shea. "I told you, I want to protect and keep Trina safe. She is my everything. You should let me handle this and take care of Dr. Shea."

"I don't think that is a good idea. I don't want to, but I

will kill them both if I have to. I won't let you hurt Trina. I have to be sure that Shea can't interfere in our plans. I would sooner kill Trina than let you bring her any more suffering."

"Does Trina know that you are doing this?" Dex was horrified to see the amount of bloodstains on the floor beneath where Shea hung.

"Trina doesn't know what I do. I make sure of that. I just like to make sure she remembers me from time to time. She forgets how much she misses me. I don't let her remember what he did to us."

"He who? Who hurt you? I will make it stop. Let me help you. I love her." Dex held his hand up to Johnny and slowly started to lower his weapon.

Sincerity burned in his eyes. His feelings for Trina were the closest thing to love he had experienced in a really long time, and his head was spinning from the reality of the situation.

He couldn't even imagine what had happened to the woman that would cause such psychosis. His heart hurt for her, but at least three women were dead, and one of the most important people in his life was hanging only feet from him with her life in the balance.

"I can't tell you, she can't find out, she can't remember. Coming here was bad. It was really bad. It has been so hard to keep her from the truth. I can't let her find me."

"Fuck this shit. I am getting her down, Dex." Johnny kept his gun pointed at Trina and moved closer to Shea.

"Dex, don't let him," she pleaded with him.

Dex had to think fast. All four of them were roughly equal distances from each other. Johnny had longer legs, but Lina could easily leap forward and plunge her gut hook into Shea's abdomen. She also could take her own life with a quick swipe of the blade.

He would take her out if he had to, but he wanted to help her. She was sick, deranged, and clearly not mentally sound. There could never be anything between them, but he truly did want to protect Trina from whatever was happening to her.

"Johnny, hold off." Dex stepped closer to him and Shea.

They needed to check Shea's pulse and get her down. He was shocked that their backup had not arrived yet. He knew that the paramedics were going to need to assess Shea as soon as they could. Trina or Lina was no doctor, who knew what level of drugs she had pumped into Shea. If Shea didn't die from the blade that Trina wielded, she was still in danger of an overdose, or the potential complications from the medication.

It clicked, in that moment, that the medications must have been whatever she was supposed to be taking for her sleepwalking. Maybe she'd stopped taking it when she moved to Hawk Creek, not thinking she would need it anymore.

Dex wanted to at least get between Trina and Shea. If he could block the path to Shea's body, then they would have a better chance of disarming Trina.

As he drew closer, he watched her lower the blade from her neck. He was glad he was making headway with her and gaining her trust enough to know that he didn't want to hurt her. His gun was still out, but he was no longer aiming it in her direction. He knew Johnny had that covered.

"Dex, I'm sorry," Lina said as her eyes wilted and her brows sloped inward. "I don't completely believe you. I can't let you hurt her. I will take her with me before I let her feel that pain again."

Dex was about to respond to calm her worries and her concerns, but the words couldn't find their way to his tongue fast enough.

She raised her hands, bending her elbows in a way to bring her fisted hands up toward her face. The movements happened so fast that it was hard for Dex to raise his weapon in defense of her actions.

She thrust the blade of the gut hook into her abdomen with astonishing speed.

Dex leaped into action in an attempt to stop her. He was too far to reach her so he aimed his weapon at her shoulder in an attempt to knock her hands off the blade.

He didn't see the coiled hose on the ground in front of him and tripped forward as his finger pulled back on the trigger. Although he caught his balance at the last minute, avoiding face planting on the filthy dirt floor, his shot went off. Everything happened in a few mere seconds, but he felt as if time had slowed down. He watched her crumble as if she was in slow motion.

Trina doubled over and dropped the blade as she fell back from the impact of the bullet. He knew without even having to look that he'd missed his intended target. He'd lost control of the trajectory, and there was nothing he could do about it. He dropped his gun and started to run.

He turned at the same time yelling to Johnny, "Get her down!"

Dex rushed to Trina's side, unsure of how much damage she had made with the gut hook. He had to consider the stab wound might not matter because, from the amount of blood staining her cream colored dress, he knew that he'd shot her in the belly. If he'd hit her spleen or liver, there was nothing he would be able to do for her. Even if the paramedics were already there, she only had a few minutes at best.

He turned to check on Shea and Johnny as Johnny struggled to get her down from the harness on the come-a-long.

Hearing Shea grunt, Dex knew she was coming to, and

he shouted, "Shit, Johnny. Disengage and release the free spool lever or cut the fucking harness." He kneeled down beside Trina as she held her stomach.

"Dex?" she whispered. "What happened? Where am I?"

"You're home, Trina. I am here with you." He didn't know what to say to her. He knew she was dying. He couldn't protect her from herself or from him.

"I can't feel my legs. I'm so cold." Her voice was soft and strained.

Dex watched the color draining away from her face and scooped her up in his arms. He laid her head on his lap and stroked her hair.

"I am so sorry, Trina. It is Trina right?" he asked her, not sure if she was the woman he had fallen for.

"Who else would I be?"

"Lina?" He gazed into her eyes searching for the truth. Confused by how things had gone so wrong.

"I remember..." A tear escaped the corner of her eye and rolled along the side of her temple into her ear.

He could hear Shea and Johnny behind them. Johnny was asking her if she was okay, and Dex could see out of the corner of his eye that he was holding her up.

"Oh my God, what happened?" Shea could barely speak, her words were so slurred. "You have to put pressure on it."

Shea was a doctor who took her oath seriously. It didn't

matter that she knew Trina had been about to take her life just minutes before, she still tried to push forward to assist Dex with the dying woman in front of her.

Johnny tried to stop her but knew it was useless. He didn't want her to hurt herself, but he wasn't sure how coherent she was, so he helped her over to where Dex was holding Trina.

Dex didn't want to tell Shea that he knew her efforts would be useless in front of Trina. He just wanted to make her as comfortable as possible in her final moments.

"I wish I had known. I would have done anything to help you," he whispered to her.

"Please, you have to find my sister and make sure that her story is told and she gets a proper burial. I am so sorry. I didn't know this was happening to me. It was my father."

Dex felt her arms releasing, she had little to no control left. She was slipping away fast. Shea had taken her shirt off and pressed it against Trina's abdomen in a futile attempt to stop or control the bleeding.

Dex leaned in and whispered in Trina's ear. "You were worth all the love in the world and so was your sister."

"The wood...pile..." the words were barely audible and they were her last.

Made in United States
North Haven, CT
23 March 2024